Temple Legacy

VALLE DE MÉXICO 1519

Temple Legacy

• TALES OF OLD MEXICO •

JAMES RYAN

Channing Way Publications

First Edition
Date of first printing, June 2023

This book is a work of fiction. The names, characters, events and dialogue in this book are drawn from the author's imagination and are not to be construed as real. Any resemblance to actual events or to persons, living or dead, is entirely coincidental and not intended by the author.

Ryan, James, author
Teopancalli: The Temple / by James Ryan – 1st ed.
Library of Congress Control Number: 2023910376
(eBook) ISBN 979-8-9879213-4-0
(Trade) ISBN 979-8-9879213-3-3
(Hardcover) 979-8-9879213-5-7

Printed in the United States of America

For Sean and Alex.

With thanks to Robert Donovan

for allowing me to bend his ear.

CONTENTS

They undertake nothing without first offering sacrifice there.

Hernan Cortes in a letter to
Emporer Charles V

PLAZA MAYOR

October 1754 Ciudad de México

As he knelt in front of the cathedral doors, the bright moonlight cast his pale blue shadow on the steps. But he was oblivious to this. He didn't notice the moonlight or the evening breeze that swirled around him. He was so hot, and it would take time for him to cool down.

It was one of those cloudless nights when the visibility was unlimited. Above and beyond the cathedral, the snowcapped volcano, Popocatépetl, was magnified by the calm, clear atmosphere. The sun wouldn't rise for another two hours, and he was alone. None of this worried him. He wasn't going anywhere.

Two women entered the Plaza Mayor, which was bordered on one side by the cathedral. "At least it isn't raining. I appreciate the dry days," said Estella, carrying her bundle of *petates* on a wood-frame pack strapped to her back.

"This time is the driest part of the year," said Guadalupe. "Just wait 'til June."

The women were walking toward the *baratillo* in the plaza. One could purchase anything there, from Estella and Guadalupe's woven mats and baskets to tools, clothing, and dry goods—everything a person could imagine. Estella and Guadalupe were headed to their little wattle-and-daub stall where they sold their goods somewhere amid the maze of the hundreds of other wattle-and-daub stands that made up the market.

It was early, but the unique aroma of the market was already present. It would bloom as soon as the sun rose. Similar to several places in the city, the marketplace was an open sewer, and the Acequia Real, which passed in front of the viceroy's palace on the square's east side, was fouled by human excrement.

Estella was accustomed to the smell of the market. But this morning, something else was in the air. She and Guadalupe made their way down the last row of stalls toward their own. Yes, she noticed something different in the air—a strange odor she didn't recognize, a sickly-sweet smell.

Approaching their stall, Estella caught the outline of a small man on the cathedral steps. When she came closer, she noticed it wasn't a tiny man but a man on his knees, posed like a boxer with his arms held up in front of him and bent at the elbows. Then the smell intensified. It was nauseating, honeyed, and putrid like nothing she'd encountered. She moved nearer, and then she saw him.

Her cry started low and guttural and stuck in her throat. She was unable to muster it. She turned from the figure and ran back to her friend. Finally, her cry exploded into an ear-shattering scream of pure horror. There, kneeling in front of the cathedral, were the smoldering remains of what used to be a man, blackened and cracked, with what was left of his life-sustaining fluids slowly seeping out of cavities that had once been his ears, eyes, nose, and mouth.

An hour later, only a few streets over, Don Diego de Santiago was beginning to wake. The early morning sun snuck through the curtains into his bedroom, cutting a sharp narrow swath of amber light across the linens of his bed as he struggled to open his eyes. Turning his head away from the morning sun, he heard his housemaid, Maria, gently knocking at his bedroom door. In a soft, even voice, he responded, "*Adelante*!"

The door opened, and Maria tiptoed into the room. A woman in her midforties, Maria was short, dark, and big-breasted with a broad face and nose. If one word could characterize Maria's build, it would be "sturdy." She had worked for Don Diego from the day he had acquired the house four years earlier. Her kind eyes masked a formidable personality. Forceful and determined, she went through life with a resolute sense of purpose. She ran a tight ship and would brook no condescension from anyone—master, merchant, or medico. Diego honored it and, on occasion, defended it.

In the *casta* system of racial "purity" in Nuevo España, Maria Rosales was considered *criollo*. Her parents were both Spanish, but she was born outside of Spain. To be ranked as a peninsular, the top caste, one had to be of the *sangre pura*, born on the peninsular de España.

Taking the hour of the day into consideration, Maria said in a hushed voice, "Don Diego, the boy Esteban is downstairs. He says he has news for you. Something about a dead man in the Plaza Mayor."

"Thank you, Maria. Please tell little Esteban I will see him shortly, and, if you would be so kind, I'll take my *xocolatl* in the drawing room."

"Very well, señor." Maria departed.

Diego rarely saw anyone or did anything in the morning before he'd had his first mug of what he called "the beverage of the gods." *Xocolatl* came from an ancient recipe and was prepared with water, cocoa, chili, vanilla, cinnamon, and honey. In the past, it was reserved for the Indio royals and elites, but the Aztecs also gave it to their warriors before battle to give them strength. Diego became addicted to it shortly after he arrived in Mexico five years ago.

He started to dress. The sunlight in the room had grown brighter. He looked across the room to his bed and what lay just below the ornate oak headboard. Covered to the waist, her brown skin contrasting with the white linens, was a silent study in beauty. *Madre Mia! I would be happy all my life with that woman. If only.*

Diego was in a hurry, though, so he quietly finished dressing and left the room. He descended the stairs to the inner courtyard, crossing it to the entryway, and then went into the adjacent drawing room. Esteban was there waiting.

Esteban was one of the *informantes* who brought Diego news about goings-on in the city, particularly criminal ones. Without fail, these informants were always ahead of any official information distributed by the Audiencia, and they were raw and reliable.

Appointed by the king, the Audiencia was the highest seat of civil and criminal justice in Nueva España, rendering final judgment in all cases, civil or criminal. Diego acted as the fiscal or crown prosecutor for criminal affairs.

Esteban was a dark and swarthy lad. Small for his age, he moved about with a pronounced limp. Born a mestizo, his father Spanish and his mother Indio, he was a denizen of the city's crowded back streets but could always be found loitering in the baratillo. Though it was known as the secondhand market, that term could be interpreted in two ways. First, the vendors there sold used or excess goods. "Secondhand" could also mean the goods were previously owned by one pair of hands but somehow found their way to a second pair. The baratillo was the center of the world in which Esteban lived. Although an orphan, he managed on his wits and had a particular talent for finding things before they were lost.

A murder? Don Diego thought to himself. There were enough murders in Mexico City, and he wouldn't necessarily involve himself with them. Still, as the victim was found in front of the viceregal palace and the holy Cathedral of the Assumption of the Most Blessed Virgin Mary into Heaven, it was worthy of his attention. He hoped there would be no ecclesiastical investigation. From a spiritual perspective, the church shared equal authority and responsibility with the government for keeping order in the New World.

"Good morning, *hombrecito*. What news requires my attention so early in the morning?"

"Respectfully, Don Diego, a most unholy creature was found in the Plaza Mayor by the *baratilleros* when they arrived this morning. Señor, I have seen it, and it is something so profane it could only have been the work of *el diablo* himself." A mixture of amusement and disbelief registered on Don Diego's face.

Maria brought Diego his steaming mug of *xocolatl*. He took a long draft, closing and then opening his eyes. He felt renewed. He asked Maria to look after his guest upstairs and to apologize to her, but he had to leave on urgent business. Diego felt guilty. He hadn't spoken to her, and he knew she would be angry at him for leaving her alone, but he had no choice. Today was different, and he had to move quickly to the plaza. Then, sadly, with indifference, he told himself she would survive. Maria said nothing and, giving a curt bow, exited the room. She thought he was being irresponsible, and it wasn't her place to apologize for him. Diego could tell she was peeved. *I suppose I have two tempers to calm later.*

"Well, Esteban," Diego said, placing his hand on the boy's shoulder, "I suppose we must go there and have a look, *sí*?"

Esteban smiled, enjoying the sense of importance working with the *fiscal del crimen* gave him. "*Sí*, señor! *Sí*."

Diego fastened his sword belt, and they were off.

Don Diego followed Esteban to the plaza. Diego's home and the Plaza Mayor were in the city's center, in a borough known as Cuauhtémoc. Cuauhtémoc became the leader of the Aztecs after the death of Moctezuma II, and both the Indios and the Spanish revered and admired him as a great warrior and king. Diego walked just behind the boy. Looking at him, he couldn't help reflecting on the good life he'd been blessed with.

Diego was born in Galicia in 1725 to a lower-ranking noble family and was therefore entitled to the honorific hidalgo. As a young man, Diego distinguished himself in Italy at the Battle of Velletri, fighting the Austrians. Afterward, he hungered for adventure and riches.

His father's oldest friend had moved to Mexico in Nueva España and wrote of the opportunities for both in the New World. In 1749, Diego migrated to the Ciudad de México, where he finished his law degree at the *Real y Pontificia Universidad de México*. Admittedly, his family and their government connections helped secure his position with the Audiencia as the *fiscal del crimen* for Mexico. Diego enjoyed the perks that came with the office—his comfortable house in the city center, a maid, and a more than adequate salary of 6,000 pesos a year. Diego's situation also afforded him an equally valuable level of prestige and visibility in Mexico City society and its political circles.

"Señor Santiago?"

"Yes, Esteban?"

"May I ask a question of you?"

"Certainly, Esteban. What would you like to know?"

"Your *amiga*, her name is Elena, yes?"

"Ah, my *amiga*." Diego emphasized *amiga*. "Yes, yes, Esteban, her name is indeed Elena."

"I guess I already knew. It's just that she—"

"Yes, Esteban?"

"It's just that, well, when I see her in the marketplace or with you, she is—" He paused. "Very kind and speaks to me."

"Well, what would you expect? She likes you."

Excitedly, Esteban stammered, "She does?"

"Of course! You're a bright young man."

"Then I must confess, señor. Someday, when I'm older, I would like to marry Señorita Elena."

"You would? That's commendable. You have my blessings."

All at once, the boy saw himself taller and with nice clothes, a handsome young man, walking straight and true with not the slightest sign of a limp. In his imagination, it was all true. "That is wonderful, Señor Santiago. I am very happy."

Diego smiled and watched as the boy, chest puffed out, quickened the pace.

It was nearly seven o'clock when Diego and Esteban entered the plaza. Business in the market was just getting started. A crowd of onlookers was gathered around the burned body. Don Diego gestured to one of the soldiers surrounding the body, identified himself, and ordered him to cordon off the space surrounding the corpse.

The sickly smell caught Diego off guard. His first reaction was to remove his kerchief and cover his nose and mouth. He had seen his share of the dead and dying, but, without question, the condition of this corpse and the setting it was in made this a unique situation.

According to the witnesses—Estella and her companion—the figure was just as it had been when the women discovered it. Diego crouched lower and inspected the body. Whatever clothes, personal effects, or jewelry it may have had were gone, as were the nose, ears, and eyes, all burned away. The figure seemed to be male. There wasn't any way of determining which *casta* he or she had sprung from.

Of one thing Diego was positive. The murder had not

taken place here in the plaza. There was no evidence of spent fuel or burn marks on the pavement. The immolation must have occurred elsewhere and the body moved to the plaza later. *Why? If the murder took place elsewhere, why place the body here?*

Diego instructed the soldiers to carefully place the body on a litter and take it to the Hospital de Indios. "Tell them my name. No one should be allowed to see the body without my approval."

Turning to the boy, Diego said, "Esteban, please ask the Monk to meet me at the hospital at noon. He should be awake by then."

"*Sí*, señor. May I ask that you provide me with a few *centavos* so I can go by the pulquería on the way to purchase a *jarra* of *pulque* for the good monk?"

Diego gave the boy a half smile. "You have a fine head on your shoulders, Esteban. That would be wise. He'll undoubtedly need it to clear the cobwebs, and we want him at his best when he examines this unfortunate soul's worldly remains. For now, Esteban, I must report to the alcalde with the Audiencia."

Diego gave Esteban twenty centavos and sent him on his way. He wished he could do more for the boy. He liked Esteban, and Esteban was bright and trustworthy. After all, his observation had been entirely correct. What they saw this morning was unnatural and indeed seemed to have been the work of *el diablo*.

Don Felipe de Carceres was Diego's favorite among the alcaldes *del crimen*. Caceres was the lifelong friend of Diego's father and had helped Diego gain his footing when he arrived in Mexico City. Caceres had also supported his appointment to the Audiencia.

Caceres smiled. "Ah, if it isn't Don Diego de Santiago, the most available bachelor in Mexico City and the greatest burden in my life." His smile changed to a frown.

"Uncle! I, a burden? Have I not supported your work in numerous cases, all ending favorably through your prudent application of justice and the law?" Diego grinned and continued. "As to my availability as a bachelor, the right woman hasn't appeared yet."

Only Don Felipe could make such a personal point to Diego. Diego addressed him affectionately as "Uncle" as he cared deeply for the man. The familiarity was welcomed by Caceres, who was equally fond of Diego.

"That is not what I've heard, and I am very concerned, Diego. What of this half-caste woman my people have told me about?"

Carceres was also born in Galicia and had served with Diego's father in the military. Fifteen years ago, King Phillip V appointed him captain alcalde of the *acordada* in Mexico. The purpose of the *acordada* was to eliminate the endemic banditry in the countryside and bring justice to the rural areas of Mexico. Caceres had succeeded in this endeavor.

He was offered the alcalde *del crimen* position with the Audiencia, so he resigned from his commission with the *acordada* and moved to Mexico City with his wife and son. Tragically, both had perished in a typhus epidemic six years ago. He never recovered from his loss and had remained a bachelor. Diego filled the space left by his son's death.

"People, Uncle? You mean spies. In any case, Elena is just an acquaintance. That's all."

"Acquainted with your bed, you mean. I worry, Diego. If someone had a mind to, they could expose you as a fornicator and ruin your reputation. Unwed sexual relations—and with a mestizo! I'm sorry, Diego, whether you're single or not, if this got out, your marriage to a respectable Spanish woman of good breeding would most assuredly be out of the question."

As Caceres moved back to sit at his desk, Diego bent forward, looking directly at him. "Uncle, I appreciate your concern, but this is entirely my affair. Now, I've come to discuss a serious situation. One you should be aware of."

"Very well, Diego. What brought you to me today, and what makes it so important?"

"This morning, a body was discovered in the Plaza Mayor. It was in front of the cathedral, amid the baratillo."

"A dead man in the baratillo? Though concerning, it doesn't seem that remarkable considering the makeup of that group."

"It's the condition of the body that's remarkable, dear uncle. The man had been burned alive and then moved to the plaza sometime in the night. I had the corpse moved to the Hospital de Indios for safekeeping. What's puzzling is the motivation behind this foul deed. Considering where the body was left, it could be political, religious, or an act of terror aimed at God knows who. I'm meeting the Monk at the hospital at noon. He'll perform an examination that he calls an autopsy. We might discover something that will answer some of these questions."

Caceres thought for a moment, then looked incredulously at Diego. "I have the same questions, but tell me, how do you know this immolation took place while he was still living?"

"By the positioning of his limbs. As he burned and struggled, the muscles contracted and remained in place, taut and bent at the elbows and knees. This would not have occurred had he been already dead."

"Incredible," muttered Caceres. "Who else is working with you?"

"No one officially. Just the Monk, Benito de Avila."

Caceres paced about the room, pondering, then turned to Diego. "Bring that *criollo* captain friend of yours in on this. He's smart and can be forceful yet diplomatic should anyone prove to be less than forthcoming during your investigation. What's his name?"

"De Anza. Pedro de Anza. I may need your help with that. He's currently attached to one of the *oidores*, de Vega."

"I'll talk to de Vega and ask him to have de Anza report to you in the morning."

"Very well, Uncle. I'll send you word of anything we discover at the hospital."

Caceres placed his hands on Diego's shoulders and looked him in the eyes. "Excellent, my boy, but please be careful when it comes to that acquaintance of yours. It could cause you trouble. And just one more thing."

"Yes, Uncle?"

"I'll see you at the viceroy's reception on Saturday, correct? His Excellency is supposed to have some special guests."

Diego bowed, stared at his feet, and said in one long breath, "Yes, Uncle. I'll be there."

Diego arrived at the hospital just as the clock tower across the way chimed twelve. It was only six blocks from his home on the Calle San Ildefonso. The day had turned hot and muggy, which was strange for this time of year. He hoped the Monk would be on time so he could get out of the sun. He glanced down the Avenida San Juan de Letrán to see the Monk lumbering along in his direction. His long *capa* swayed from side to side as he walked. A broad smile broke on his face as he recognized Don Diego.

"Buenos días, Don Diego. I understand you have come across something out of the ordinary you would like me to comment on."

"*Sí, mi viejo* amigo, very much out of the ordinary."

Benito de Avila—or the Monk, as he was known—was a large man. Tall and bulky but not fat, he seemed to plod along like an ox. Appearances aside, Diego had seen him move with incredible speed and agility when needed. His head was crowned with a mop of sandy brown hair with only a hint of gray at his temples. A noticeable bald spot toward the back of his skull gave him the appearance of a monk, but this was not the sole reason for his sobriquet. His large, rounded face housed two hazel eyes and a bulbous nose that looked as though it had been broken on multiple occasions sitting above an equally large mouth he used perhaps a bit too injudiciously.

Diego knew the Monk was in his early forties. Though not a practicing *Padre de la Iglesia*, it was rumored he was once a Jesuit priest who had been defrocked for reasons unknown to Diego. He had a mind as keen as any Diego had ever encountered, with extensive knowledge of medicine, the arts, philosophy, and science. His last and less visible distinction was he had the strength of a bull.

Diego and the Monk entered the hospital and made their way through the colonnades to the back of the building. They had both been there before on previous cases. An attendant unlocked the door for them. They walked down the few stairs, leaving the hot, humid atmosphere to enter a cool, almost cold space with a stone floor, white stucco walls, and a curved ceiling. The room was bereft of light save for two barred windows sitting high on the wall opposite them. Fortunately, this time of day provided all the light they would require. The room was empty except for two tables topped with cut marble slabs. On one stood—or knelt—the victim, positioned just as he had been in the plaza.

"He looks smaller than when I saw him this morning," Diego said.

The Monk commented, "Yes, not surprising. He's still issuing fluids. For one who has been dead this long, an appreciable amount of heat still radiates from the remains. And you are correct—it is a 'he.' There's vestigial evidence of a penis still visible. He must have been very well-endowed for that to have survived what he must have gone through. Almost his entire epidermis has been carbonized."

From beneath his cloak, the Monk produced a canvas roll with two leather bindings, which he untied. Inside were his tools. They looked like something you'd find in a carpenter's toolbox, except for the knives, one long and one short, both of which looked extremely sharp.

"So, you will carry out this autopsy you spoke of?" queried Diego.

"Yes. It could provide us with more facts and dispel some speculation."

"From what I've heard, autopsies seem barbaric."

"Nonsense, Diego. An autopsy is merely the application of scientific means to determine the time and exact cause of death and what, if anything, preceded death, like a struggle or other injuries that may not be immediately evident. It could also be useful to know what this man ate before his death. We can roughly estimate his time of death depending on what's left in his stomach. Frankly, there's a lot he can still tell us."

The corpse was bent, so it was difficult for Benito to put it on its back. He had to break the legs for it to lie flat. Once the corpse was in position, Benito deftly executed a long incision three inches deep from the sternum down to the groin. Diego reacted immediately with three quick movements of bending, vomiting, and simultaneously trying to turn away, but he fell short of completing the third.

"Good god, man! Do you mind?" howled the Monk. "My sandals don't matter, but this is a new cloak."

Diego took a minute to gather himself. He left the room and went to the fountain in the courtyard. There, he dashed water on his face, took four or five deep breaths, and returned.

"Apologies, Benito. I don't know why I wasn't prepared for that."

"No matter," said the Monk. "Look here. This outer char is hard and deep with a clear delineation between the epidermis that has been completely carbonized and what is left of the abdominal sack that contains his organs. It must have been intensely hot for this to happen so quickly and efficiently."

"*Dios mío!*" Diego said. "What could do such a thing?"

"I'm not sure. Considering he's still warm to the touch,

he must have been very hot when he was left in the plaza. I can't think of anything in the vicinity that could produce such intense heat. Perhaps a smelter or crucible, but it would have to be large enough to fit a man."

Diego asked if there was any way of confirming the man's race.

"No. His outer shell has been completely obliterated, and all humans are the same on the inside."

Benito worked for about another hour, examining the body and bones for any other signs of damage or injury. Last, he reviewed the contents of the stomach. It was nearly empty except for the final meal of what looked to be mushrooms and, surprisingly enough, the intact remains of a toad. "Well, apart from the mystery of how this man burned, there are signs of additional injuries. Both the humeri were fractured, pulled backward away from the scapula. It's the sort of injury that might result from being hung by your arms while they were tied behind your back. Regarding his last meal, I'll have to investigate that a little further to see what else I can uncover."

The Monk looked at Diego and smiled. "One other detail has been overlooked."

"What's that, Benito?"

The Monk's smile disappeared. "His heart is missing."

Walking home, Diego mulled over the conversation that had followed the revelation that the man had probably been brutally tortured before immolation.

"Tortured and then burned alive. Seems to fit with the methods used in the Inquisition." That's what he had told Benito.

Benito quickly retorted, "No. The Inquisition practices their atrocious deeds in public. They do not need to skulk about dumping bodies here or there at night."

"I suppose you're right, Benito."

There had never been anything clandestine in the actions of the Inquisition. For anyone accused of crimes against God and the Church, the Palace of the Inquisition—or the *Casa Chata,* as it was known—was a frightening proposition. Interrogations entailed relentless physical torment and excoriation until a confession was secured. That was followed by a public confession, or *auto de fe,* and an execution of judgment.

The most common judgment, an *abjuration de formali,* was issued to a penitent first offender and involved wearing the *sanbenito*—the garment of shame—in public for a period commensurate to the offense. In the worst case, the offender would wear the *sanbenito* and a dunce cap for years, and, once removed, they would be put on display in the offender's parish church in perpetuity—a reminder of the perpetrator's shame and the continued shame for their family. The most extreme judgment was reserved for the relapsed heretic. If supported by eyewitness testimony, the penalty was death by fire.

Benito had pointed out that the plaza, or somewhere near there, was the site of the Aztec Templo Mayor. At the height of their reign, the Aztecs sacrificed tens of thousands of people in public every year. Most of the sacrifices were to Huitzilopochtli, their god of war. It was a daily routine meant to ensure the sun would rise and cross the sky. Multiple other rites appropriate to the day also appeared on the Aztecs' ritual calendar. All of them involved death—most ending with hearts being ripped out. Depending on the festival and the god or gods being praised, the rites could include amputation, decapitation, burning, and cannibalism. Dogs, deer, jaguars, hummingbirds, and even butterflies fell victim. The Aztecs were a bloodthirsty lot—or at least their gods were, and the Aztecs had many.

Diego was always impressed with the knowledge Benito possessed. The Monk said this temple of the Aztecs, the Templo Mayor, had been lost to time. Cortes had it razed with all the other buildings of the Aztec capital. He used the stones to build a new Spanish city for God and the Spanish crown, a city of palaces, government and ecclesiastical offices, churches, and the first cathedral.

Diego found himself standing in front of his home. It had been an incredibly long day. He was ready for supper, a long hot bath, and a good night's sleep. He worried, though, about the dreams that might accompany the sleep.

Elena Bautista was vexed. Sometimes Diego could be so cruel. This was the second time he had abandoned her in his bed to be thrown out by his housemaid. Well, not thrown out. Maria had been considerate in both instances. She understood Elena's feelings had been hurt and how awkward it was to hear Diego had left for the day and she should probably go. *Next time!* Elena shouted to herself. She wondered whether there should be a next time but didn't think about it too long. There would be a next time because she loved Diego with all her heart despite his sometimes callous disregard of her emotions. With her confidence waning and insecurity bubbling up within her, she thought, *I think he loves me and finds me attractive.*

Elena was attractive, to be sure, but not in the alabaster fashion of the Spanish women in the royal court. At five foot six, she was olive-skinned with long, tawny hair and a not altogether slim waist. Taken together with the other attributes of her figure, she had a decided appeal. She inspected herself in the mirror—green-brown eyes with a little of each color in both, slightly curved nose, and well-proportioned mouth. The men on the Alameda would whistle and comment as she walked past, so she thought that some part of her seemed agreeable to males. She was satisfied with her firm, medium-sized breasts that stood up on their own. Turning back and forth, she scrutinized the image in the mirror. Grimacing at her reflection, she thought it was not immediately apparent, but she was still easily identifiable as mestizo. Her heart wouldn't listen to what her head kept telling her. Diego was out of her reach.

She'd met Diego at the marketplace six months before. There was an instant spark, and the attraction grew over time. They strolled together through the park and took carriage rides in the countryside. Soon they were dining together almost every evening. Eventually, they found themselves in love. It was so wonderful, so magical.

Once again, doubt snuck in as she thought, *I think he loves me.*

Elena finished dressing. There was a brisk knock on her door.

"Elena. Are you there?" It was Ana Lopez, her friend since childhood. Squat and a bit dowdy, Ana had a vibrant, gregarious personality that always made Elena cheerful when they were together. Elena opened the door and admitted Ana.

"Buenos días, Ana."

Ana didn't return the greeting but said, "Hurry, Elena. We don't want to be late, and there's lots to do this morning."

Ana and Elena were employed by Condesa Dona Andrea de Montoya. She owned an enormous mansion in the city, where they spent their time as ladies-in-waiting to the *condesa's* daughter, Dama Isabel.

"Patience, Ana. I'm nearly ready."

Ana chided her. "Moving a little slow this morning. No doubt you were out riding again last night."

Elena gave her a half smile and rolled her eyes to the ceiling. "Keep a civil tongue, Ana! Not that it's any of your business, but I just got home an hour ago.

"Ah, you were with your handsome caballero again. Isn't this the third time this week? *Ay! Venga!* Don't you realize that man will disappear one of these days? You'll have wasted precious time with him when you could've been out finding a good man to marry you."

"You don't understand. We love each other, Ana."

Ana moved closer to Elena, waving her finger and raising her voice. "He's a hidalgo, *aristócrata*! He won't marry you. He's Spanish-born. He'll marry some *Cachopin* cow just off the boat. We're mestizo. Lower than the *criollos*. It just doesn't happen."

Elena fought back her anger and didn't want Ana to see the tears welling up in her eyes, revealing her doubt. "Counting you, there are already plenty of cows in Mexico, and, if you haven't noticed, there are more mestizos than Spanish in Mexico City. Someday we'll run this country."

Ana could tell she'd gone too far. She backed away a

little, then softly said, "*Bueno. Bueno.* I'm sorry. Now let's go. You know the bitch will be in a mood today. She's in a fit preparing to pimp her daughter at the viceroy's reception Saturday. *Vamos!*"

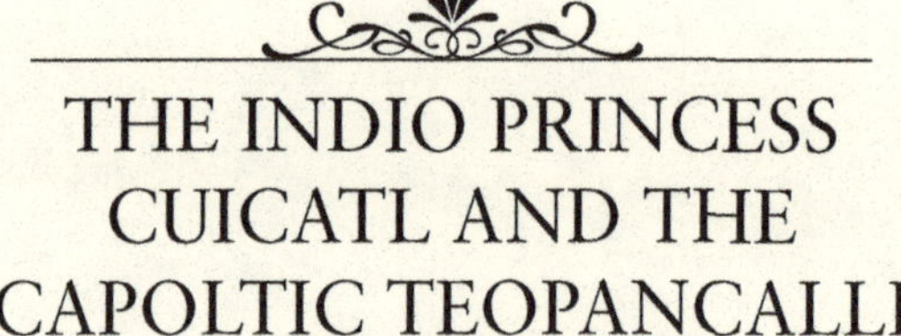

THE INDIO PRINCESS CUICATL AND THE CAPOLTIC TEOPANCALLI

August 1521 Tenochtitlan

MOCTEZUMA II WAS dead. Cuauhtémoc had succeeded him and fought bravely against Hernan Cortes, only to be captured by Cortes and installed as a puppet emperor. Cortes would later execute Cuauhtémoc for allegedly plotting against him.

Isabel was the favorite daughter of Moctezuma and her mother, Teotlalco, a Nahua princess of the Ecatepec city-state. Isabel became consort and then bride to two other men before her third marriage to Cuauhtémoc. She had arguably reigned as the last empress of the Mexica people.

As the Spanish Conquest raged, Moctezuma, foreseeing his fate, implored Cortes to treat his favorite daughters well, and he had—maybe a little too well. In the case of Isabel, she became pregnant with his child shortly after moving into his palace. Soon after Cortes became aware of her pregnancy, he quickly married her to Alonso de Grado, an officer who had been with Cortes since they arrived in the New World. Grado, Isabel, and their daughter, Lenora, would become a dynasty. That was Isabel's story.

Cuicatl had a different story as she sat and dwelled bitterly over her fate. She too was the emperor's daughter, but she was never destined to reign. Yes, she was a daughter of the emperor, but how many other daughters and sons were born to Moctezuma and any one of the thousand women who shared his bed—princesses given as tribute from neighboring tribes, women seized in battle, courtesans, and whores? Her mother was a princess of low-level nobility. That hardly registered with Moctezuma. She was a dalliance, soon forgotten. He would never see this daughter, and even if he did, he would not realize it.

Moctezuma advised his offspring not destined for nobility to "learn well the way of the artisans." That would be Cuicatl's future, a potter or a weaver of baskets or blankets. She coveted rank, but though artisans were respected for their skills, they held no form of rank that distinguished them in society. For Cuicatl, artisanship could never replace status as a royal princess. She was left to live in the house of her mother and two sisters she detested, doomed to marry a man of equal mediocrity.

The thought of all this nauseated her. It ground at her spirit. Slowly but assuredly, she forged a deep-seated hatred of all society and the men who condemned her to this fate. Eventually, she decided the world and the people in it were to be punished and exploited for her own gain—not for material goods, but for the sweet revenge she saw as her due. Cold, cruel, and calculating, Cuicatl would inflict as much pain and suffering as she possibly could. Her desire for revenge became all-encompassing. It burned into her soul and became part of her persona.

Cuicatl thought of this as a spiritual awakening, the way of life and death as she perceived them. Her understanding of truth, justice, and the value of human life became increasingly twisted each year. It became something so horrible and inhuman that it took on its own identity that was her and yet again separate from her. *Separate and divine*, she thought to herself. She began to nurture this other part of herself as a sacred being, a goddess she and all people should worship. Cuicatl attended the daily ritual sacrifices at the temple. There were thousands. She was learning the varieties of sacrifices in the Aztec traditions as they were prescribed to each god and festival in the Aztec calendar. This was when she incorporated the Aztec goddess Xochiquetzal into her myth. It was Xochiquetzal that was that separate and the same aspect of her personality.

Then came the Conquest. The war lasted almost two years. Finally, Cortes and his Indio allies, the Tlaxcalans, succeeded in their siege of Tenochtitlan. The Tlaxcalans hated the Aztecs and would have their retribution. After the fall of Tenochtitlan, an orgy of murder, rape, and looting ensued that lasted for days. Cuicatl's mother did her best to hide Cuicatl and her sisters, to no avail. A group of seven Tlaxcalans cornered them in their home and savagely beat them. The Tlaxcalans then took turns with the women. Later in the evening, during the nightmarish violence and depravity, Cuicatl saw her chance to escape.

She was on her back under a large, oafish Indio who

was crushing her with his weight. Blinded by his lust, he didn't notice as she reached around him and took the sharp obsidian blade from the sheath on his belt. She was small, but that was to her advantage. She managed to maneuver her arms under him, bringing them level with her shoulders. With a firm grip on the handle of the razor-sharp blade and using both hands, she thrust the knife upward into the man's throat with all her might and twisted it. His head tilted downward as if he could squeeze the gushing wound in his throat closed. Their eyes met. She thought the expression on his face almost comical as his lifeblood flooded from the wound onto her and then the floor. It didn't take long for him to die.

While the others were still occupied with Cuicatl's family, she took her chance. Slowly, she squirmed out from underneath him. Once freed from his weight, she crawled over his body and through the door into the night. None of the dead man's comrades noticed her escape. There was already so much blood on the floor that they couldn't tell that a good deal of it was his. Not until the morning did they realize he hadn't just passed out from the drink.

Once outside, Cuicatl moved as fast as she could. The city was in flames. She made her way to the lakeside, hidden by the smoke and chaos. Rows of fishermen's reed canoes sat tied up on the shore. She untied one of the canoes, slipped into it, and pushed off into the water. The lake was crowded with hundreds of war canoes, both Tlaxcalan and Aztec, along with the Spanish brigantines they had constructed for the battle.

Slowly, making it seem as though the canoe was only drifting with all the others, Cuicatl paddled with her arm as she lay flat in the boat. After what seemed like an eternity, the sounds of chaos in the city faded. Still fearful she'd be spotted, she lifted her head to look over the side of the canoe. Across the lake in the distance, she saw Tenochtitlan burning. She had escaped the carnage. She spent the night paddling across Lake Texcoco, praying the canoe wouldn't capsize. The water was deep in this part of the lake, and she couldn't swim. Her arms ached from paddling, but fear drove her on. She didn't rest. Finally, east of the city, she reached an island known as Tepetzinco. She struggled to pull the boat out of the water and onto the beach, and then she collapsed to the ground and slept. This would be her home until fate took her elsewhere.

Cuicatl stayed away from the few local villagers and confined herself to the island's southwestern shore. In the following days, she scavenged for food and managed on a diet of tubers, insects, and the occasional *axolotl* she caught with her hands in the shallow water. There were plenty of fish in the lake, but for now, she hadn't the skills to capture them. She knew the island was also home to a hot spring, but she shied away from that part of the island. The Aztecs had built a small temple there to Chalchiuhtlicue, the water goddess. It didn't look as though it was used much, but she feared the Spaniards might seek it out.

She explored the area around her portion of the island, looking further up the hill for some natural defense from the wind and a place to keep herself out of view of the fishermen. She caught sight of what looked to be a suitable spot, a ledge on the hillside about twenty feet up and seventy-five feet from the shore. It was an easy climb, and plenty of reeds were growing by the beach. The surface of the ledge had a triangular shape that went back another twenty feet away from the lake. This would be a good place to build her little wattle-and-daub hut.

Cuicatl started to clean out the brush in the far pocket of the triangle. She cleared an outline of what would be the floor of her jacales. Then she glimpsed a small opening at the back and to one side. Curious by nature, she thought, *This must be some creature's home dug out of the rock*. The only animals she'd seen, though, were deer, mice, and a few rats. *They did not make this opening. It must be a natural breach where these two rock faces come together.* Curiosity getting the better of her, she decided to explore. The opening was barely large enough, but she managed to squeeze through it. It seemed to open into a larger space she couldn't see. *If this proves to be bigger, it would be a better home than anything I could build. Better to build the jacales first. I can investigate this later.* She carefully positioned the small hut, hiding the rock opening from view. It took four days to cobble together a hut large enough to comfortably lie in, though not quite tall enough to stand in.

Her proficiency for foraging improved, and she added seeds and some wild greens she saw the locals harvesting. With food and shelter secured, she turned her attention back to the opening. Cuicatl fashioned a torch with dried grasses and some bitumen she'd found further along the hillside. It took her the better part of the morning to collect the correct type of dry, green wood and cut it to size for a *tletlahuitolli*. Fortunately, she had brought the Tlaxcalans' obsidian blade with her. Cutting the wood would have been tricky without it. After a minute's drilling, she had created enough friction to start a flame. The dried grass caught first, and, once the bitumen caught, she had a glowing torch.

Once again she squeezed her way through the entrance, holding the torch out in front of her. *The passage ahead looks large*, she said to herself as she crawled forward. It opened to something spacious enough for her to stand. Cuicatl stood and took a few tentative steps forward. The walls and floor were smooth, and the passage almost round. *It's all the same sort of rock.* She ran her hand along semi-smooth, grayish-black walls. She noticed the passage angled slightly downward. *If I lose the light from my torch, I could feel my way back to the entrance.*

Cuicatl had traveled more than thirty paces down the tunnel when it started to widen even further. *The ceiling is higher here.* The light continued. She kept climbing until she realized she was in a large cavern. It was a cold, empty place. Checking her torch, she noticed the flame was flickering back in the direction from which she had entered. *The way the air moves in this chamber, I suppose if I built a fire, I wouldn't have to worry about smoke choking me.* She was sure she'd found a place she could retreat to in bad weather.

She was afraid to stay too long, not knowing how long her torch might last. She returned to the entrance and crept back through and out. *I can dig this entrance out further. The rock here is more like gravel, not solid like the stone in the passageway.*

Over the following weeks, she continued to improve the opening and visited the cavern many times. She found the cavern extended more than a hundred feet before it met a passage like the entrance at the other end. She reckoned the room to be seventy feet wide and at least thirty feet high near its midpoint. *This will be my temple. The Capoltic Teopancalli of Xochiquetzal. Here, I will perform sacred rituals and minister to my followers, teaching them and practicing the secret doctrine of the Capoltic Teopancalli.*

Cuicatl's curiosity compelled her to explore the tunnel beyond the temple. *The goddess has blessed me and has shown me her holy temple. What else exists in her dark realm?* She came to a branch in the tunnel and followed it to her left. Not too much further along, she met another. For the first time, she understood she could easily get lost depending on how many branches there might be. So she improvised and on the next trip took bits of dried reed and dropped them as she walked. This was necessary because she encountered many more branches as she explored deeper into the earth. She always carried a satchel she'd fashioned containing her fire bow and dried grass, and she took further precautions against finding herself in the dark by storing spare torches along the way. But she was never afraid. The goddess worked in mysterious ways. All this was preordained for her to discover.

Cuicatl became familiar with the routes and mapped them. She started leaving clay figures as markers indicating precisely where she was in the maze of passages based on the characters she had molded. Her maps could pinpoint her position at any point in the tunnel network. *I'm passing the bird marker now. When I come to the deer marker, I know if I go left, I'll find the cat, or to the right I'll come to the tree figure.* When she came to forks she hadn't explored either left or right, or both, she marked them with an X on her map and placed a disc-like figure with an X scratched on it at the beginning of the passage.

Cuicatl came across the river during one of her trips. She heard it before she saw it—the sound of rushing water coming from ahead of her in the tunnel. It grew louder as she entered yet another cavern. It was one of the larger of the eight caverns she'd discovered. This hollowed-out chamber was different from the others, however. She saw it was just an open space between three colossal rock faces.

The space was humid and filled with the smell of sulfur. To one side, the floor angled down along a shallow slope. At the bottom, she could see a crevice with a fast-moving stream of hot water flowing from left to right. She felt the steam rising from it and billowing in the cooler air of the cavern.

I better be careful. This slope is very slick. I'll never get back out if I slide down into that. The water, she realized, was the source of the sulfur smell. She followed the stream, which ran for about thirty more feet. There the angled slope decreased until it was even with the rest of the cavern's floor. That was where the torrent of water exited the cavern and moved back to its underground route. She could get closer now without fear of slipping. Lying on her belly and holding onto an outcrop with her right hand, she reached over to the stream with her left and then quickly pulled her hand back. "*Ay, yai!*" The water was scalding hot.

As Cuicatl walked back over its length, she realized this was just a crack in the floor exposing only a portion of what must be a subterranean river hidden behind the rock face. *This must be the water source that makes its way to the surface and into the temple of Chalchiuhtlicue.*

Months went by before Cuicatl finally stopped exploring. *This labyrinth of tunnels and caverns goes on forever. I must turn my attention to serving the goddess mother.*

So, a few days later, she walked into the village and introduced herself as the high priestess Cuicatl, servant of Xochiquetzal, goddess of beauty and love. She was here to lift the village out of its poverty and save it from the Spanish invaders. She told the villagers it was only a matter of time before the Spaniards came and enslaved them all.

The villagers had become aware of Cuicatl months before. They knew she was living in her little jacales and believed she was a recluse who had somehow come to their village from some other island. Now the islanders thought she was *cuaquepi*. Over the course of days and weeks, however, they listened to her and became interested in her talks about the goddess and the church of the Capoltic Teopancalli. They were especially interested in the rewards she said would come to them.

It was apparent Cuicatl had a gift. She was charismatic and charming, yet forceful when she needed to be. She never faltered or showed a hint of doubt in what she preached. Her eyes held her audience in place as she spoke.

Cuicatl wanted to grow the number of her followers. At the same time, she wanted to keep control of the "purity" of the faith. She accepted nonbelievers but would not tolerate revisions or reductions of the sacred word. She understood that, by herself, it would be difficult to stand up to the native patriarchal leadership. A tight inner circle of true believers could act as her lieutenants and impose physical enforcement when called for.

Cuicatl didn't reveal her secrets concerning the underworld and its vast network of tunnels and caverns right away. Everything had to be in place first. She would find those in the island's population she could trust implicitly and establish her inner circle. She identified two characteristics necessary to be considered for this role—reasonable intelligence and unquestioning gullibility.

Once she had established her inner circle and was sure of their total commitment and loyalty, she would reveal her "true nature" to them alone. She was two beings incarnate—Cuicatl, high priestess of Xochiquetzal, and Xochiquetzal herself. If the disciple gave themselves over to that concept, she would reveal the hidden kingdom beneath them. These individuals would learn her doctrine, proclaim the word, and propagate the faith.

She went slowly. Over the course of six months, she identified three trusted and devoted acolytes. Now it was time to recruit the next group. They would ensure the permanence of the order. As before, she sought a specific set of characteristics for these followers. Now, aside from gullibility, she sought low intelligence and physical strength.

These would be her enforcers of the faith, *ejecutores de la fe,* as her ancestors would later call them. When necessary, they would quash any naysayers, but not blatantly at first. She had to be very selective of those she thought needed an "intervention." The following had to grow until the ratio of true believers to everyone else was about one to three. That would be enough of a power base to allow her to apply more open pressure on those who contradicted the sacred word. She knew there would always be a part of the population who wouldn't accept her doctrine. She didn't need to convert them, but she must and would dominate them.

It had nothing to do with Cuicatl or the goddess, but the Spanish never did come—a point she consistently raised as proof of her divinity. Because they had little interest in the island, over time, she would come to control communication and traffic on and off the island, thus assuring opinions contrary to her teachings would not be permitted to taint sacred doctrine on Tepetzinco.

Eventually, with a small army of followers, she built out and consecrated that first cavern she had discovered as the Capoltic Teopancalli for the worship of Xochiquetzal. It had a crude stone block dais with a wooden altar, *ocotl* torches placed in a semicircle around the dais, and nothing else. It was nothing compared to what it would later develop into during her lifetime. The temple would be transformed, filling the entire cavern with a mosaic tiled floor, paintings and statues of Xochiquetzal in all her manifestations, depictions of the sacrificial rites, and an impressive altar of three enormous blocks of green onyx.

Cuicatl purposefully denied access to tunnels beyond the temple, maintaining the mystery of what lay beyond. She knew this would enhance the personal mythos surrounding her priesthood. She would keep the river to herself until she thought of how to incorporate it into her story of Xochiquetzal.

The first sacrifices were modest affairs—slaughtering goats, feasting on their flesh, and drinking their blood. Cuicatl did this repeatedly, a hundred times at least, accurately reciting the mass until, mesmerized, everyone could recite their lines back to her without error.

The first human sacrifice was an unlucky fisherman from another island whose boat had capsized in the lake. Half dead already, he washed up onto the shore near the village. Being from another island, he was immediately held suspect by the villagers.

Some hesitated at first. But then they said, "She is the high priestess. Does she not have the authority to do such things in the goddess's name?" Attentively, they followed the words and motions of the mass just as they had been taught. Somewhere between the end of the screams and Cuicatl holding up the still-beating heart in offering, they willingly accepted the bloodlust and never questioned her again. Soon enough, the cavern was running red with the blood of the chosen. Now Cuicatl's disciples could taste the blood. Not long after that, they descended to the final rung and tasted the flesh.

Once Cuicatl was satisfied with her success and had established the dominance of the Capoltic Teopancalli with the islanders, she decided to explore the tunnels again. She traveled them enough to notice that those that branched to the south were warmer than those that ran north. One day as she continued along one of the southbound passages, she stumbled across something she had never noticed.

She was taking a new route for the first time and noticed it had grown warmer, as she expected, but then, as she entered a new cavern, Cuicatl felt it was noticeably warmer, almost hot. The cavern was about half the size of the temple. The floor was irregular and filled with jet-black swirls of motionless rock angled up like a wave all along the right side. Cuicatl counted seven fissures stretching from where she was standing to the other end of the cavern. They grew in height, each fissure larger than its predecessor. The closest was about six feet high and a foot wide, ratcheting up to the last crevice. That one stood to the full height of the cavern, twenty-five feet with a gaping eight-foot-wide opening.

A glow of red-tinted light filled the far end of the cavern. The temperature rose as Cuicatl walked along and inspected each of the fissures. Each was dark and filled with the same sort of rock to a depth of about a foot below its opening. The seventh and largest frightened Cuicatl. The scarlet light intensified as she grew nearer. She heard a low, deep rumble like a slow rockslide perceived from a distance. Both that sound and the temperature increased as she approached. She distinctly felt the rumble now beneath her feet like she was standing on the back of an enormous growling monstrosity. The sulfur smell she had experienced in the river cavern was present. Only this time, it was much more intense.

Mother Goddess! What magic is this? As she stood in front of the seventh fissure and looked down into it, she saw a reddish-gold flow of fire. *Mother Goddess, it burns my eyes to gaze upon you. I beseech you. I am humble in your presence. Protect me, your servant, and teach me that I may know the power of your being.*

Cuicatl didn't know she was staring into an exposed lava tube, part of a miles-long system emanating from and around the volcano called Popocatépetl, the smoking mountain, thirty-eight miles southeast of the island. Cuicatl decided this cavern would become a place of offering to Xochiquetzal along with the temple or *lugar de ofrenda* as it would be called later. She was delighted with her discovery.

Aside from surviving the Conquest, discovering the underground chambers and *lugar de ofrenda*, and founding her sect, all of that would likely have ended with Cuicatl's death—that is, had it not been for Gaspar de Montoya, a conquistador in the army of Hernan Cortes.

While de Montoya was reconnoitering Lake Texcoco and its islands, he came across Cuicatl living in her simple wattle-and-daub hut. He noticed her dress was too lovely to be that of a humble Indio girl, and she wore more elegant jewelry than someone who lived in a fishing village. He didn't know what to make of her, alone, living in a jacales on a desolate island. It didn't matter, though, because de Montoya was smitten with her at first sight, with her tall, straight form, black hair falling nearly to her waist, and large brown eyes that looked directly into his soul.

Cuicatl told her following she had summoned the Spaniard and would use him to spread the faith far and wide. De Montoya took her for his bride. Cuicatl became Imelda de Montoya. They used the *encomienda* he had been granted after the Conquest to amass a fortune in Michoacán. They maintained a home on Tepetzinco, and Cuicatl (Imelda) lived there most of the year. She told Gaspar she could never let go of her home and the village where she grew up, the place where they had fallen in love.

She never told him of the Capoltic Teopancalli and her alter ego. With the help of her followers, she concealed the entrance to the passage. Later, a more substantial and secure access was constructed behind the house they built on the hillside.

They built a hacienda in Michoacán just outside of Morelia. Gaspar pursued ranching and farming using the Indio labor deeded him through the *encomienda*. The *encomienda* not only granted de Montoya the land but also provided him with some two hundred villages and the work of the Indios who lived in them, a vassal state of his own.

Gaspar was a brutal landlord who managed through violence, fear, and intimidation. This worked out perfectly for Imelda, who co-opted that terror to convince the more gullible she had a way for them to survive and thrive. Her legions grew as she maintained her base in Michoacán while transplanting selected devotees to Tepetzinco. For ten generations, this continued in Michoacán and on the island in the waters of Lake Texcoco—until one of Imelda's descendants, the reigning high priestess of the Capoltic Teopancalli, made a discovery that would transport the cult to the very heart of the empire's new world.

CAPTAIN PEDRO DE ANZA

October 1754 Ciudad de México

A LITTLE BEFORE NINE in the morning, Captain Pedro de Anza made his way to the office of Don Diego de Santiago in the Palacio del Virrey. De Anza was born in the city of Arizpe in Nuevo Navarre. He had begun his military career in Mexico City after attending the Coligeo San Ildefonso, but he was quickly reassigned to Altar in Sonora, where he spent three years working to quell the Pima unrest. His commanders quickly recognized his extraordinary abilities, and their dispatches caught the eye of Viceroy Francisco de Guemes Horacasitas, who had him posted with the Audiencia.

Tall and broad-shouldered, with piercing brown eyes, a hooked nose, and a heavy black beard, he was every inch a soldier. He was an expert swordsman and liked wearing his black tricorn cockade rakishly askew with a blue ostrich feather trailing behind. He dressed flamboyantly, wearing a blue greatcoat cut to the knee, a large brass belt buckle, and black knee-high leather boots. The way he swaggered with his sword gleaming in the sun, he might have been taken for a buccaneer, but he didn't care. He loved the attention it brought him from the *doncellas* in the square. It could be said that the captain was a bit of a show-off.

"Buenos días, Don Diego." He doffed his hat and bowed slightly as he entered the office of the court's criminal attorney.

"Come, come now, Pedro, that's not the way to greet an old friend. How in God's name have you been? Well, I imagine well, judging by the weight you've put on." De Anza shot a glance of mock resentment at him. Diego began to laugh. "Just kidding, Captain. It is truly good to see you again."

De Anza's face lit up with a broad smile. "Yes, Diego, good to see you as well, although you seem shorter since last we met." They both laughed as de Anza sat next to Diego's desk.

They had worked together before. A year ago, they raided a warehouse in Veracruz run by a corrupt customs inspector. They liberated 100,000 pesos worth of undeclared trade goods from Spain and 30,000 pesos in cochineal that would have found its way out of the country equally unaccounted for.

Diego apprised de Anza of the previous day's events and the speculations made by himself and the Monk.

"All this speaks of witchcraft or some other form of dark magic," said de Anza.

Diego was surprised by de Anza's superstition but nodded in agreement while dismissing the idea of any preternatural force being behind the deed. "Leaving the corpse in the plaza could serve one of three purposes—warning, threat, or revenge," he replied.

De Anza stared into the space just beyond where Don Diego was sitting for a moment, then looked at him directly. "There is a fourth purpose."

"And what is that?" asked Diego.

"Fear!" returned de Anza.

Diego reached across his desk for a packet of cigarillos and offered one to de Anza. "I get these from a little shop by the Teatro Comedias. The woman who owns it gets her tobacco from Orizaba." They lit up and sat for a while, deeply inhaling the rich smoke.

Diego said, "Fear. Yes, Pedro. I overlooked that. But this act wouldn't affect the church, the viceroy, or his government, if they even noticed it all. No, I think we can eliminate them. So, who is left?"

"If not the church or the government, it would have to be either the *baratilleros* or the Indios. It was left in the market, and the *baratilleros* know they are not wanted in the plaza. So, possibly it was left to threaten them. However, if striking fear is the intent, then it would have to be the Indios. Their pagan superstitions would make them particularly vulnerable to such an act."

"Yes, that's true. But a lot of money trades hands in the market, a healthy amount of it graft and protection money. Perhaps a rival group is sending a signal. But I would say that any other group powerful enough to try and take control of the illegal business in the baratillo would take some other action to threaten the status quo besides dumping a burned corpse in their midst. Still, we'll need to investigate further before we can rule out the baratillo as the target."

De Anza added, "We still need to understand why and to what end the Indios would be affected before we can rule them out."

"Very true, Pedro, so we will work under both premises and follow up. For the Indios, that would mean speaking to someone acquainted with native beliefs, and for the *baratilleros*—"

De Anza stopped him short. "*El jefe de baratilleros. Alavaro Yaotl*!"

Condesa Dona Andrea de Montoya y Michoacán was as beautiful and serene as she was cold and calculating beneath her benign appearance. She was the doyenne of Mexico City society, invitations to her soirees were highly coveted, and her attendance at other's gatherings was hotly sought after.

La Condesa glanced in the hall mirror as she paced from one end of it to the other. She was pleased with what she saw. Nearing fifty, she exemplified a woman of high breeding. She wore only the latest fashions from Paris and maintained a figure that was the envy of all the ladies in this year's social register. Maybe a tinge of gray was showing in her expertly coiffed black hair, but her complexion still possessed the blush of youth.

Every eligible bachelor in Mexico knew of her, many of whom had courted her without success. She said she could love no man other than her departed husband, Count Renato de Montoya y Michoacán. The fact was that she didn't wish to marry again. Her marriage to Renato was all that was required of her to fulfill her duties as wife and mother.

Now, however, her ability to maintain her outward

serenity was deeply strained. La Condesa was troubled. She was under pressure to sell the hacienda near Morelia. Her finances were stretched to the limit. Notes were coming due, and she wasn't sure her income was sufficient to cover those and meet her other expenses.

The *encomienda* granted to her ancestor had been a gold mine for the family. Over the years, it had provided funds to build their hacienda, enter mining and mercantile businesses, and procure the title of Count de Montoya y Michoacán. However, investments made by the previous two counts had proven unwise. The Montoyas had sold their mining interests to grow their import-export venture.

Their number one export was cochineal. Cochineal was the second largest export from Mexico after silver, highly prized for the true red color it provided as a dye in textiles, cosmetics, and foods. Nothing could match it. Unfortunately, the return on investment in the export business could run into years, and financing the venture required third-party loans besides a considerable personal investment. It was a disaster for the Montoya family.

One year, the Montoyas had imported silk from the Philippines, only to find on arrival that the market had taken a downturn and a glut of silk was sitting in merchants' warehouses. The merchants cut prices to move their inventory, and the buy offers to the Montoyas sank below breakeven. They took a beating. In another year, an export shipment of cochineal went missing, presumably lost at sea. The following year, a ship carrying their import goods was lost to pirates.

After paying off their debtors, the Montoyas found themselves nearly destitute with no more funds to launch a new venture. They were forced to scrape by with the farming income. It was hit or miss from then on, depending on the harvest. All that was left of a once vast fortune were the few assets still in their possession, which included the hacienda in Michoacán, the palatial home in Mexico City, and little else. The mansion across from the cathedral and adjacent to the archbishop's palace was valuable, but the cost of upkeep was painful. Worse still, if this decline continued, and should La Condesa default on her debts, she would be forced by law to surrender the *encomienda*. It could never be restored.

La Condesa had eight children—five boys, three girls. Her husband had died when she was twenty-six years old. Now she was forty-seven, and only two of the five boys remained alive. Both were living in Spain. It had long been the Montoyas' ambition to hold Spanish land and titles, but they would need to amass a good deal more wealth to accomplish that. Besides bribes and payoffs to local officials, they had to acquire the land. So far, neither of the boys had accumulated anything close to what was necessary.

The eldest daughter, Elena, died shortly after birth. The next oldest, Gabriela, was much like her mother—ambitious, lusting for life, and willing to work for what she wanted. The youngest daughter, Isabel, well, Isabel was exceptional.

With all that was going on in her life, La Condesa was buoyed by one dark secret she kept from the world around her, hidden from her deceased husband, her sons, and her network of friends and associates. Condesa Dona Andrea de Montoya, aristocrat, beautiful patrician, and mistress of society, was, in a word, evil.

Cuicatl the Tenth—as she was known to her

followers—had inherited the cult from her mother and had been indoctrinated in its teachings and rituals from birth. The rituals were still based on the worship of the Aztec goddess Xochiquetzal. La Condesa now presided over the cabal, conducting the required blood sacrifices using the words and motions handed down for generations and taught to her by her mother.

She learned how to keep the cult stable and manage her disciples. From birth, the children were taken from their parents and brought up by the sect. In an unending stream of proselytization, the tenets of the cult were drummed into them. As they grew older, any rebellious behavior was answered with segregation from the community. They would be kept alone, not allowed to sleep, and driven to near starvation until they repented and embraced the teachings. By adulthood, most of the islanders would gladly die for the cult. Many did, happily, offering themselves up as sacrificial victims. Terror kept most others in check. Those who didn't openly conform would either become reluctant oblations in the blood ritual or simply disappear.

La Condesa trusted Gabriela to reign in her place over Tepetzinco. Eventually, she would inherit the position of high priestess. Gabriela was a formidable woman and possessed all the traits of her mother. La Condesa was not only confident in Gabriela's ability to sustain and guide the Capoltic Teopancalli but also thought Gabriela would someday expand its influence over all of Mexico. Other than Gabriela, La Condesa trusted only one other person in her orbit to carry out her directives without fail—her majordomo, Giraldo Arias de Angamuco. He steadfastly obeyed the edicts of his *condesa*. He dared not betray her.

It was a terror Giraldo had never lived without. His family had ancient ties to the Montoyas, going back generations to the time of Cuicatl. He was skinny and thin-lipped, a sixty-year-old weasel of a man with a pale and mottled complexion. Vain and supercilious, he was in the habit of wearing his powdered wig all day, every day, to hide his bald, scabby pate.

As La Condesa was taking another self-admiring glance in the mirror, Giraldo appeared at the end of the hall. "Giraldo. Where have you been all morning?" La Condesa said, not turning her gaze from the mirror. "We must be sure all preparations are complete for our appearance at the viceroy's reception tomorrow. Has Isabel's dress arrived?"

"Yes, *mi dama. La modista* is with your daughter as we speak, checking the final alterations."

"She must be the ultimate vision of beauty, grace, and splendor. I have confirmation from our agent in the palace that Miguel Torres will be in attendance."

Miguel Torres was the wealthiest man in Mexico and Nueva España. Early in his life, he had been a successful merchant. Then, in his thirties, he had invested in the silver mines of Pachuca, and his fortune skyrocketed. *This is the man who will marry my Isabel and provide the capital necessary to ensure our family's continuation far into the future. My future. Miguel Torres will see Isabel this Saturday, and he will fall in love when he does. I will see to that.*

"Giraldo, do we have the small anteroom next to the ballroom in the palace to ourselves? We cannot be disturbed. No one must have access to that room except those we've discussed."

"Yes, *mi dama*. Our agent, Alejandro, bribed the head steward and told staff the room was being redecorated and would not be available until the Monday after the reception. All the furniture has been moved out except for what we need. The room will be held vacant and for our use exclusively."

La Condesa spoke sharply. "Nothing can go wrong. After the viceroy's toast, I will usher Isabel into the chamber. Only one person may follow her—Miguel Torres! Do you understand?"

"Yes, Dama de Montoya. Only Miguel Torres."

"On another topic, tell me, Giraldo, is there any news about our admonition left in the plaza the other evening? I expect the recusants will think twice before trying to foster dissent within the faith. You're sure you've identified the leaders?"

Giraldo liked the sense of importance the question gave him. *She needs me. I'm vital to her cause.*

"Giraldo! Wake up! Have you singled out the other individuals we consider threats to the order?"

"Er, yes, yes, *mi dama*. There were only three—the one we placed in the plaza and another man and a woman."

"Very well," said La Condesa. "We'll sacrifice the man but not the woman for the time being. She isn't a candidate for the *teixiptlatini*. We need someone pure of heart for that role to ensure the offering is untainted."

The *teixiptlatini* assumed the persona of Xochiquetzal for one month. She dressed and was worshipped as the goddess mother. In the final ceremony, she would be sacrificed to Xochiquetzal, her skin flayed from her body and worn by the priest attendant, who would then proceed with a ritualistic dance, praising the goddess.

La Condesa turned away from the mirror. "I will go to Tepetzinco and visit the ancient one. He has the critical component necessary for our plan's success. Arrange my transport immediately!" Giraldo acknowledged his mistress's command and left her as she returned her gaze to the mirror.

Isabel de Montoya y Michoacán was twenty-five years old and stunningly beautiful. One could say a singular beauty and not be overstating it. Five foot five with unblemished skin and jet-black hair, she possessed a perfect figure, full-bosomed and narrow-waisted with an admirable derriere. Yet her beauty was not all that was distinctive about Isabel.

To be sure, measuring a specific quality in a human being is difficult. It is subjective, and there are no established benchmarks. However, if a scale existed, Isabel could rank as the dullest, most boring, and most insipid woman ever to walk the planet. Five minutes with Isabel could seem like an eternity. She was a facade with nothing behind it, a face staring with a blank expression, a mind that begged no explanation and employed no curiosity. She had lived a life without once raising an eyebrow. She was woman incapable of interrogative speech, the antithesis of Socrates.

Born in Michoacán, Isabel was brought up and educated by the sisters of the *San Francisco de Tzintzuntzan* convent. She rarely had contact with her mother and hardly knew her father. Exhibiting a careless attitude, she seemed to glide through life. It wasn't that Isabel was unintelligent, but she was supremely disinterested in practically everything. She would neither start nor end a conversation unless, of course, it was with herself. Without questions put to her directly, she would rarely speak at all.

Despite this, Isabel did possess one other unique and genuinely remarkable characteristic that set her apart from other girls—her sex drive. She wasn't a nymphomaniac by the clinical definition. She wasn't compulsive or addicted to sex, but once engaged in the act, she was almost inhuman in her gusto. There was no constraint to her enthusiasm, an unstoppable force with her true anima exposed and driving a seemingly unquenchable appetite.

Once, when Isabel was a young woman, a youthful gardener cornered her behind a topiary of Saint John the Baptist in the convent's garden. His libido played out quickly. She, however, hadn't even gotten started. Her absence at dinner initiated a search. The nuns found her and the boy under the topiary. Isabel was sitting with her head tilted upward, her teeth clenched, still rocking. The nuns had to pull her off. The boy nearly suffocated. The sisters awarded her the title *la Bestia* and, from that point forward, they isolated her from the male population at the convent.

Each of us has our cross to bear. This was Isabel's. Oddly, it did not raise a concern with her mother, La Condesa. She would have it no other way, for, in her mind, the beautiful Isabel had one purpose and one purpose only.

"I have prepared the item you requested, Your Holiness." The wizened arm of the old man reached out. He grimaced with pain as he tried to control the dry, parchment-covered collection of bones that was his hand. He kept his tenuous grip long enough to deliver the stained white cup to his mistress. La Condesa took the cup from him. It was fashioned from a prenatal human skull she knew to be female, a sacred receptacle that imbued its life force and power to the philter contained within it, a philter not to be underestimated in terms of its potency.

"I pour this into his drink, and then what?" asked La Condesa.

"Then the charm will be cast. Any man who drinks this and sees a woman wearing the necklace of Cuicatl with its green topaz set within it will be beguiled by her mystique and under her power. It is not a love philter. Such a thing does not exist. But that woman will have a dominating influence over the man. He will only believe he is in love."

"And how long will this last?" asked La Condesa.

"It's difficult to say, Your Holiness. It will depend on the man. It could be weeks or months. But he must encounter the necklace and its wearer immediately after drinking the potion. The jewel's radiance identifies the *objeto de su obsesión.*"

La Condesa pondered the length of the drug's effect for a moment. She knew it wasn't magic. *It must last only long enough for the marriage banns to be read. Miguel Torres is a gentleman. He won't back out once the charm has lost its potency.*

The old man added, "Be aware. The taste is impossible to conceal. He will think he has drunk something foul. Indeed he has. But that will pass very quickly, and shortly he will be overwhelmed by a sense of extreme euphoria, which will transform to obsession for the one wearing the necklace. He will be drawn in by the radiant green glow of the topaz."

La Condesa felt ready. *By the end of tomorrow evening, Don Torres will be infatuated with Isabel. All Isabel or I need to do then is press the engagement. Once the priest has proclaimed the marriage at mass, the deed will be done. His wealth will be mine to control!*

Don Diego called for Maria as he walked through the front door of his home. A sound came from the rear of the house, and, shortly after, he saw Maria shuffling toward him across the courtyard from the kitchen. "Buenas noches, Maria. Is there a chance I could get breakfast early tomorrow morning? I have an early appointment. It's been a long day, and I'll be retiring soon."

Maria had a look of disapproval on her face as she replied. "*Sí*, but perhaps you'd want to speak to your guest. She arrived not five minutes ago."

"Guest?" Diego replied.

Maria answered sternly. "*Sí*, Señorita Bautista. You know, the woman you left in your bed yesterday morning."

Diego dared not confront Maria on this topic for fear of her withering response and because he knew she held the moral high ground. "I see. Thank you, Maria."

Diego opened the door to the drawing room to see Elena standing next to his bookcase, holding a volume of poems. "Buenas noches, Elena."

"Diego," she replied.

"I'm sorry I had to leave you without saying goodbye yesterday morning. There was urgent business. I had to leave quickly. Eh, a situation in the plaza." He moved toward her, and it was at that moment he saw the tears in her eyes.

She said, "I suppose that's something I should get used to. Whatever works with your schedule. A mestizo lady-in-waiting and the gentleman attorney. I'm a fool, Diego."

"No, no, Elena. You know how I feel about you. You're wonderful, everything I've ever dreamed of, but—"

"But what, Diego? We can never work. You can never marry me, a mestizo, an Indio."

"That's not it," Diego said, cradling her face in his hand and looking into her eyes. "You know I love you, and, in my heart, I believe you love me."

"I do love you, Diego."

"Then please be patient. I want you more than anything else in the world. Give me time so I can find a way for us to be together. Together forever." He drew her close and kissed her, softly at first and then harder as she responded. They fled upstairs, and their passionate lovemaking stretched late into the evening, alternating between tender, lingering kisses and devouring each other. He was sure. This time he would not leave her alone in the morning.

The following day found them naked in each other's arms. They woke, and he whispered, "I love you." Elena smiled and closed her arms around him. Diego said, "I must meet my colleagues at the palace this morning. That incident in the plaza I told you about."

"Incident?" queried Elena.

"I didn't want to frighten you, but a disturbing murder occurred Thursday morning. It's why I had to leave so quickly. I'm only involved in this because of the location and nature of the killing. The body was found on the cathedral steps. The poor man had been burned alive."

"Sounds horrible."

"It was. I'm hoping we can bring the perpetrators to justice soon."

Diego traced his fingers over the tanned skin of her shoulder. He was obsessed with her skin's soft cocoa color, its flawless texture, its scent, and, yes, its flavor. He continued lightly down her perfect arm until he reached the ever-present turquoise bracelet—an Indio bracelet with eight azure-colored turquoise stones strung together on twisted silver strands. Two clasps at either end secured it to a simple leather tie that fit her wrist. Elena had told him it was her grandmother's and had been handed down in the family for generations. Diego kissed her shoulder, tasting its warmth.

He raised his head and said, "Elena, there is one other thing. I promised my uncle I would attend the viceroy's evening reception. I'm sorry I didn't mention it before, but I only found out yesterday myself."

Elena smiled at him. "Well, it's a small world, Diego. My mistress, Dama Isabel de Montoya, and her mother, La Condesa, will also be there."

"I'd rather not go," said Diego.

Elena smiled at him again, laughing as she pulled the bed linens over their heads. "I wish you wouldn't." They were late for breakfast.

AN EVENING WITH THE VICEROY

THE MONK WAS a few minutes late to meet with de Anza and Don Diego in Diego's office. Diego and de Anza looked refreshed while the Monk looked bedraggled with his bloodshot eyes and disheveled hair.

The Monk looked at Diego. "You wouldn't have anything tucked away in here for a suffering catechumen, would you, Brother Santiago?"

Diego gave him a straight-lipped smile and produced a bottle of tequila and a glass from a cabinet behind his desk. He gestured to de Anza as if to ask if he'd like one. De Anza silently shook his head.

"Bless you, my son," said the Monk. "Your place in God's heaven is assured." Then he downed two quick shots and handed the bottle back to Diego.

Catechumen. Whenever Benito spoke of himself in the third person, he referred to himself as a novitiate or postulant. Diego suspected he'd been ordained in the church at one time.

De Anza did not think much of the Monk and wondered why Diego placed so much stock in him. To de Anza, the Monk was just a big clumsy drunk and worse.

Don Diego quickly brought Benito up to date, summarizing his discussion with de Anza of the day before.

The Monk leaned forward. "Sounds like a reasonable plan. Do you want me to look into the possible motives behind the Indios as the target?"

"That would be me. I've got it," said de Anza.

"Benito, we need to follow up on the baratillo being the target. The killer is possibly someone trying to move in on the illegal trade or to clear the plaza," said Diego.

"It's been tried," said the Monk. "Sixty years ago, after the riot of '92, they succeeded, but it took an army. Once they cleared the plaza and tried to replace the baratillo with the merchants' exchange—the *Parian*—but the *baratilleros* slowly filtered back in. It seems only the royals wanted them gone, and they failed."

De Anza spoke next. "Still, what if this was aimed at Yaotl and his *matones*?"

Benito said, "Much money is involved. Merchants in the baratillo speak on their behalf when necessary."

"Yes," said Diego. "They parlay with the *ayuntamiento*, politicos, and the other merchants. The politicos want to keep the people happy and need the merchants' support in elections. The *ayuntamiento* collects its rent and turns a blind eye to what goes on under the surface. The merchants work with them to funnel contraband through the market and Alavaro."

A look of disgust came over Diego's face. "He hangs

back and collects his *quinto real*. There isn't a peso's worth of business that goes through the market from which Alavaro doesn't collect his twenty centavos in protection money. Fear and intimidation are his stock in trade. You either pay or your stall suspiciously burns down, or, worse, you lose a couple of fingers, perhaps your life. No, the more we discuss it, the more I'm beginning to believe the *baratilleros*, good or bad, are not the target here. It must be the Indios."

"Perhaps," the Monk interjected. "And perhaps Yaotl can shed some light on this even if it is the Indios. He may know who could have placed that unfortunate soul in the plaza. I don't like him, but he knows what goes on there, and we can only speculate. What do you think, amigos?"

De Anza scowled. "Listen, Monk, I may agree you've got something there, but I am not your amigo."

Diego was startled at de Anza's outburst. He tried to gloss over it by quickly commenting, "So, it's resolved. We talk to Alavaro. Benito, I think you're best suited for that task. Yaotl probably wouldn't feel comfortable or want to be seen with two representatives of His Majesty's government. Yes?"

"Well, er, yes, I suppose that's true," said the Monk, a little taken aback at de Anza's hostility. "Probably best I wait until after dark. The night market, the *tianguillo*, attracts his shadier clientele. It's when he cuts deals with the other crime bosses in the city. He's bound to be present."

"Good," Diego said. "Now, how do we answer the question of the Indios?"

"I'll go see Padre Aranda at the university," said de Anza. "He knows the Indios' concerns and struggles better than anyone. He has connections in every barrio in the city. If there's anything he doesn't know, he'll put me in touch with someone who does."

"Excellent, Pedro, Benito," said Diego.

With that, the Monk rose. "I'll tell my informants I'm trying to get in touch with Alavaro this evening. I don't think it will be difficult to find him there. He's a brash character and doesn't hide in the shadows."

The Monk departed. Diego turned to de Anza. "What was that about? You've only just met him. Why so antagonistic?"

"I don't know him," de Anza replied, "but I know of him. He was a Jesuit padre at the mission in Altar when I was there with the Catalan volunteers fighting the Pimas. He was well known and respected then." De Anza assumed a mocking tone as he finished the sentence.

"Then you know the story behind Benito de Avila."

"Yes, I know it, and I tell you, I have no respect for that man. He should rot in hell, and I'm sure he will." An angry look came over his face. Whatever he was about to say, Diego wasn't sure he wanted to hear it.

De Anza started, "I'd been in Altar for a little over a year when it happened. Things had settled with the Pima, and we had good relations with the Papago tribe. The mission had established itself with a permanent stone church, a refectory, gardens, workshops, and an Indio school. Padre de Avila taught in the school and ran the *clínica medico* seeing to the health of the *misioneros*, soldiers, settlers, and Indios.

"A young Indio woman assisted him in the *clínica*. Her family had been killed in an Apache raid when she was young. All were brutally murdered, and she was left for dead. The padre taught her Spanish and the basics of medicine. She was very bright, a capable assistant, and beautiful as well." De Anza paused, controlling the anger in his voice. "God knows we are all men, Diego, but he was a man of the cloth." He took a few seconds, then continued. "They were caught together one evening in his cell, fornicating, brazen in their nakedness. They were arrested and locked in the stockade.

"The Inquisition tribunal may be here in Mexico City, but there are also commissioners throughout Nueva España, and there was one in Altar. The inquisitors interrogated them for three weeks. You know what unspeakable methods they employ in their search for confessions. The padre and the Indio were judged, and a private *auto de fe* was held with just the inquisitors, the mission pastor, and the commandant of the presidio. De Avila was defrocked, flogged, and sentenced to a year's hard labor. The Indio woman, however, was thought to be a witch who had enticed and entrapped the Jesuit priest. She was flogged then strangled to death in his presence."

Diego was stunned. He had known Benito for years and knew him to be a good man. The story de Anza recounted was nightmarish. A man was ruined and a woman was murdered for being human. Diego was sure Benito and the woman were in love and it was more than just some lascivious act they had committed.

"I understand your revulsion, Pedro, but I know Benito to be a kind, caring person. There was no equanimity in their punishments, but can you imagine how he must suffer every day of his life?"

"His punishment is still ahead of him," said de Anza. "God will see to it."

Diego said nothing after that. De Anza stood and left

the office. Diego just sat there in silence. All he could think of was Elena.

De Anza walked down the Calle de Justo Sierra toward the front of the school. He felt nostalgic as he recalled his days at the Colegio San Ildefonso. He was grateful for the education the Jesuit priests provided him. They had a more objective worldview than the Franciscan and Dominican orders. He was introduced to the sciences, art, world history, and Latin and Greek and graduated with a liberal arts degree. He was young and hopeful then, his days filled with warmth and sunshine. His military career had changed all that. He was no longer the idealistic young man he had once been, and cynicism informed his outlook much more than it had in his youth.

It would be good to see his old history professor and friend Padre Pablo Aranda. The padre was originally from Valladolid in the Yucatán and was impressed by the Maya and their culture. Over many years as an academic scholar, he produced volumes of works documenting many of the native Indio peoples, their histories, and their cultures. No one in Mexico knew more about the Nahuatl than he.

De Anza walked through the arcade and took the stairs up to the second level, where Aranda kept a small office. He was semiretired now and no longer taught but continued to pursue his scholarly work.

Aranda greeted de Anza as he appeared at the door. "Pedro! Pedro! How wonderful to see you, my son." He extended the crucifix attached to his rosary, and de Anza kissed it.

"Padre Santo, it is no less wonderful for me. Have

I come at a bad time?" Aranda was a small man in his declining years, but he stood straight, and his smiling eyes belied a man still keen and engaged.

"Pedro, my dear son. At this point in my life, all I have is time. I can well afford to spare you some. But please, let us sit outside. It grows warm this time of day in my study." They moved to a small bench in a shady section of the second-floor arcade. "Now, Pedro, how can I help you?"

"Padre, something has happened. A death—no, a murder—and my colleagues and I are trying to understand its motive."

"This wouldn't have anything to do with the scorched figure found in the Plaza Mayor, would it?"

De Anza was amazed. "Padre, how could you know?"

Aranda tilted his head a little, "Pedro, Mexico City is indeed a large city, but in some respects, it is still quite small. Word travels fast in my channels, especially when something like that occurs."

De Anza nodded and asked, "And you believe this is a result of some ritual based on pagan belief?"

"Burned alive with his heart torn out? That is not the modus operandi of your common street thug or hired killer. I'm familiar with the practice, and I'm sure the people behind this don't think they are pagans. Let me tell you what I know.

"You are aware of Mexico's history, and that of Mexico City. It was the former capital of the Aztecs. That civilization lasted hundreds of years, but its culture and other tribes in the Valle de México are much older and go back thousands of years. Kings, governments, and buildings disappear, but cultures are inherited by the people and last much longer. The Indios still speak the Nahuatl language, and many, not just the Aztecs, still pay respect to the old gods and goddesses.

"Much has changed for these people since the Conquest. Now the Indios are considered vassals of His Royal Highness and citizens of Nuevo España. Almost all of them have converted to the Catholic faith. They have their own government patterned after ours. Several of their old customs and beliefs still exist in the open, however, and have only been modified by us Christians. I'm saying, Pedro, that culture endures, and the Indio people of Mexico City are good Christians and very religious. Beneath that, traces of the old culture still exist. I'm afraid their superstitions also do. Religion is a strength, but superstition is a weakness and can be exploited. I believe this unholy act was intended to frighten the Indios who still hold on to some of those superstitions—not all Indios, but a significant number of them."

"Who would that be?"

"Long ago, while researching my histories of the tribal peoples and their cultures, I became aware of underground cults operating in the native communities. They're mostly short-lived, coming into existence, then, after a time, fading away. One seems to have survived over many years. Perhaps hundreds. The reason cults exist is not surprising. In most cases, they answer a need current dogma doesn't—a promised cure to ills, social or spiritual.

"They thrive on the poorly educated, the superstitious, and the gullible. Often, they form around one or a few charismatic personalities, promising an answer to all these needs and more. In some instances, drugs can be involved, typically reserved for a *teopixqui* or Nahuatl shaman. The sect feeds the participants mushrooms before a rite or ritual to induce an out-of-body or spiritual effect.

"Cults are held together with a mixture of guilt, fear, intimidation, and hope. Yes, Pedro, hope. The people drawn to these sects often have none and are desperate to find it. That can overcome many doubts."

"Padre, do you think it possible this group was responsible for the victim in the plaza?"

"More than possible. Probable. It was either a message or a reprisal, maybe both."

De Anza had to process for a minute. It seemed bizarre to him that something as odd as Aranda described could still exist.

"Thank you, Padre. This information has been most helpful. I'll share it with my colleagues."

"No need to thank me. I wish you had more time to catch me up on what you've been doing since your time here at the school. If memory serves, this marks only the third visit in all these years. I'm old, and many friends have departed this world." Aranda affected a sad, downward smile. "I'll tell you what. I will make some inquiries through my sources. Come back in a few days, and I'll tell you what I've learned. Bargain?"

"Bargain," said de Anza.

Then the priest rose and, facing de Anza, said, "May the blessings of the Lord be upon you, Pedro. *Vaya con Dios.*"

As the sun sank behind the *Portal de Mercaderes*, its shadow was extending further into the plaza, and the stone face of the viceroy's palace took on the reddish hue of its dying light.

The Monk was standing at the east end of the *ayuntamiento*, waiting for the street rascal, Esteban, to arrive. It was the Monk who had introduced Esteban to Diego. The child was one of dozens the Monk looked after at his self-proclaimed mission.

It wasn't a proper mission. For one thing, it had no roof. It was only a location. Walking southwest from the Plaza Mayor to the Indio barrio of San Juan Moyotla, you would find it in one corner of the Plaza de San Juan. Even without a building, it was well known, and the Monk never failed to receive his flock there three days a week from noon until three in the afternoon. On some days, upward of a hundred hungry, sick, and barely clothed children would come looking for something to eat, medical assistance, or someplace to sit for a while, knowing they were safe there.

The visits started at noon because the Monk spent the first part of the day hungover from the night before. He would get his morning *pulque* and shake off the cobwebs. By noon, he would be in his spot in the plaza, distributing food and speaking to each of those who had come to him. Most were not seeking spiritual assistance. Their needs were much more secular in nature. He would not preach or quote any of the Gospels, but he would share the parables of Jesus if they applied to the questions the children might have. To all of them, he was indeed a holy man.

"Buenas noches, Padre!" The Monk nearly jumped out of his skin as the boy appeared from out of nowhere directly behind him. The Monk had told the boys repeatedly he was not a padre, but they persisted, and he eventually gave up. With a disdainful look on his face, the Monk chastised the boy.

"Esteban. Must you always startle me like that?" The boy looked back at him, hurt but not afraid. The Monk put a hand on Esteban's shoulder. "Don't fret, *hombrecito*. It's just that I was deep in thought, and you gave me a turn."

"I'm sorry, Padre."

"Don't worry, Esteban. I'm over it. Now we have work to do." He had agreed that either Diego or the captain attempting to contact Yaotl would prove useless. He wasn't sure his attempt would be fruitful, but he had said he would try.

Yaotl was known to occupy a shaded area around a small *taquería* on the eastern edge of the plaza, where he would hold court in full view of the viceregal palace. For his protection, he had sentries posted all around the plaza and was accompanied by his inner circle of associates and five bodyguards. If the Monk were to march straight up to Yaotl, he would most likely be stopped before he got close. His best bet was to send the boy ahead to ask for an appointment. That showed respect. Esteban was well known in the baratillo. The Monk was proven correct when Esteban returned and told him Yaotl would receive him. *Receive me?*

The Monk started across the plaza with Esteban at his side. As he came close to the unsavory group, the bodyguards instinctively tightened their ranks. Benito might be dressed as a monk, but his imposing stature and build were not to be ignored.

"Buenas noches, Señor Yaotl. I am Benito Avila. I am seeking your help. I won't take much of your time." Usually, the Monk would suspend judgment on a person until he had a chance to get to know them a little, but all that was going through his mind now was, *This does not look like a nice man.* Yaotl was short and stout, bordering on fat. He had an enormous round, flat face with beady eyes, two upturned nostrils, and an unnaturally small mouth, none of which seemed to protrude from his flat face. It was as though his features were carved into his melon head. This was not his stand-out physical feature, however. A long, deep scar ran from his upper right temple diagonally across and down his face and nose, ending at the bottom left of his jaw. Again, the Monk thought, *This does not look like a nice man.*

Yaotl spoke, revealing a severe lisp as he did. "What is it you want, thinior Avila?"

"I believe you heard about the murdered man found in the plaza Thursday morning."

Yaotl smiled for the first time. The Monk couldn't help thinking, *Does that hurt?*

"Of course, I heard. Nothing goes on in this city, let alone the plaza, I do not hear about."

"That's fortunate. If you're aware of it, you might be able to tell me a bit more about it."

"Why should I know anything more about it? You think I'm involved?"

The Monk chose his next words carefully. "Apologies, señor. I didn't mean to imply you were. But, as you say, you know much of what transpires in this city. Perhaps you were privy to some proximate bit of knowledge."

The smile disappeared from Yaotl's pie-like face. "Listen. I know who you are, padre who's not a padre, and I know you work with that *fiscal del crimen* Santiago. Tell the bastard if he wants to know something, he can come here and ask for himself. I don't know anything about any dead man." Yaotl cocked his head and said with finality, "I'm afraid our time together is ended." The largest of the five bodyguards came up to the Monk and grasped his upper left arm.

"You have a firm grip, señor," the Monk said and slowly put his hand on the man's opposite shoulder. They held that pose briefly as the man looked threateningly into the Monk's eyes. The Monk looked straight back at him, gave him a half smile, and began to squeeze. The man smiled back at first but shortly broke out into a grimace and then, almost as quickly, fell to his knees in agony.

The Monk released his grip, looked at Yaotl, and said, "Buenas noches, señor."

Yaotl looked back at the Monk and, in a low, hostile tone, said, "Buenas noches, thinior."

Juan Francisco de Guemes y Horacasitas, the viceroy of Nueva España, strode into the *Palacio del Virrey* reception hall, resplendent in his viceregal attire. He was the living expression of King Ferdinand VI's presence in Nuevo España. De Guemes had been viceroy for eight years. He was seventy-three years old. Only a few knew he was planning to resign and return to Spain in the coming year. He was secure in his reputation, and not many would argue he hadn't performed well during his tenure as viceroy.

He whispered to his secretary standing next to him, "*Dios me salve*, Alfonso! Tell me there's a way to reduce the number of these infernal receptions. I've grown tired of highbrow *peninsulares* fawning over me, not to mention the same contingent of sycophants present at all these affairs."

Alfonso whispered back, "I'm afraid little can be done, Your Eminence. It is expected. Your office demands you entertain the more elevated of the king's vassals with your presence aside from official state visits—the wealthy scions of the old families and the ascendant merchants and businesspeople, men like Miguel Torres over there."

"Where, Alfonso?"

"There, standing at the entrance. He must have just arrived. They call him the silver king. I'm told he is spoken of in His Majesty's court. Torres has been generous in his endowments and has gained much recognition through them."

Guemes gave a short sigh. "I suppose you're right, Alfonso, but I have to say I will not miss this."

So, as the viceroy stood in place, smiling his most regal smile, the reception line slowly made its way past him. The men bowed, and the ladies curtsied. They smiled and mentioned how delighted they were to be in his company. All the while, Guemes dreamed of his upcoming hunting trip in Cuernavaca.

In his turn, Miguel Torres addressed the viceroy, bowed, and said, "So happy to see you, Your Eminence. I so look forward to your visit to my hacienda. I won't forget our bet when you bring down the stag with the best rack of antlers. Five hundred pesos to the charity of your choice."

The viceroy smiled. "Miguel, I have already begun to regret that bet. Please, let me introduce you to my private secretary, Alfonso Delgado. Alfonso, this is Don Miguel Torres." He added with a smile and a theatrical flourish, "The silver king!"

Torres laughed. Alfonso meekly said it was a pleasure.

"Miguel, your man can talk to Alfonso about the travel arrangements." Delgado felt the fool that Guemes hadn't let on he was already acquainted with Torres.

"Of course," said Torres, nodding to Alfonso as he moved on.

Guemes enjoyed chatting with a few of the seventy or so people attending the reception. He brightened when he saw Don Felipe de Carceres making his way across the room.

"Your Eminence. Good evening."

"Don Felipe. A pleasure beyond your comprehension. I was just about to leap from the balcony."

De Caceres laughed. "Come now, Francisco. It can't be all that bad. These things usually break up early. Besides, I understand La Condesa de Montoya is in attendance. She is an absolute vision, and she brought her daughter Isabel."

"Felipe, you know I'm a married man. Maria would hardly think well of me if she knew I was discussing the single women here this evening."

Felipe nudged him. "It doesn't hurt to look. By the way, I'd like to introduce you to the son of my old friend. He's one of the *fiscal de crimen* and works with me from time to time. Don Diego de Santiago."

"Yes, I've heard of him. I understand he's prosecuted several important cases and brought a substantial amount of silver back into the treasury. It would be a pleasure to meet him."

Just at that moment, as if presaged, Carceres saw Dona Andrea and Isabel de Montoya approaching them. Carceres quickly managed a half bow and spoke. "Condesa de Montoya. What a pleasure it is to see you once again."

"And you, Don Felipe. I trust you've been well. May I introduce my daughter Isabel?"

Isabel smiled and curtseyed but did not speak.

The viceroy bowed to Isabel, took Dona Andrea's hand, and kissed it. "I was telling Don Felipe that these functions, while sometimes a bit dull, have their moments of sunshine. You, dear lady, have provided such a moment."

Don Felipe thought, *What would Maria say to that line?*

"Your Eminence is an unabashed flatterer, but I thank you all the same. Please say hello to Maria Josefa on my behalf."

Guemes coughed slightly. "Er, well, yes, of course."

Don Felipe said, "Dama Isabel, I must remark on your stunning necklace. Is that a topaz?"

Dona Andrea spoke for her daughter. "Yes. It's a family heirloom going back to the sixteenth century. I told Isabel she could wear it for this special occasion."

"Unique," said Carceres. "The color and reflection are amazing, almost mesmerizing. In any case, I was just about to introduce my good friend Don Diego de Santiago to His Eminence. I'm sure he would be equally pleased to meet you, ladies." They smiled and nodded simultaneously as Carceres stepped away to fetch Diego.

Guemes recovered from the *dama*'s quip and asked, "Condesa, are you and your daughter staying in the city, or will you be returning to Michoacán for the holidays?"

"We'll be here through the end of the year. The holidays are much more festive in the city compared to the countryside. The parties are so provincial in Michoacán. I'll take advantage of the parties to introduce Isabel to Mexico City's polite society."

Don Diego was speaking with Miguel Torres when Felipe found him. Torres was enjoying his conversation with Diego, so they both accompanied him back to the viceroy's group.

As the group exchanged introductions, no one noticed the Montoyas' majordomo, Giraldo Arias de Angamuco, was standing at the rear of the room. Next to him was their spy in the palace, Alejandro Hernandez. He had many responsibilities in the palace, but this evening he had juggled the roster to ensure he served as a steward for the reception.

Angamuco spoke to him out of the side of his mouth. "This is our opportunity. Remember—as you serve the drinks, be sure Torres gets the glass with the tick mark on the bottom. Immediately after the toast, La Condesa will feign a dizzy spell, and she and Dama Isabel will retire to the antechamber. Then I'll tell Torres La Condesa wishes to speak with him privately and guide him to the chamber. Again, no one else is to enter that room. Understand?"

"*Sí*, Giraldo, *claro*."

La Condesa ingratiated herself with de Santiago and Torres, beaming as she spoke. "Señor Torres, I think everyone in Mexico is familiar with your reputation for generosity—the mission you funded in Sonora, the schools in Oaxaca, not to mention the convent in Cuernavaca."

Torres demurred. "I cannot take the credit for all these things, my dear *condesa*. It's God's will, and I only act as his humble servant on Earth."

Diego interjected. "Please, señor, you must temper your humility somewhat and accept a margin of the gratitude everyone feels for these beneficent gestures."

Torres raised his hand and waved the compliment

aside. "If anything, we must thank La Condesa and her lovely daughter for gracing us with their beauty and Viceroy de Guemes for hosting this evening." Isabel, not used to this level of social gatherings or to compliments such as Torres', blushed and looked embarrassed.

Diego thought, *Yes, what a comely young woman.* He felt a little sinful as he surveyed her ample décolletage.

Dona Andrea, seeing the cue from Angamuco and knowing this was her chance, said, "Yes, we must thank our esteemed viceroy. May I propose a toast?"

Felipe agreed heartily and motioned for the wine steward. Hernandez approached, and Felipe said, "I think champagne for this toast. Steward, would you kindly accommodate us?"

Without expression, Alejandro simply said, "*Sí*, señor." He walked away and was back shortly with six glasses of champagne.

Dona Andrea unconsciously pursed her lips and readied herself for the dance she had choreographed in advance for herself, Isabel, and Torres.

Alejandro approached the group and skillfully offered the six glasses on the tray. He circled the group, keeping the one meant for Torres closest to him. Each took their glass from the tray until only two remained, Diego's and Torres'. Diego reached to take his glass. Suddenly, a very large woman in a bell-shaped ball gown barreled past them and bumped into Diego. Instead of grasping his drink, he knocked it over, sending it and its contents to the floor.

"A thousand pardons! What an oaf I am," declared Diego.

Attempting to deflect some of Diego's embarrassment,

Torres took his glass and handed it to Diego. "Please take mine." He turned and asked the steward to bring another glass.

Dona Andrea was enraged. *What should I do now? That man Santiago will drink the philter meant for Torres. I must get Isabel and the necklace away from here.*

Too late, Torres grabbed a glass from another passing steward and laughingly said, "This will do." Raising his glass, he said, "If I may be so bold, Condesa, I propose a toast to the ladies and to His Eminence Juan Francisco de Guemes y Horacasitas, forty-first viceroy of New Spain. Good health and long may he reign!"

There was no way for Dona Andrea to stop this as together they raised their glasses.

As Diego drank, he immediately tasted what he thought at first was an off vintage. Still, as he swallowed, the taste swiftly evolved into something sickening, and he instantly felt faint. He looked down at his glass and was about to comment when he looked up. There, nestled in the décolletage he had admired just moments before, was the gleaming green topaz.

The topaz seemed to radiate a light of its own. Glinting shafts of alternating green and gold emanated from the jewel in every direction, reflecting on the soft curves of Isabel's breasts. Then, not knowing how long he had stared at the gem, bewitched by the illumination, he looked up to see Isabel. Her dark eyes were wide and fixed on Diego's.

THE MORNING AFTER

DON DIEGO DE Santiago woke at six the following day to a fearsome hangover. At least, that's what it felt like. He tried to put together the events of the previous evening. He remembered Isabel, the topaz, and then nothing. *No, wait.* He remembered hearing Don Felipe's voice.

"Diego, Diego, what's wrong? Summon a doctor!"

After that, he had just flashes of memories. A few people helped him walk, he was riding in a carriage, and then Maria Rosales, his housemaid, screamed hysterically, "Dieguito! Oh, Dieguito. What has happened to him? Oh, Diego." It was all a mishmash.

A few hours later, after some ministering from Maria with cold compresses and two mugs of *xocolatl*, he remembered the dream that came to him in the night. It had to have been a dream.

He was climbing a broad and steep stone staircase with narrow steps. He was afraid he would fall back down the stairs if he didn't watch his step. Then he did. He didn't feel himself tumble down the stone steps. Instead, he felt like he was falling through space and watching the staircase melt away.

Minutes passed, and he was still falling. He closed his eyes. Opening them, he found himself floating in an aquamarine pool of water. It was warm and pleasant. He was tranquil and wanted to remain in the water's warm embrace.

He heard someone softly calling his name and saw a figure in the distance lit from above. It was Isabel standing in the water up to her navel. She was naked save for a glittering headdress of gold and turquoise with a tall fan of blue-green quetzal feathers. She looked like a goddess.

Isabel brought her arms straight out in front of her, upturned palms beckoning Diego toward her. He didn't have to move on his own. A current was carrying him slowly toward her. Then it began to gain speed. Now Isabel was gone, and he was moving faster and faster. He was hurtling toward a horizon ahead of him. He heard the thunderous crash of water cascading over a precipice like an enormous waterfall. The cool air formed by the convection of the falling water flew over him, and fine droplets of water rained over his body. He sensed the abyss ahead of him. He was getting closer, moving faster and faster. He bolted upright in bed and as quickly fell back and slept. That was all he could remember. *It must have been a fever dream.*

Diego had to talk to de Carceres. Felipe could fill in the parts of the evening lost to him. He summoned Maria and asked her to send word to him, Benito, and de Anza to come to the house.

She said, "No need. They're both downstairs, along with the alcalde of Carceres. He brought you home last night and hasn't left."

"Why didn't you tell me earlier, Maria?"

"It was obvious you needed more time to clear your head, and the alcalde told me not to hurry you. You would come when you were ready. The other two just arrived. Do you want them to come up?"

"No, thank you, Maria. Please tell them I will be down shortly." Diego, his head still aching, began to dress.

Don Felipe's face was grave with concern when Diego walked into the drawing room. Still weak, he smiled briefly, walked to one of the oversized chairs by the fireplace, and sat.

"Don Felipe, thank you for looking after me. I have no idea what came over me. Frankly, I don't recall what occurred last night."

Carceres recounted the event. "Well, we all drank to the viceroy, and you, well, you got this sour look on your face that disappeared in just a few seconds. Then you froze, half stooped, and stared at young Isabel's, ahem, bosom. That went on long enough for everyone to take notice. Honestly, it was awkward. I was about to admonish you when you raised your head and locked eyes with Isabel. You kept that gaze for some seconds, then blurted out, 'I love you.'"

"Oh?"

"Just that, my boy. You told Isabel de Montoya you loved her."

"I don't remember having said that." It was Diego's turn to feel a bit awkward.

"You stood and continued your stare for a few seconds

more, then collapsed to the floor. Everyone was aghast. Torres and I managed to get you onto a divan. It didn't look like you would come around, so some of the viceroy's guards carried you down to my carriage, and we drove you here. The driver, Maria, and I got you up the stairs and into bed."

Benito said, "Don Carceres is leaving out a few other details he shared with the captain and me before you came down." He looked at Carceres. "Are you going to tell him, señor?"

Carceres began again. "Well, Diego, I may not be as skilled an investigator as you, but once I had a moment to think, I remembered your sour look. I returned to where the six of us had been standing and found your glass where you dropped it. I have it here."

Benito reached out his hand. "May I look at that?"

"Of course. I think you'll find, as I did, that whatever was in the glass Diego drank from was more than just champagne."

Benito sniffed the glass and turned away with a wince.

Carceres continued. "It was obvious to me that glass was originally intended for Señor Torres, and it was only because of that clumsy woman and Señor Torres' polite gesture that you, Diego, ended up drinking it. I've left orders with the Audiencia to locate the steward who served us and have him brought in for questioning."

"I am duly impressed, Uncle. Your reasoning is sound. Is it possible someone was trying to poison Señor Torres?"

"Yes. But I can't say for certain why. We should be grateful you're sitting before us and not lying in the morgue."

Since they were all assembled, Benito told them Yaotl

had nothing to contribute and denied any knowledge of how the burned man found his way into the plaza. "Which doesn't mean he isn't hiding something. I would say he is still a suspect."

De Anza outlined the information Padre Aranda had offered.

Benito found this particularly interesting. "That supports the theory that it was a warning to the Indios and the baratillo wasn't the target. If I'm correct about some of the autopsy findings, there's also a connection to what the padre mentioned about drugs."

They looked at one another as Maria entered the room with the tea service.

Carceres spoke again. "Well, if I may summarize, we have a mostly carbonized body without its heart left in the Plaza Mayor with a toad in its stomach, a scholarly padre who claims secret cabals function somewhere in the city, and a young man poisoned in the presence of the viceroy with a drink perhaps meant for someone else, that someone being the wealthiest man in New Spain. Does that about sum it up?"

"There is just one more thing, gentlemen," interjected Diego, looking up from his chair. "I am in love with Isabel de Montoya."

Maria dropped the service.

After Maria had served a hearty breakfast, the men discussed their next steps. Everyone was concerned about Diego. He seemed lucid but was convinced Isabel de Montoya was the only woman in the world for him. Diego was desperate to see her, yet it seemed easy to restrain him. A simple no would suffice. His eyes would lower, and he'd take on the countenance of a child told he could not go to the park that day. They decided Diego would stay at Don Carceres' home while they continued their investigation. De Anza was to follow up with Padre Aranda. The Monk said he would take the glass from the reception and confer with someone familiar with native pharmacopoeia.

La Condesa couldn't sleep and rose early. All she could think about was how badly her plan for the reception had been bungled—she was fuming as she descended the stairs and walked across the hall to the library.

The library was well stocked with novels, histories, books on nature and science, and biographies. Noticeably missing were any books by or about women. She blamed her husband for that, and there he stood to the right of the broad stone fireplace, a full-length portrait of the man himself, her deceased husband, Renato. *Cockerel*, she thought to herself.

She took a lamp from the writing desk, lit it, and walked over to the painting. Reaching just behind the gilded frame midpoint from the floor, she felt for the lever that released the painting, allowing it to swing out from its left. The portrait opened. Dona Andrea stepped through the door, pulling it closed behind her as she did.

She was standing on a small landing atop a stairwell. She descended the twelve steps to a basement room. The north foundation wall of the mansion was just eight feet ahead. The room smelled of whatever lives, dies, and rots in cellars. The air was damp and condensing on the stone walls and glistened in her lantern's light.

She saw a figure standing in the shadows to her left. She stepped forward and scornfully shouted. "Ass!

Son of a worm." Her lantern illuminated Angamuco's craggy countenance.

"*Mi dama*. It could not be avoided. That woman—"

"Shut up! And I am not your *dama*. I am your goddess, so you should be on your knees."

"Yes, m-my queen," Giraldo stuttered and fell to his knees.

La Condesa thought out loud. "We'll have to try again. I don't know of any other way. It will be dangerous. That fool of a *fiscal* will have professed his love for my daughter to everyone by now."

"We could kill him, my queen. He could meet with an accident."

"Idiot. That would only serve to draw more attention. No. The tincture will wear off in time. Young men fall in and out of love every day. No, we'll let that run its course. But having Torres fall in love similarly and suddenly, so soon after the *fiscal*, would raise suspicion. Nevertheless, we need to get the *fiscal* out of the way for a time. I don't want him rooting around my daughter and bringing attention to her."

Angamuco said nothing. *Best to keep quiet.*

"Are the preparations for the ceremony coming along?"

"Yes, my queen. Would you like to see?"

"Yes! What do you think? Or do you think at all?"

Giraldo turned to avert her cold stare. *Cow! I'm not responsible for the woman running into the* fiscal *and the old man's philter taking such immediate effect. There was supposed to be enough time to maneuver Torres into the antechamber. The poor bastard Santiago. He collapsed like a sack of shit. That wasn't my fault either.* He smiled to himself. *Now he thinks he's in love with that brainless daughter of hers.*

It was twenty years ago. As the foundations for the mansion were excavated, the architects made the discovery. It was a startling find. Dona Andrea thought this was her destiny fulfilled. The ruins of the Aztec *Templo Mayor* were situated directly beneath the northern half of the mansion.

Almost exhausting her funds, La Condesa paid a small fortune to excavate the temple and create a subbasement, concealing it from the outside world. The entire effort lasted over two years. She would end up having to collude with Yaotl on several kidnap-and-ransom schemes to subsidize the effort.

Most of the temple that existed at the time of the Conquest was destroyed, but earlier versions of the temple lay underneath. There had been two earlier versions. It was the first construction they found; two-thirds were still intact once it was dug out.

Once new pylons were driven and the foundation supports put in place, the subbasement was complete. The result was fantastic—a large, vaulted room with a restored pyramid fifty feet in height and eighty feet across at the base. The rear of the temple was still partially buried. Front to back, one could still walk thirty feet on either side before running into a wall of earth and rubble. Most importantly, the top platform, completed at those dimensions, included the two reconstructed, smaller temples to Tlaloc and Huitzilopochtli, with another ten feet open to the ceiling beyond that. The chamber was lit with large cauldrons filled with oil on the top platform and a series of torches on either side of the two stairways leading up to the platform. Large air shafts rising to the roof of the mansion provided circulation. Within a year of the mansion's completion, all the architects, tradesmen, and artisans involved in the effort mysteriously disappeared or died in accidents.

For security, the mansion was staffed entirely with followers from Tepetzinco. They would perform all the maintenance and upkeep for the mansion and temple. They had access to the temple through a secret passage inside the servants' entrance. Staff could come and go without notice. That said, the doorway that opened to a gated yard at the mansion's rear was heavily guarded.

"We still require a suitable sacrifice for next Sunday," she said to Angamuco.

"The female Indio in the cells is still available."

"Of course not! Haven't I told you before? She is an apostate and therefore impure. The sacrifice doesn't require a follower, but one who has denounced the faith will not do. No, we need another." Dona Andrea thought again. "But tell me, Giraldo, how old is this woman?"

"Nineteen, my queen."

"Is she a pretty little thing? Wait. I don't trust your opinion. I'll have a look for myself. Should she prove charming enough, this is what I want you to do."

After she had finished and left the temple, Giraldo thought, *This is what you want me to do, eh? Oh, the things you've had me do.* The majordomo was in his sixtieth year on the planet. He had been with the family since birth and inherited his position from his father, Don Sebastian Angamuco. Growing up in Michoacán, he had witnessed the countless horrific acts of violence committed by the previous *condesa* before he formally took his father's position as majordomo. When he started, he worked for Dona Andrea's mother, La Condesa Maria Teresa de Montoya. In his mind, he could barely separate the two. Each was as cruel and wicked as the other. It was in their nature, their bloodline, a bequeathed mark of evil on their souls, though Angamuco still debated with himself as to whether they possessed souls.

Maria Teresa differed from Dona Andrea only in her sexual proclivity. To Dona Andrea, men and women were toys to be used and discarded. She didn't have the transcendent drive of Isabel, but she made up for that with the sheer number of partners. Maria Teresa's thirst was for a fusion of cruelty, copulation, and murder. She had a secret penchant for capitalizing on her physical beauty to lure men into bed. Once she had sated her lust, they would be killed in one grisly fashion or another, if not by her own hands, then with the assistance of her cadre of thugs. Every one of them was as sadistic as she. One lover, post coitus, was beaten unconscious only to wake and find himself sewn tightly into a wet cowskin and left in the sun to slowly suffocate as the hide dried and constricted, crushing his lungs.

Giraldo had spent a lifetime in this world of violence and depravity, and it had taken its toll. He was unable to engage in any level of intimacy with others. What he had observed from his two mistresses' behavior had all but eliminated his trust in people. He remained friendless throughout his sixty years, and, during most of that time, he self-medicated with copious amounts of alcohol. He was a miserable man consumed by self-hatred.

Angamuco was across from Don Diego's house, standing in the shadows, when he saw, to his surprise, Elena Bautista walking up the avenue and then stopping at the front door of the *fiscal*'s house. *Why would one of Dama Isabel's ladies-in-waiting be visiting the home of the fiscal?* She lifted the brass door knocker and brought it down twice on the heavy oaken door. After a few moments, the door opened. Maria appeared and, with a turn and a motion of her hand, ushered Elena inside.

"Buenos días, Maria," said Elena, smiling pleasantly. "I hadn't heard from Diego, so I thought I'd come by to see how his evening with the viceroy went. My mistress was there as well with her mother. Their gowns were beautiful, and the jewelry was like nothing I'd ever seen." She was genuinely excited and wanted to hear more about the reception from Diego.

Maria thought for a moment. She couldn't tell the girl the truth—Diego had left with Don Carceres only an hour before. It would break her heart. That was Señor Santiago's responsibility, not hers. Quick like a rabbit, she came up with a lie.

"I'm so sorry, child, but Señor Santiago fell ill last evening at the reception, so his uncle, Señor Carceres, took him to his home to look after him. They sent a messenger earlier this morning to tell me."

"Oh no, Maria, is he seriously ill? Did they say what might be ailing him?"

Maria knew Don Diego was in no danger and had recovered physically. She didn't want to alarm Elena. "The messenger said he was feeling better, but they thought it best that he stay with his uncle so they can keep an eye on him for a while longer. I'm sure he'll be fine."

Elena wanted to see Diego, but that was out of the question. "Maria, when he comes home, will you tell him I hope he is well and I-I hope to see him soon?"

"Of course, my child. I'll tell him just as soon as he gets back. Now, don't you worry. I'm sure you'll see him soon." Maria thought perhaps she shouldn't have said that, but she was sincerely fond of the girl and felt terrible about lying. Elena was so sweet and obviously in love with her master.

"Thank you, Maria. Please tell him I will be home this evening, and-and thank you again. Goodbye, Maria."

Elena turned toward the door. Maria reached ahead of her and opened it. "Goodbye, Elena!" She closed the door behind the girl. "Poor child. Men! They can be such turds."

Giraldo watched as Elena exited the house and walked away in the same direction from whence she had come. *Could she be a spy? Does Santiago suspect something?*

Initially, La Condesa had intended to leave the lifeless body of the Indio woman they had in their custody in the *fiscal*'s bed. That would keep him distracted and away from Isabel. Giraldo had come to reconnoiter the house and its surroundings. He intended to return later to carry out his queen's instructions. But now? *La Condesa must know of this!*

La Condesa pondered the news Giraldo had just given her. *What is the connection? Was she sent to spy on me? But why? Don Santiago drinking the elixir was a mistake, and, up to that point, there was no reason for anyone to suspect me of anything.* She looked at Giraldo as he sat at a reading table in the library of her mansion. *Such a worm. But I suppose he has been useful to me and kept my secrets all these years.*

"Giraldo, how long did the girl visit this morning?"

"Perhaps ten, fifteen minutes, *mi dama*."

"And you know for certain Santiago was not at home?"

"Yes, *mi dama*. We've watched him since he and Don Carceres left the reception. Carceres took him home and stayed with him through the evening. Then two others arrived around eight o'clock. Two hours later, they all left, Carceres taking Santiago with him. One of my men followed them to his home."

La Condesa thought for a moment. "Bring Isabel's other domestic, Ana, to me. Now!"

A few minutes later, Giraldo returned to the library. He had the mestizo girl, Ana, with him. She was visibly nervous, perhaps even frightened. She took a few paces into the library, stopped, and dropped a curtsey.

"Buenos días, my child."

"Dama de Montoya," stammered Ana.

La Condesa gestured to Ana. "Come, sit by me on the settee. Don't be shy."

Ana did as she was told, walked timidly toward the settee, and sat on one end of the divan facing Dona Andrea.

"My daughter says she is very pleased with your attendance."

"Thank you, *mi dama*," whispered Ana.

"She also complimented Señorita Bautista. Isn't that right, Giraldo?"

The emotionless majordomo, sitting across from them in a small chair, made no sign of acknowledgment.

La Condesa sat upright, smiled broadly, and then

inquired, "Ana, you are friends with Señorita Bautista. Isn't that the case?"

"*Sí, mi dama*. Since we were children."

"Two attractive young *doncellas* such as yourselves must captivate many handsome young men. Yes?"

Ana blushed vividly and was dumbstruck.

"Come, come, my child. I'm sure that must be true. Don't you have a beau of your own?"

Feeling obliged to say something, Ana responded, "*Sí, mi dama*."

"And what is your young man's name?"

"Jaime. He works in the *mercado*."

"So nice. Tell me, does Señorita Bautista also have a young admirer?"

"*Sí*. She does."

"And her beau works in the *mercado* with Jaime?"

Ana giggled.

"Why would that make you laugh, Ana? Maybe he cleans the horse droppings off the streets or empties toilets."

Ana was shocked and answered defensively. "No, *mi dama*. He is a very important man and does important work."

"Of course, of course, my child. I'm sure. And what important work might that be?"

"He is a *fiscal* and works in the Audiencia."

"Really?" Dona Andrea feigned disbelief. "Please excuse me, but a woman of the señorita's station involved with a man of that rank seems unbelievable."

Ana excitedly agreed. "*Sí, sí, mi dama*. I have told her many times he would let her go any time and forget her in an instant. She is stupid to believe that man will marry her."

Dona Andrea leaned back on the settee and reflected. *So it's only a coincidence and she is a trifle of the demimonde. He suspects nothing of us. But this girl cannot share our inquiries.*

"Well, Ana, I've enjoyed our little chat. You are such a sweet girl. I have a treat for you, and I'm sure you will want to tell Señorita Bautista all about it. Giraldo! Please show Ana the treat I have for her, and thank you again, my child. You've shared so much."

Dona Andrea stood and took Ana by the hand. Ana rose from the settee as La Condesa led her across the room to Giraldo, now stationed by Renato's portrait. Ana knew something wasn't right. Fear grew in the pit of her stomach. Freeing herself from La Condesa's grasp, she turned toward the door and ran. Giraldo grabbed her by her hair, jerking her head back and stopping her forward motion. She started to let out a scream but was caught short by a blow to the back of her skull from a truncheon Giraldo produced from his coat. The library reeled around her as she crashed to the floor. Ana would not wake for some time.

SOR JUANA AND THE MONK

THE MONK HAD been mindful to keep his drinking down the evening before. He wanted to be presentable for his meeting this morning. So it was that at the ungodly hour of nine o'clock in the morning, the Monk found himself near the convent of Santa Teresa La Antigua at a little bar café.

Sor Juana Ines de la Montes was a Carmelite nun at the convent. She had grown up in the countryside south of Mexico City. As a child, she cultivated an avid curiosity about the world around her, especially the flora in its boundless forms. She spent her days hiking near her home, collecting and cataloging all her specimens, and producing accurate, detailed drawings of each. Like many scientists of the age, she began with this hobbyist's approach, but through diligence and erudition, she had garnered a reputation as an expert in her field of botany.

Diminutive in stature, Sor Juana Ines had inexhaustible energy witnessed in her inability to sit still. She was always flitting about like a bird, unsure where to perch. If you managed to engage her in a conversation that held her interest, though, she could keep perfectly still. A young woman in her early thirties, she had taken the veil when she was twenty. The Carmelites at the convent of Santa Teresa La Antigua were liberal thinkers, and she was allowed to continue her education along with her other duties. With a bit of politicking and arm-twisting, the Mother Superior had leveraged her connections with the *Real y Pontificia Universidad de México*, namely Bishop Juan Jose Eguiara y Eguren, the rector at the school, to allow Juana Ines to sit in on some of the classes and lectures.

Sor Juana met the Monk about a block from the convent at the Café Dos Loros on the Calle de Bilbao. It was popular with the students at the university and a meeting place they had frequented for some time. The formalities had long since fallen away.

"Benito, you look well today."

He knew she was referring to the fact he did not look hungover. "Hello, Juana. You are looking especially lovely today."

"Please. Little Esteban mentioned you need some advice."

"I do, but perhaps we could meet later as well, before you have to be locked up." He grinned. She would have punched him in the shoulder if they weren't in a public place. Their affair had been going on for a little over a year. They found conversation effortless and genuinely enjoyed each other's company. It was purely platonic at first. Then, after a while, the physical attraction became undeniable.

"I like being locked up. It keeps me safely away from

people like you. Now, seriously, I understand you have something intriguing for me to look at."

"This may challenge your intellect. I have three items from two different places that could be connected." With that, Benito produced a small cloth satchel, placed it on the table, and carefully withdrew the contents. He opened the handkerchief containing the autopsy results.

A look of disgust came over Juana's face. "Benito, what have you brought me? Aside from the glass, the rest looks like something you scraped off the street in front of a pulquería."

"That, my dear Juana, is what I found in a dead man's stomach during an autopsy two days ago. The champagne glass was taken from the viceroy's reception Saturday evening. The *fiscal de crimen*, Don Diego de Santiago, drank from it, and, well, I'll tell you the rest later."

"Well, Benito, I can give you one answer fairly quickly. I can see that is a toad, and the remaining under-digested bits there are mushrooms."

"This I know," said Benito sarcastically.

"Well, how about I tell you just what kind of mushrooms they are?"

"You can do that with the naked eye? You don't need your microscope?"

"They are discernible as is, Benito. They are what's known as *Psilocybe aztecorum*, a mushroom that grows on the slopes of Popocatépetl. They are a type of hallucinogenic fungus. Its habitat is limited to that region, and you won't find it anywhere else. The toad will take more time. I know people at the colegio who could help with that. Tell me, how did an entire toad end up in this person's stomach?"

Benito told her how they found him and that they suspected he was a victim of a horrible sacrificial rite.

"It's possible someone had mercy on this person and force-fed him the toad ahead of his execution. It looks like something I encountered in Sonora. If so, an entire toad would likely have killed him."

"Good Lord, Benito! That's ghastly."

"Yes, dear Juana, the world can be cruel."

Juana drifted for a moment but swiftly came back to attention. "What about the glass?"

Benito picked up the glass and looked at it. "As I mentioned, Don Diego drank from this glass. It was supposed to be a champagne toast between himself, Viceroy de Guemes, Don Felipe de Carceres, Miguel Torres, La Condesa de Montoya, and her daughter Isabel. We believe the glass was meant for Torres, a rich mining magnate. You can still smell the residue of whatever was served to him. I am told Diego drank to the toast, grimaced for a second, went into a stoop across from Isabel de Montoya, and stood leering at her bosom for five or six seconds more. He raised his head, staring her in the face, and blurted out a declaration of love. Then, straightaway, the poor boy crumpled to the floor in a heap."

Sor Juana couldn't help but giggle. "Well, if whatever was in there was plant-based, and there's some residual matter, I might have a chance of identifying it. For that, yes, I will need my microscope."

"How exactly would you do that, dear sister?" inquired Benito with a smart-aleck tone.

"I'll employ a method invented by an Englishman named Hooke. I have a copy of his *Micrographia* that discusses the makeup of plant tissues. I also have the

Aztec book of herbal medicines *Libellus de Medicinalibus Indorum Herbis* translated from Nahuatl right here in Mexico City by Juan Badiano over two hundred years ago." Juana smiled broadly at Benito with the same smart-aleck look. "Then, of course, there is my compendium of over two thousand native plants."

Benito raised both palms in a signal of surrender. "This is why I sought you out. Well, part of the reason."

Benito slowly pushed his hand out across the tabletop toward hers, and she swiftly slapped it away. "You were right to do so. I'll try to work on this today. I'll confirm the mushroom identification and see what I can tease out of what little remains in the glass."

"And let's not forget our amphibian friend. As I said, I have my theory about that."

"I'll take it to the colegio this afternoon," she replied.

Benito packed up the satchel and gave it to Sor Juana as they rose.

"Well, then, Benito, I will send Esteban once I have something."

"Thank you, dear sister."

They rose, turned from the table, and walked side by side. Sor Juan Ines, keeping her eyes forward, reached with her right hand and clasped Benito's left hand, just briefly, before turning away.

The news from Padre Aranda was startling and greatly concerned de Anza. After polling his contacts, the padre was told about two Indios, a man and his woman, who had escaped an underworld sanctuary. This underworld sanctuary was home to an evil priestess. The Indio man told stories of a vast, dark city illuminated by fire. Hundreds of people lived there. The man and his woman had been captured several months ago and taken to this place. They were kept in a cold, dimly lit space with several other captives. The number of captives rose and fell over time but never exceeded twelve. It was a mixture of men, women, Indios, mestizos, and blacks.

De Anza asked, "No Spanish?"

"Curiously, no, Pedro. My guess is that might draw attention."

All these people were taken from the outside world in the same way, waylaid as they walked a country road or snatched from the city's streets at night. Their captors called them supplicants. New supplicants would arrive, and others would leave. The ones who left never came back. Allegedly, the high priestess lived in this underground world and worshipped a horrible goddess, offering blood sacrifices and ritual immolation to appease it.

One day, a man told the guards minding the supplicants he needed a man and a woman. The man and woman were close to the prison's doorway, so, entirely by chance, the guards grabbed them and pushed them over to the man.

The two left with him. He led them down a series of long passageways. He told them as they walked he no longer believed the truths he had been taught all his life. He said the religion they practiced was an abomination and needed to be stamped out. After walking through miles of dark and narrow passages, they came to an archway. A staircase lay just beyond. He led the two up to what looked like a dead end. The way was blocked on all three sides by rock walls.

He produced two blindfolds and told them that, to return to the world above, they must wear them. They did as they were told. The man reached forward and pressed hard on one of the rocks in the wall. They could feel a cool breeze, and there was fresh air. He continued to lead them blindfolded through what felt like and smelled like a grassy field. They stopped. The Indios heard water lapping on a beach. He placed them in a canoe.

They made their way over the water for hours, finally reaching a far shore. The man helped them out of the canoe and told them to wait. They again did as they were told. An hour passed before the Indio woman gathered enough courage to slip off her blindfold. She tugged at her partner to do the same. They were standing next to the lake and could see the city lights some three miles distant.

"Padre," asked de Anza, "where can I find these two? Do you know?"

"They have disappeared, my son. That, by itself, has caused a great deal of anxiety in the community, only to be followed by the discovery of that poor soul in the plaza. As I told you, I've heard many tales of secret religious orders, cults, and sects, and rumors of all sorts of murderous cabals. But they were just that—rumors and folktales told to scare children in their beds. This is the first time someone has claimed to have witnessed it."

"Padre, if all we have to go on is rumors, then let's hear them. Maybe some of them fit together."

"Yes, Pedro. I will tell you what I've heard." So Padre Aranda told a story he had thought apocryphal until now.

"The high priestess dwells in an underworld kingdom and worships the old Aztec goddess Xochiquetzal."

The padre proceeded to go into graphic detail about

how the sacrifices were performed. This included removing still-beating human hearts, flaying the skin from still-breathing sacrificial victims, and a third practice that involved burning the victim and excising the heart.

"That poor fellow in the plaza is an example of that," said Aranda.

De Anza was sickened by what he heard and had to pause for a moment. Recovering his composure, he asked, "And what of the man in the Plaza Mayor, Padre?"

"The Indios said that as they made their break across the lake, the man told them others besides himself have rejected that faith. They believe the man in the plaza was one of these apostates, possibly the same man who aided them in their escape. He was placed there in reprisal for the escape and as a warning of what happens to recusants. The two hapless Indios thought telling their story might protect them. This does not seem to have been the case."

"Was there anything else?"

"Yes. They said the place where they were held captive was home to a sacred fire. They also said the temple could be accessed only by water, and they heard the high priestess was both beautiful and regal.

ELENA'S DISTRESS

THE MANSION HAD sent word to Elena she was not needed today. Thinking there was an opportunity for her and her friend to share the day, Elena went to the small room Ana kept off the street and next to the *mercado* where her boyfriend, Jaime, worked. She hadn't seen Ana since Saturday evening, and she wasn't home when Ana came by Sunday night.

She knocked on the door, half expecting Jaime to answer. There was no response. She went around the corner and went into the *mercado*, where she found Jaime unloading fruit from a cart and stacking it on a table display.

"Hola, Jaime."

"Hola, Elena," he said, flashing a smile.

"I'm looking for Ana. Do you know where she is?"

"I'm not sure. She's not at home?"

"No. Did you see her at her place last night?"

"No. She wasn't there when I went by. I thought she was with you."

"No. I'm beginning to worry. I suppose we both could have missed her if she was out shopping."

"Ana doesn't have a *peso* to her name. She told me she has nothing until she gets paid this week."

Now Elena was even more worried and thought about what she should do next.

"Thank you, Jaime."

"*Adiós*, Elena," he said as she turned and left the shop.

This isn't like Ana. She wouldn't wander off for days at a time without telling me. Aye yai yai, Ana! First Diego gets sick, and now what? Elena was beginning to feel desperate. She convinced herself she had to see Diego. If something terrible had happened, Diego would know what to do. That meant going to the home of Don Felipe de Carceres, the alcalde.

She vacillated. Hadn't Maria said he was feeling much better? With that, she decided this was the best course of action. She started for the home of the alcalde, unable to get Ana's disappearance out of her thoughts.

"Pardon, Don Carceres. A woman at the door claims to know Don Santiago and wishes to see him."

Carceres could guess who it was, especially since she had come to his front door without an appointment or announcement. "Javier, did this woman mention her name?"

"*Sí*, señor. She said her name is Elena Bautista."

"I'll be down in a minute, Javier. Please show the señorita to the sitting room."

Don Felipe was at a loss. *I can't lie to the girl. Diego seems perfectly healthy except for his obsession with*

Isabel de Montoya. I'll tell her the truth as we understand it and let her come to her conclusions. I told Diego this woman would mean trouble for him. Why is it I'm the one dealing with her?

"Buenos días, Señorita Bautista. I am Don Felipe de Carceres, alcalde *de crimen* with the Audiencia."

Elena curtsied. "Buenos días, Don Carceres. I'm a friend of Don Diego de Santiago. Maria told me of his affliction and that he was recuperating here."

"Yes. That is correct. Diego and I are very close. I knew his father in Spain and have known Diego since he was a boy. Señorita, I know who you are and why you are here. To be completely candid, I must say I disapprove of your relationship with Diego."

"I'm sorry you feel that way, Don Carceres, but what goes on between Diego and myself is just that. I came to speak with Diego. So, if you would be so kind, could you inform him of my presence? I would be most grateful."

"Voicing my concern about your and Diego's relationship is only a statement for the record. I agree it is none of my business outside of my affection for Diego."

"Thank you for that clarification, but I must respectfully repeat my request. Would you kindly inform Diego I am here and wish to see him?"

"You appear to be an intelligent young woman. Please, sit and give me a minute or two. It would help if you were prepared."

Don Felipe offered her a chair. She sat, and he took a chair directly opposite her.

"Diego has, for the most part, recovered from his sickness. I suppose you could call it that. Captain de Anza,

Benito de Avila, and I suspect he was poisoned. Apparently by mistake, but poisoned nonetheless."

Elena's eyes widened in surprise. "Poisoned! By whom? And why do you say he has mostly recovered?"

"We do not know who it was yet. There is a decidedly bizarre aspect to this, and I must ask you to be calm." Don Felipe recounted the scene Saturday evening at the reception, skipping the part where Diego seemed to be staring at Isabel de Montoya's cleavage. "Then his head rose, and, seeing Señorita de Montoya, he stated the following: 'I love you.'"

Elena's face went blank. "He said what?"

"Trust me, señorita, it befuddled everyone present, and, within a second of saying that, he fainted. I took him home and have stayed with him since. He appeared in good health yesterday morning, and, together with the captain and de Avila, we discussed the event. Once more, he stated, without qualification, that he was in love with Isabel de Montoya."

"But how does this happen? He'd never met her before."

"That, my dear señorita, is what we are trying to understand."

Elena struggled to hold back the tears. *Am I losing my Diego?*

"One could surmise this peculiarity in his character is related to whatever was in his champagne glass other than champagne. At this very moment, the captain and de Avila are working to ascertain what that was."

Elena sat staring into her lap. She was confused. After some time, her head rose, and she asked Don Felipe, "May I see Diego now?"

Don Felipe could tell this girl was struggling with her

emotions. Whether or not he approved of their affair, he couldn't help but feel sorry for them both. They were the victims of an appalling crime. "I'll tell him you're here."

Carceres left the room and returned a minute later with Diego. Diego walked into the room and swiftly across it, took Elena into his arms, and kissed her. "My darling. I'm sorry this terrible circumstance has separated us. I do feel better now. I'll be returning home this afternoon." Still in his embrace, Elena wasn't quite sure how to react.

"That's good, Diego. I'm relieved you will be home soon."

Diego lowered his voice to a whisper. "Yes, my love. I've missed your touch and yearned for your warm caress. I will blanket your body in kisses and respond to your every desire." This did not sound like Diego. Diego was a man of action, not words, when it came to lovemaking.

"Diego."

"Yes, my sweet."

"Don Carceres mentioned Isabel. Isabel de Montoya." Elena pronounced de Montoya with a raised accent on the last syllable.

Diego's face melted. "Oh, yes, Isabel. I love her with all my heart."

Elena threw her arms down, breaking their embrace, took two steps back, and asked, "How can you say that? How can you say that when you just said what you said?"

"Because I do."

Don Carceres stepped in, taking Elena by the arm. "I've asked my man Javier to bring tea. Won't that be nice?" He took Elena aside. Diego still stood there non-plussed, trying to fathom what had riled her so.

Don Carceres whispered to Elena, "Do you see now?

It's like some spell or charm has possessed him. He can be sincere with you while simultaneously playing out this romantic fantasy concerning Dama Isabel."

"The words he spoke to me were not Diego's. He never speaks like that."

Carceres walked Elena into the foyer. "Diego will go home this afternoon. I told him he must stay home for a day or so and have instructed Maria to keep a close eye on him and send me word if he tries to leave. Benito Avila will stay with him tonight. What's strange is, he doesn't think anything is wrong. He conducts himself as he always has. He converses normally and seems to grasp everything said to him. It's as though mentioning her name triggers this inexplicable response."

"I know how dear you are to Diego. I hope that with good care, he will recover. That is, unless—unless it's permanent."

"I'm sure that's not the case. As you say, we'll take good care of him and see what comes of the investigation into the contents of the glass."

Elena felt hopeful again and remembered Ana. "I feel so selfish. I was going to see him when he returned home, but my friend went missing. That's not like her. It's why I came to your home. I don't have anyone but Diego to turn to."

"Can I help, señorita? I do have certain connections."

"Well, it all seems so odd, so coincidental. When Diego told me he was going to the reception, I laughed because my mistress was also invited. Dama Isabel and her mother, La Condesa Dona Andrea."

This caught Carceres' attention. "You're employed by the Montoyas?"

"Yes. Both myself and Ana."

"And it's Ana who has gone missing?"

"Yes. I haven't seen her since Saturday evening."

Carceres followed the thread. "Señorita, what do you and Ana do for La Condesa?"

"We attend Dama Isabel exclusively, but two days every week, she is attended by just one of us while the other has the day to ourselves."

"I see. I'll ask one of my men to make inquiries. May I ask, what is Ana's surname?"

"Lopez. Ana Lopez. We both have rooms near the Alameda."

"I will contact you should I discover anything, and please let me know should she turn up. I'm sure she's fine and will probably be waiting for you when you return home."

"Oh, I do hope so, and thank you, Don Carceres. You've been most kind."

"Not at all, and I must say it was a pleasure meeting you." Carceres made a quick bow, and Elena departed.

Felipe, de Anza, and Benito had agreed to meet at Diego de Santiago's home for dinner. Felipe had accompanied Diego home earlier that afternoon. As they gathered in the drawing room, their discussions had an almost funereal atmosphere. Diego was there, in body, and spoke in a normal tone, but everyone knew some sinister effect was acting on his psyche. No one spoke of Isabel de Montoya.

They went over the findings of the day. Felipe told them the steward from the reception, a man named Alejandro Hernandez, had disappeared. "When my men spoke to the kitchen staff, they said he hadn't shown up for work yesterday or today. They checked the small room he shares with two other men. They hadn't seen him since Saturday before he left for the palace."

De Anza told his incredible story of the two Indio runaways. He told them about the temple and the female deity, and described the grisly details surrounding sacrificial rites performed to appease her goddess. "Most interesting were the three clues the Indios left before they disappeared again. The temple could be accessed only by water, it was home to a sacred fire, and the high priestess was both beautiful and regal."

"With hundreds of followers," interjected Felipe. "How could such a thing be kept secret?"

"Easily," said Benito. "As the padre stated, there had long been rumors. Many Indios are uneducated and superstitious. Some continue to worship these ancient gods. Many of the Aztec festivals are still celebrated, albeit with Christianized replacements. The *Basílica de nuestra Señora de Guadalupe*, built on Tepeyac Hill, was also the place of Aztec worship of the goddess Tonantzin, or Mother Earth. Then there's *Día de Los Muertos*, which was moved to coincide with the Catholic All Souls' Day. The Indios are still attuned to this spirit world. We Spanish are blind to these things because of our indifference to their culture."

Felipe got Benito's point. "I understand. It's hidden only for want of seeing what's right in front of us."

"Yes," said Benito. "But our eyes are open now, and this understanding may help us expose this monstrous sect the padre has told us about. We must pursue this abomination and destroy it utterly. The problem is, we still know so very little about it."

De Anza spoke up. "Let's try to piece together the fragments of information we do have. At least it's a start. We know the sacrifice left in the plaza was still extremely hot, so he couldn't have been there long. Wherever this temple is, it couldn't have been too far."

De Anza went to the bookshelf, withdrew *Atlas of New Spain*, and placed it on the desk. He thumbed through it until he came to a plate depicting the *Valle de Mexico*.

"I think I know where you're going with this, Captain," said Benito. "But if you're going to judge the place of execution based on the cooling rate of the body and travel time, I have a more precise determinant for the time of death. You could substitute that in your calculation in place of the cooling rate."

"That's exactly what I was going to propose, Monk. Tell us, how would you determine the time of death?"

"Two findings made during the autopsy I performed with Diego here."

"I only observed," said Diego.

"And what's an autopsy?" asked de Anza.

Benito went on to explain what an autopsy was and its purpose.

"That's disgusting," said de Anza.

"No, that's science. Though it had nothing to do with the time of death, we also observed the man had been tortured before he was executed by binding his hands behind his back and hoisting him off the ground by his wrists. But back to my point. First, I took his temperature. Second, I examined the contents of his stomach.

"Postmortem, internal body temperature begins to cool by one and a half degrees per hour. That is, at a stable ambient temperature. Since he was effectively cooked to death, I adjusted the cooling rate to one degree per hour, allowing for the elevated external body temperature. At noon I measured eighty-four degrees. That places the time of death around midnight. The Indio women discovered the body at six. We don't know the exact time it was placed there, but let's say four thirty. That leaves four and a half hours to load up the body and convey it to the plaza."

"That's amazing!" voiced Felipe. "We should incorporate this method in all of our murder investigations."

"It wouldn't be a bad idea," said Benito. "Next, we examined the stomach contents, and admittedly, this measurement involved some judgment calls. One can digest a light meal in one to three hours. You also need to factor in the volume and contents—in this case, mushrooms and the toad. The fact that they were still in his stomach indicates his difficulty digesting these items. Knowing the body temperature and assuming he didn't eat them between midnight and four thirty supports a time of death between eleven Wednesday night and midnight Thursday."

"Bravo, Benito. Well done." Felipe was obviously impressed with the scientific methods Benito employed.

"Thank you," Benito said, "but I think the captain has the next step figured out."

"Okay," said de Anza, "let's say a four thirty arrival in the plaza and time of death of eleven that night. Traveling at roughly three miles an hour, that's 16.5 miles." De Anza took a compass, placed one leg in the Plaza Mayor, and according to the map scale, set the second leg, set the radius, and drew a circle. He stepped back, assessing the challenge. "That's a little over 860 square miles in area. That's a lot to cover, considering only four of us."

Don Felipe said, "Let's whittle that down. Remember

the clue said the temple was accessible only by water. So, if we assume we were not just crossing a moat, it would be somewhere in the lake. We can confine our search to the parts of the circle's arc in the lake. In other words, the islands."

"That's true, but it still leaves us with every island in Texcoco within sixteen miles," remarked Benito.

"I make that to be nineteen islands," said de Anza. "I suppose we at least have a list. So that would be north to Atepehuacan and south to Tepepilco."

"Yes, dear captain, but causeways connect nine islands to the city, either directly or via one of the other islands." Benito beamed.

"Seven islands. Gentlemen, our search area has become much more manageable. Now, Benito, what have you learned?" asked de Carceres.

"I've spoken with Sor Juana Ines de la Montes at the convent of Santa Teresa La Antigua. She is an expert on plants and their medicinal purposes. She took the glass to see if she could identify the residue. Hopefully, the sister can tell us something in the morning.

"She identified one of the contents of the dead man's stomach—the mushrooms are *Psilocybe aztecorum*. She'll confirm that with the sample I gave her. It's a hallucinogen."

"And what about the toad?" asked Diego.

"She's going to ask a colleague at the colegio. I have my own opinion, however. I believe it's a type of river toad. The skin produces another type of stupefying drug as a defense."

Benito saw de Anza nodding. He had learned of this in Sonora, as Benito had. "One important difference from the mushrooms is that the toad's venom can kill you in large enough amounts. An entire toad—and these are not small—would be deadly. It had to have been forced down his throat, perhaps as an act of mercy after he had ingested the mushrooms and before he was put to the flame."

Diego seemed to wake up. "Are you saying those things are responsible for me blacking out at the reception the other evening?"

"Not necessarily. We still don't know what was in the glass," responded Benito. "But a hallucinogen might have been part of it. Remember, these are two separate incidents. We have nothing that links the drugs in the dead man's stomach to the incident at the reception with Diego. Do you know what is meant by the term *hallucination*?"

Diego said, "I've heard it before. Doesn't it mean one goes mad?"

"Not quite," said Benito. "A hallucination is an unfounded or mistaken impression—a delusion. It's perceiving something that doesn't exist, a chimera. Do you think that was what happened to you, my friend?"

Diego thought for a moment. "I don't believe so."

Benito saw Diego was still confused and decided not to pursue it further.

At seven thirty, they sat down together for dinner. Señora Reyes had set out a sumptuous feast of fresh tortillas, roasted corn, grilled chicken in a green pumpkin seed sauce, a fish-and-rice *cazuela*, and a seared lamb dish with *pasilla* peppers and honey.

Diego presented the wine for the meal. "I hope, my friends, that you will like this. It's a Tempranillo Garnacha blend grown in Aguascalientes. A bit young but ready."

Don Felipe answered, "I'm sure it will be wonderful, Diego." He paused a moment, then continued. "I know toasts have been problematic of late, but I'll propose one anyway." He raised his glass. "To our host and a man I love like a son, Don Diego de Santiago. *Salud*!" They each raised their glasses and drank.

Don Felipe turned to Benito. "You raised a good point earlier. You said nothing connected the dead man to Diego's poisoning. I must ask, is that true, gentlemen?"

De Anza spoke first. "I see nothing that connects them. Whatever Diego drank was intended for Miguel Torres. Tell me, assuming he had drunk the concoction rather than Diego, would he have reacted the same way as Diego? I mean, with the señorita, that is."

"This is a very potent brew of which we know nothing yet," Benito responded. "Suffice it to say that everyone may respond differently."

"But let's assume it had precisely the same outcome, and Señor Torres professed an abiding love for Isabel de Montoya," said de Anza. "I think I see a clear motive."

"Marrying your daughter off to the wealthiest man in Nueva España? I would agree, Pedro," said Felipe. "A strong motive."

Felipe had grown more suspicious since his encounter with Elena that morning. That Elena was connected to both Diego and the house of Montoya was, he believed, only a coincidence. He doubted the Montoyas had arranged her *affaire de cour* with Diego. His discussion with Elena that morning had left him with the impression that the girl was a sincere and caring person. Coincidence or not, though, there was the matter of her missing friend. That raised his curiosity, but still he couldn't make any connection.

Benito asked, "What do we know about La Condesa besides her beauty and affluence?"

"Not much!" said Don Felipe. "Her family goes back to the Conquest. The wealth was established through an *encomienda* of considerable size and value. The patriarch married an attractive Indio woman, an alleged daughter of Moctezuma. That's about all. We need to know more."

"I agree. I'll see what I can unearth," said de Anza. "Don Felipe, I'd like to request a cadre of soldiers to assist with exploring the seven islands."

"Certainly. I'll look to secure that in the morning. Diego, I think you should accompany the captain." Diego nodded in agreement.

With that, Don Felipe and de Anza departed. Benito took a spare bedroom, and Diego, still a bit confused with all the talk of Isabel and Miguel Torres, ascended the stairs to his own.

Diego was having the same dream. He was floating toward Isabel, who was bare-breasted with her multicolored crown of feathers and outstretched arms, beckoning him. Then he saw it nestled between her breasts—the large green teardrop topaz suspended by a delicate gold chain. Its light captivated him as it had before. Once again, the glittering green and gold light was reflecting off her skin, and though the gem was fixed in its place, myriad sparks of light spun out of it. It held his gaze, and he couldn't look away as it drew him into its warm embrace. He swam in its glow, never wanting to leave the light. It whispered to him. "Diego. Diego." Slowly, not wanting to let go, he awoke in bed, lying on his back. It felt like he couldn't move. Something was weighing him down. A candle burned on the nightstand beside the bed, softly illuminating the room. His eyes slowly adjusted to the light.

Once everything came into focus, he looked down and saw a woman lying on top of him, her face turned to the side.

She looked up, and he saw who it was. "Elena?"

"Yes, Diego." Putting both her hands on his bare chest, she pushed up and away until her naked body was perpendicular to his. Sitting astride him, she looked downward with her eyes, keeping her head straight, and in a low, husky tone whispered, "I thought you needed something to remind you of me." She took both his hands and cupped them over her breasts, moving them in a slow, rhythmic, circular motion. "Something personal from me to you." Her hips began a forward-and-back grind as she kept her body upright. She started taking short, quick breaths. Was he still in a dream? Perhaps he was, and this was all in his mind. Without any doubt, though, the rest of him was indisputably awake and paying full attention.

Diego felt better than he had in days. He and Elena cuddled in the morning, then rose to see that Maria had prepared a hearty breakfast of eggs, fresh bread, ham, potatoes, and fruit juice. Still in their robes, they ate at the kitchen table, taking advantage of the warm oven to hold off the morning's chill. Maria smiled to herself. She wished the two could find some way to be together.

Diego met Captain de Anza in his office at the *Audiencia*.

"I have to say I'm blessed to have a woman like Maria in the house. That meal last night was near perfect. She takes good care of me. I'm a lucky man," Diego boasted.

"*Sí*, my brother, you've done well for yourself."

"Smoke?" offered the captain. "I stopped by my shop on Madero Street where the ladies role the best cigarillos." He threw the packet on the desk.

Diego saw they were the Two Crown brand. He'd heard of them, which was something considering the hundreds of shops in the city. The tobacco monopoly ran most, but there were a few independent artisans. Diego reached for the packet and took one as de Anza lit his. Diego leaned forward to share de Anza's match, then sat back. Exhaling a thick plume of smoke, he addressed the captain.

"Pedro, I'd like to thank you for the care you've given me over the past few days. I admit I haven't been myself. It was like I was awake and alert but looking through a fog. Whatever it is, I feel it lifting bit by bit." Diego thought for a second, then said, "Elena came by last night after you left."

"That's good, Diego. From what I've heard, she's a good woman with a fine head on her shoulders."

"Yes, she's wonderful."

"Let's look at the map," said de Anza, "and see if we can outline our approach for tomorrow's mission. Don Felipe has secured twelve men from the Regimiento de México to assist in the search."

Diego spread out a map on his desk and secured it with a paperweight and inkwell.

De Anza said, "None of these islands are that large. It should take only two days to cover them all. Do you think we should split them up with two men assigned to each?"

"No. I want to see each myself. Not that I'm any more discerning than the rest. It's more for my peace of mind, so I'm satisfied with the results, good or bad. We'll visit all the islands as one group, fan out in twos, and search end to end."

"*Bueno*," said de Anza. "I suggest we cover the six islands to the south tomorrow. The furthest island, Tepepilco, is only twelve miles from where we stand now. We'll start with Zacatlalmanco, then Ixtacalmanco, Nextiplan, Atlazolpa, and Ixtapalapa, and finish with Tepepilco. Tomorrow we'll explore the seventh, Tepetzinco."

"That seems fine to me. However, we may be saving the best for the last."

"Why is that, my friend?"

"Its history—or legend—is similar to the rituals we're interested in. Tepetzinco is where Huitzilopochtli, the sun god and the god of war, had his nephew Copil murdered by the Mexica. They cut out his heart and threw it into the lake."

"Really? The more I hear about these people, the less I like them." De Anza thought to himself, *Hweet see lo Poch tlee*. He spoke a little Nahuatl but still struggled with some of the pronunciations.

"What's more, it's also where Moctezuma would go to take advantage of the restorative waters of a hot spring that bubbles from the base of the hill."

"Well," said de Anza, grinning, "if we don't find anything, we can always take a dip."

"Fine, then. That's the plan. We'll meet at eight tomorrow morning at the Alhondiga dock. I have a meeting in ten minutes with Don Felipe. We can meet later with him and Benito."

De Anza sighed. "Yes, when he wakes up. As for me, I'm afraid I'll be spending my day right here and at the *ayuntamiento* going through the city records. I want to see what I can find about La Condesa and the family's move here from Michoacán."

Ana was wet and cold. Her thin straw mattress sat on a damp stone floor. She wasn't sure how long she'd been here, and, so far, her companions, an Indio couple, hadn't spoken a word. The woman looked young, perhaps in her early twenties. The man looked older, about twenty-eight or thirty by Ana's reckoning. Occasionally they'd shoot a glance her way, but the few times she'd tried to speak with them, they remained mute.

A small iron gate separated them from the torchlit corridor outside their cell. As well as cold and frightened to her core, Ana was hungry. The last time she had eaten was Sunday morning before leaving for the mansion. She dozed for a while. When she opened her eyes, the Indio girl was standing in front of her, hand outstretched and holding half of a tortilla.

Ana reached slowly and took it from the girl. "Gracias."

A weak smile formed on the girl's face. "*Bienvenido.*"

Ana could tell she was struggling with the word. Her Spanish wasn't good.

"My name is Ana."

"They call me Flaquita." Ana could tell why. She was small and slender, but not skinny. Ana envied her figure, wishing she wasn't quite so sturdy. "Him Manolito," the girl said, pointing to the man. Ana looked over, and the man nodded.

So they do feed us, Ana thought and then asked aloud, "Why am I here? What is going to happen to me?" The girl stared, puzzled, unable to take in everything Ana had said. Ana knew this and apologized. "I'm sorry. I don't expect you to know." The girl smiled again and returned to the man's side. Savoring the tortilla, Ana resumed her quiet meditation and tried not to weep.

Benito and Sor Juana Ines sat at their regular table in the café, drinking hot chocolate. Sor Juana enjoyed her extra cinnamon while the Monk enjoyed the fortification provided by two ounces of tequila.

"Benito, why do you poison yourself every evening?"

"I'm bored," he offered, knowing that was not the complete truth. The pain he suffered wouldn't go away with the drink, but the drink did blur it for a time.

"I think I have some good news for you and your friend Señor Santiago."

Benito's eyebrows lifted. "We could use some good news. It's been difficult working with Diego these past couple of days. He's inimitable in every aspect, but mention that Montoya woman's name, and he'll lapse into a kind of stupor, professing his undying love. It's sickening."

"Well, first, the results of the samples you gave me from your autopsy are confirmed. The mushrooms were indeed *Psilocybe aztecorum*. My colleague at the colegio said the toad specimen you provided was a type of amphibian known as *Bufo alvarius*. It secretes venom from its back that contains a potent hallucinogen. It can be fatal in the right amounts."

"Like an entire toad?"

"Without question, Benito."

"Now, the good news regarding your friend. His condition will eventually wear off."

"Fantastic! When?"

"That's difficult to say. It depends on the individual's size, constitution, strength, and the amount of the drug ingested. It could be today. It could be a week from now."

"God, let it be soon. So, what was it? Is there a way to hasten his recovery?"

Juana shook her head. "I don't know. I'm sorry, but there is so much we don't understand about these drugs. Like your pulque, it works on the brain but in a much more profound fashion. The glass contained remnants of the same mushroom you found in your subject's stomach. It affected his senses and behavior. The interesting tidbit is that the mixture in the glass contained not just mushroom fragments but an extraction of that same fungus. An extract would provide an intensely stronger effect. We're lucky that whoever prepared this mixture didn't employ more sophisticated methods. I'm sure the chemicals used were not very concentrated, and I suspect other aspects of the extraction were not very well controlled. Processes in use today would result in a nearly pure extract without any leftovers from the original plant. We were fortunate there were residual bits of plant, or I could never have identified them. There are a few other findings."

"What other findings?" Benito was fascinated and hung on Juana's every word.

"There was a second drug in the glass, which also seems to have been an extract. I was able to identify the plant under the microscope. It's a climbing vine the Indios call *coaxihuitl* or snake plant. The seeds of its flowers contain the drug used in the extraction. I'm sure the final draft had a ratio of two parts fungus extract to one snake plant extract."

Benito had a hundred questions. "So, my dear Juana, what do these drugs do?"

"Good question, because that leads to my second finding. You'll need to bear with me. It's more of a theory than a solid finding based on data."

"Very well. I'm already amazed at what you've been able to discover from that small, dried sample left in the glass."

"Both drugs have similar effects with variations. They both create a feeling of euphoria in the subject. Now, these drugs, ingested in their natural state, like mushrooms or some seeds, can be very potent, depending on the amount. Aside from euphoria, an individual may hallucinate or become delusional. The effects would wear off in a couple of hours. I believe that, because they were extracts, the dosage in the glass may have been a hundred times more potent. The effect would be immediate upon ingestion, with a tremendously heightened sense of euphoria. Again, bear with me. Those are the facts. Now here's the theoretical part.

"I'm convinced the two-to-one ratio was meant to deliver a specific response. By that, I mean the amount and type of euphoric response, an intense sense of well-being so strong the subject would never want it to end. And it wouldn't because the dosage was so great it would take days, even weeks, before it started to diminish."

Benito was trying to imagine what it would be like to experience such a thing. "I can grasp what a sense of well-being feels like, but you're saying it would be magnified?"

"I think I can explain, Benito, but let me finish with my theory."

"Please."

"I think the intent here was to focus that exceptional degree of euphoria so it would be associated with the first person who caught his attention. If attached to a personality, that hyper sense of well-being could easily be mistaken for love. Just as he would want the feeling he was experiencing never to go away, neither would he want the person he associated it with to go away. Hence the declaration 'I love you.'"

"I don't know. I think I understand what you're saying, except for two things. First, I'm still having a hard time with this keen sense of well-being, and second, what if the first person Diego saw was the viceroy's wife or the viceroy?" He chuckled.

"I agree that's problematic. Part of the ploy would have to involve isolating both the subject and their intended."

"Well," said Benito, "we know or at least suspect Diego was not the original mark and he drank from Señor Torres' glass by mistake. There's nothing to say Isabel de Montoya was the intended. It could have been La Condesa."

"Yes, and I believe whoever produced the drug miscalculated the speed and intensity of its effect. I'm sure the plan was to isolate him with whomever immediately after the toast."

"Getting back to this amplified sense of well-being, this euphoria. How can you be so sure this overwhelming feeling that drives such behavior exists?"

Sor Juana Ines bent forward, looking Benito straight in the eye. She whispered, "Because I tried it."

Diego, Don Felipe, the Monk, and de Anza were gathered once more for dinner to compare notes. This time, they were at the home of Don Felipe de Carceres by his invitation, a new two-story home done in the baroque style. Its location on the Calle de la Palma was just a few blocks northwest of the plaza. Larger than Diego's modest home, it had a charming inner courtyard shaded by several Ficus trees. The evening was warm, so they gathered around a large oak table covered with a richly colored *mantele* woven by a local artisan. The pleasant combination of the warm evening air scented by the honeysuckle, marigolds, and *Laelia* orchids adorning the table perfectly complemented the delightful supper before them.

Don Felipe sat at the head of the table. "Gentlemen, I am pleased to have you as guests in my home this evening." He raised his glass. "To his Royal Majesty, King Ferdinand the VI."

Smiling, they all raised their glasses and drank to the king. "It was some days ago Diego made me aware of the crime in the Plaza Mayor, a criminal act that was both brutal and mysterious. Since that time, you three good gentlemen have pursued the people who committed that atrocity. And, as if that crime was not shocking enough, another act—an outrage, rather—was committed at the very heart of our government of Nueva España. A personal attack was carried out in the presence of the viceroy himself. Such an act cannot go unanswered.

"Normally, as alcalde, I would leave the prosecution of these affairs to the office of the *fiscal de crimen.*" Felipe paused, then continued, his voice echoing the humility he felt in the request he was about to make. "Humbly, I would ask, and with Don Diego's permission and the assent of you gentlemen seated at my table, to allow me to join you in your efforts. I promise you I will provide whatever assistance I can to this undertaking. I will, of course, recuse myself as alcalde in the matter."

Without hesitation, they voiced their unanimous approval. Each of them understood this was something out of the ordinary, a man of Don Felipe's position humbling himself to act as an equal. A common purpose bound them together. They would do whatever was necessary to see justice done.

After some laughter and more toasts to the effort, Felipe cleared his throat. "I'm anxious to hear what each of you has to share this evening, but uppermost in my mind is the health of my nephew, if not in blood, then by the bonds of true affection. So, tell us, Diego, how are you this evening, my dear boy?"

It wasn't difficult to see that Diego's normal, keen, energetic state of mind had returned. He stood up from his chair and said with mock sincerity, "My dear compañeros, I'm delighted this evening to report that my true and undying love for Dama Isabel de Montoya has diminished to the point of mere fondness." They all laughed, relieved to see their old friend in complete possession of his mind once again. "What's more," Diego continued, "I now remember the reception up to the point where I blacked out."

Benito smiled. "That's wonderful, Diego. Honestly, if I heard more about your 'undying love,' I would disown you. But please tell us what else you remember."

Diego turned and paced about the table. "There may

be more because it's coming to me in bits and pieces. I took the last glass from Señor Torres. Señor Torres proposed the toast, and we all drank. The taste overcame me. It was horrible. I tried to say something but couldn't get the words out. I looked down into the glass and then started to raise my head. That's when I saw it, the bright shimmering light of that jewel. I was transfixed. I couldn't take my eyes off it. It's difficult to describe how I felt. It wasn't just beautiful. It was wonderful. It was like nothing I'd experienced before. Its green light seemed warm and benevolent. I mean no blasphemy, but I felt like I had ascended into heaven. When I finally managed to look up and away, I saw what I thought to be an angelic vision. It was Isabel, with those large dark eyes.

"She drew me in. Gentlemen, I know this sounds demented, but I not only wanted to surrender myself to her but to be part of her. We were transcendent. Isabel and I together."

Diego was correct. None of the other three men could grasp what he was trying to say, but they knew Diego was trying to explain something none of them had experienced.

"The next I remember, I was waking up in my bed with no recollection of what I just now so inadequately described. I felt something like a hangover, and I was oddly disassociated from my surroundings. From that point on, if I happened to think of Isabel or someone referred to her, it would trigger that warm, almost overwhelming sense of bliss. It's interesting when I think of it. If I had been in love with Isabel, she should have been constantly in my thoughts. But she wasn't. The trigger and response were all that ever existed of our so-called love."

Benito stood and walked to the side table. Pouring

himself another glass of wine, he said, "Diego, given what you just told us, I think you all should hear what I learned from the good Sor Juana Ines today."

Leaving out the self-experiential aspect of Sor Juana's analysis, Benito detailed her confirmation of the substances found at the dead man's autopsy and the contents of the glass from the reception. He described the substances involved, their potency, and how long they might be expected to last. He allowed them to dwell on that for a moment.

They were all silent, each of them still struggling and unsure of what Diego had gone through. Benito thought this was a perfect segue to Juana's theory. "That's just the half of it. There's one other facet to this I haven't mentioned." He had their attention but was unsure how they would receive what he was about to tell them.

"After hearing what Diego told us of his experience, I think this could go a long way to explaining it. As you may or may not know, Sor Juana Ines de la Montes is considered an expert botanist. Her skill and knowledge singled out the plants and the drugs derived from them. She also presented me with a theory I thought was both amazing and far-fetched. Diego's description of events, however, has lent credibility to her wild theory."

Benito went on to outline Sor Juana's explanation of how drugs could strongly affect a human's thinking and rationality. They could induce an intense and lasting impression of comfort and well-being, mimicking something like love. With this heightened euphoria, an individual would likely associate the sensation's source with a personality, the first one they encountered after succumbing to the drug. In this case, it was Dama Isabel.

"And why Isabel de Montoya, Monk?" asked a doubtful de Anza.

"Two reasons!" interjected Felipe. "The most obvious one is that she was standing directly before him. The second, as Diego has recounted, is the brilliant green topaz. We mistakenly thought that, in his torpor, he was staring at her, er, abundance, when in fact, it was the jewel."

"You think it was premeditated, then?" asked Benito.

"Perhaps, but nothing proves that one way or the other. I'm only answering the captain's question. It is, however, suspicious. Captain, what, if anything, did you find in the *ayuntamiento* about La Condesa de Montoya's move to the city?"

"Not very much, I'm afraid. I visited the royal archives and found a copy of the original *encomienda* in Michoacán granted to her ancestor Gaspar de Montoya. He was an officer close to Hernan Cortes. The land and number of villages within it were quite substantial. Other records show the Montoyas own a hacienda in Michoacán near Morelia.

"The mansion here in the city was built twenty years ago. It's quite a large structure in a prominent section of the city next to the archbishop's palace. In actuality, it's larger than the archbishop's residence. The only noteworthy information I found was that it took nearly two years to build. I was told by the recorder, who remembers it being built, that the foundation works seemed to have taken half of that. He guessed they wanted to drive additional pylons to avoid the subsidence other buildings around it have suffered. That makes sense. You can see several buildings all across the city sinking or tilting. Though a full year to drive additional pylons is hard to explain. That's all, gentlemen. I'm sorry I don't have more to report."

"That's fine, Captain. You and Diego will be searching the islands tomorrow morning?"

"*Sí*. We're going to the six southern islands in the morning, traveling as far as Tepepilco. The day after, we'll visit Tepetzinco."

"I'm optimistic you and Diego will find this demonic temple. Hopefully, that will lead us to those responsible for the Plaza Mayor murder."

Felipe continued. "We all agree a mistake led Diego to drink from the glass meant for Señor Torres. At first, I thought it must have been a failed assassination attempt on Torres. Anyone seeing Diego's violent reaction to the poison would have thought the same. Diego, you could have just as easily died. We were lucky the attempt failed. Assuming it was an attempt on Torres' life, I can't see what motive any of the six of us in the toast would have. I told myself some other party with either a political or commercial motive must have been behind it. Anyway, here are the facts we have so far.

"Hallucinogens were employed in the plaza murder and the poisoning at the reception. Ana Lopez went missing the day after the reception. She and Señorita Bautista work as ladies-in-waiting for Dama Isabel. If Sor Juana Ines de Montes is right, a potential motive exists to drug Miguel Torres and obtain his wealth through marriage. From all of this, one might ascertain that La Condesa is a suspect, but I caution you that all of this is conjecture and coincidental at best. Unless we discover some evidence, I would consider La Condesa's involvement purely theoretical. Do you agree?" They all nodded in agreement.

"And where do we go from here, Felipe?" asked Diego.

"Back to work, gentlemen."

"You've enough money, Alavaro. Why don't you find someplace decent to live instead of this filthy hole?" Angamuco was looking for a few inches of space to sit that wasn't filthy with grime or sullied by bits of food.

Yaotl spat and pointed to an old woman sitting across the room. "If it's good enough for *mi madre*, it's good enough for me."

Giraldo decided not to pursue it further. "I need your help with something, Alavaro."

Yaotl spat again. Giraldo winced, taking his kerchief out and covering his mouth. "What?" said Yaotl.

"I need you to quietly take someone in hand and bring them to the mansion. Use the special entrance."

Yaotl smiled, and Giraldo observed his scar took on the appearance of a musical notation when he did so. "Male or female?" asked Yaotl.

"Female." Giraldo caught a repulsive leer on Yaotl's square, fat, and remarkably flat face. He wondered, if Yaotl were to turn sideways, would his facial expressions be noticeable? "She must be delivered unmolested."

Yaotl's eyes turned into slits. "What do you want her for?"

"She is to be the guest of La Condesa for a while. How much do you want?"

"What *casta* does she come from?"

"Mestizo."

"Then the same as the last two Indios put together."

Giraldo thought to bargain, but he wanted to stay on

Yaotl's good side. Secrecy was worth more than what he might save. Besides, it was La Condesa's money, not his.

"Very well. Done. But I should mention one other noteworthy item."

"What's that?"

"She is the paramour of a certain government official."

Angamuco had had Elena followed since he first saw her entering Santiago's house the night before. She and Santiago had spent the night together.

Giraldo thought through the plan. "Snatching her from Santiago's home would simultaneously present Santiago with a crisis and a dilemma. We would send a note demanding money. This would deflect any idea the kidnapping was motivated by his investigation of the plaza murder and establish the act as purely for financial gain. It must look like ransom is the sole motive. Best of all, he would need to keep it a secret. If it got out that he was having sexual relations outside of marriage and with a mestizo woman, his reputation would be ruined. He may even be called before the Inquisition."

Continuing with Alavaro, Giraldo said, "They conduct their affair in the evening. So if you do this at night, he'll either be out, or you'll need to find some excuse for him to be called away from his home. In either case, he cannot be harmed."

"Old man, you ask a lot. Who is this government official?"

"Don Diego de Santiago."

"Cabrón*!* Are you loco? A *fiscal de crimen*? They would have my balls for breakfast!" Yaotl muttered that last sentence.

"If you have added expenses and need additional compensation," said Giraldo, "we can discuss it."

"That's if I do it at all. If he had even a hint I was behind this, he'd break my legs or make me disappear."

"Perhaps I've come to the wrong person, then. I thought you were the great and feared Alavaro Yaotl, *el jefe de baratilleros.*"

Angrily, Yaotl barked, "Don't try that on me, old man." Then his expression switched to a jocular one. "This must be one special mestizo. Let us say 300 gold escudos."

Giraldo's eyes widened. It was far more than he had expected to pay. Nonetheless, it had to be done. "Half up front and the balance on delivery."

"I'll need her name and where he lives."

"Her name is Elena Bautista. He lives at this address off the plaza." Giraldo handed him a slip of paper.

"When?" said Yaotl.

"As soon as possible, and remember that no harm can come to her or the *fiscal.* Santiago must not be present when you snatch the girl."

"I will satisfy all your mistress's requirements, old man," Yaotl said, making clear he knew who pulled the strings.

Giraldo said, "Just be sure you do." With a visceral tone in his voice, he rose and departed, leaving Yaotl and his mother to themselves.

THE SOUTHERN ISLANDS

THEY GATHERED IN the cold early morning light by the Alhondiga dock, where the Acequia Real turned south to the lake. The assembled included Diego, Captain de Anza, and twelve soldiers from the Regimiento de México.

The senior officer was Sergeant Luis Trujillo, born in Mexico City and an eighteen-year military veteran. He, like most of his men, spoke Nahuatl. The native populations of these islands spoke little or no Spanish, so this would help. Diego and de Anza could describe their Nahuatl as proficient at best.

The barge for their transport down the canal and out into the lake was ready and waiting. Seven men manned the barge, bringing the entire party to twenty-one. It would be cramped, but the trip out and back was only a little over twenty-four miles.

All the islands were remnants of ancient volcanic activity. They were covered with wild green grasses, scrub oak, maguey, and prickly pear cactus. Large rocky outcrops were scattered throughout. Their first destination in the chain of six islands would be Xacatlalmanco.

The island of Xacatlalmanco and the others were home to small settlements of between fifty and two hundred Indios. Some were managed by farming the *chinampas*, but most of the people were water folk specialized in exploiting the lacustrine resources, worms, fish, salamanders, insects, and algae. They maintained nurseries for the fish and insect eggs. Those would be eaten on their own or made into a paste with the algae, then molded and dried into cakes. All these items were trade goods for the islanders to be sold or bartered for other goods in the city or with other villages.

The searchers landed on a small spit of land toward the northern end of Xacatlalmanco. To the east, there were wetlands near the shore. After the soldiers disembarked, the bargemen pushed off and headed to the island's southern tip. Per their plan, they would fan out in teams of two and walk the island north to south.

It was slow going on this first island. The sergeant and his men were told to look for structures that could act as temples of worship, caves, grottos, and anything else that would serve as the same. The search lasted over an hour, and no one saw anything worth reporting, no structures of any kind other than the modest jacales the Indios lived in. They crossed paths with an islander who lived in a small village on the eastern shore. They asked him if he had ever seen or heard of people worshipping and sacrificing to Xochiquetzal. He replied no and said the only items of worship on the island were a stone fetish representing Chalchiuhtlicue and a crucifix. Those were kept in an open shrine made of rocks stacked together. That was outside the village near the shore.

The process was repeated over the following five islands with similar results. They finished just past three o'clock in the afternoon. That found all of them, including the bargemen, sitting in the tall grass on the edge of Tepepilco's western shore. They shielded their eyes from the bright afternoon sun sitting low in the sky.

"We may as well rest for a while and eat our rations. Then we'll head back to the city," offered de Anza. Looking dejected, Diego nodded his approval and sat down next to de Anza. They sat quietly and looked out across the lake, silently eating their rations of tortillas, beans, and *tecuitlatl* cake.

"Pedro, I'm always overly optimistic when it comes to searches. I keep expecting to find what we're looking for around every corner. We turned many corners today, my friend, and nothing." Diego laughed halfheartedly.

"Don Diego, tomorrow we will go to Tepetzinco, *sí*?" asked Sergeant Trujillo.

"Yes, Sergeant. Thank you for reminding me. Though today's search was fruitless, we've at least eliminated these six islands as possible locations. Tepetzinco must therefore be the one."

"The most dangerous one," said Trujillo.

"Dangerous? Why is that, Sergeant?"

"The whirlpool. The Pantitlan. We must be wary and keep watch as we cross the lake."

"I've heard of it, but I thought it was a myth," said Diego.

"No, it's real and considered a sacred place. The Aztecs thought it was a portal that led to the underworld."

"And what made it sacred, Sergeant?"

"Every year at the height of the dry season, the old kings would make sacrifices at the temple to summon the rains and change the time of death to the time of rebirth. Then they would make a pilgrimage to the Pantitlan. The ancient ones marked the area containing the swirling waters with flags. That is what the name Pantitlan means in Nahuatl—between the flags. They'd assemble by it in their canoes and make offerings to Chalchihuidicue, the water goddess. The flags fell away long ago. That is why I say we must be wary. Once caught in the whirlpool, it's impossible to escape."

Diego looked at de Anza and then back to Trujillo. "Sergeant, you've got me thinking. We cross the deepest part of the lake on our way to Tepetzinco. Am I right?"

"*Sí*, Don Diego. The lake can get as deep as seventy fathoms on the route we take for tomorrow's journey."

"Well, then, we will be cautious, Sergeant, and each man will be on alert. Now, let's head home."

The Monk was restless. He continued to mull over what he, Diego, Felipe, and de Anza had discussed at dinner. Leaving the baratillo, he decided to stroll up the royal canal. He started with the viceroy's palace and the canal's termination point on the plaza.

It was already four in the afternoon. The baratillo was hushed, and the crowd had dwindled. Only hard bargainers remained, hoping sellers would be desperate to offload their remaining inventory. This worked for foods and flowers and perishable goods, but none of the hardware dealers would give a centavo beyond their already fixed bargaining price. They'd wait for morning.

Soon most of the *baratilleros*, hawkers of every type of item conceivable, from baskets to butcher blocks, would be packing their goods and leaving for the day, making way for the dealers of darker, prohibited items, better suited for the cover of the night market, the *tianguillo*.

The Monk thought to himself, *Diego should be returning soon from his exploration of the southern islands. If I keep moving north along the canal, I should reach the docks at the Alhondiga about the same time he and the captain are disembarking.*

This wasn't the only reason the Monk chose this route for his stroll, however. Beyond the plaza and the archbishop's palace was the enormous mansion of La Condesa de Montoya. *I don't think La Condesa would be open to entertaining a visit, and breaking in would be more de Anza's style. But it can't hurt to reconnoiter and, as they say, see what I can see.*

The Monk made his way north along the canal. As he passed the archbishop's palace, images from his past crowded his mind, memories of his time as a Jesuit priest in Sonora. He stopped beside the entrance, staring at the palace's stone walls. His thoughts again drifted back in time. What was a wall was now a window; he was looking through it and out onto a small square. He could feel the warm breeze and the scent of flowers flooding in through the window. Around the square were a series of white stucco buildings, their walls ablaze in the bright Sonoran sun. One, taller than the others, stood out. It was the mission church, his church, and next to it, the dispensary where he served as medico to the parishioners.

Then he heard a disembodied voice softly calling his name. "Padre Avila, Benito." The soft, gentle voice was soothing and familiar. It was the Pima Indio woman Aponi, a kind and gentle soul he'd known for five years. She helped him in the dispensary. Aponi was his assistant, translator, confidant, and so much more.

"Aponi," he said aloud.

A passerby broke his reverie. "I'm sorry, Padre. Were you speaking to me?" It was a young cleric dressed in a brown cassock, just going into the palace.

"Oh. No. I was just talking to myself. Apologies."

"Not at all. Is there anything I can help you with?"

"No. No. Thank you, though. I'll just be on my way." Benito, bowing slightly, turned, and continued up the canal. How he wished to God that he could forget, but he never would.

He caught sight of La Condesa's mansion ahead on the right. It was built in a style similar to Don Felipe's home but on a much grander scale, taking up the entire city block. Disgusted, he thought of how much it must have cost to construct. *And for what? A monument to someone's vanity when the money could do so much for the needy and poor of the city.*

Taking his time, he circumnavigated the mansion, noting the entrances and a few places toward the rear that were blocked off by walls. He surmised these were service entrances.

Passing them, he made his way back around to the canal. Standing there again, he looked south toward the plaza and noticed something odd.

The cathedral's walls, which ran from the plaza to where he stood, were slightly angled down, higher at the plaza. Similarly, on the other side, the viceroy and bishop's palaces were also angled slightly down. The subsidence was not surprising. The city began on a small island in the lake, but the Aztecs, and later the Spanish, had significantly expanded on that. Many of the large stone structures were, in effect, sinking.

What was odd was that, from where he stood, he could see that all the structures on the east side of the canal, starting with the palace and coming north, were angled downward except one—the mansion of La Condesa de Montoya. The northern half was perfectly level with the street, but the southern half seemed to be sagging nearly as much as the other buildings. He remembered what de Anza had said about the time it had taken to complete the building with the extra pylons. *Strange. Why is only half of the building level? I guess they didn't do such a good job of it.* The oddity nagged at him.

In unending darkness, you can hear everything, and Ana did. Shivering in the cold, she heard the breathing of her two cellmates, the scampering of rats along the stone floor, even the flickering of the torch outside and down the passageway. Unsurprisingly, she heard footsteps long before they reached her cell. As they drew nearer, fear rose in the pit of her stomach. *Oh, my sweet Jesus, keep and protect me.*

"Buenos días, mi amigos."

It's that scab of a man holding a torch. The man who struck me. Unthinkingly, she ran her fingers over the painful lump on the back of her head. The throbbing had lessened, but it was still painful to the touch.

He turned the key in the cell's lock. "I have news, my pretty one."

Ana wasn't sure if he was referring to her or the Indio girl huddled with her man across from her. Then it became apparent as he moved through the cell to Ana.

"I wonder. Do you know whether it is day or night?" A thin-lipped smile curled on his pockmarked face. "It's daytime, and it will soon be nightfall. The news I bring, dear Ana, is that La Condesa, in her magnanimity, has given you to me." The smile broadened, revealing his bent and yellowed teeth. "I've prepared a different accommodation for you. I think you'll find it much more to your liking. It's an improvement over your present surroundings."

Madre de Dios. What does this scum have in mind?

Angamuco offered his hand. "Come, child. Come back into the light and say goodbye to your amigos. You won't be seeing them again." Ana slowly rose, and, as she did, the throbbing returned. She was weak, having barely eaten in whatever amount of time it had been since she woke in this nightmare.

Ana worked up the courage to speak. "Where are you taking me?"

"Why, to your new home. I'm sure you'll like it, and it's not just your home but *our* home." He had put his arm around her to help her walk. Ana could smell the stench of alcohol on his breath.

"Please. Can't you let me go? I promise not to tell. I—" Ana went silent. She wasn't stupid. She realized he was not going to free her and she was wasting her breath. *I'll play along. Yes, I'll do that until I see my opportunity. Merciful God, watch over me until then.*

They left the cell and walked down the passageway

until they came to a staircase leading up. As she was climbing the stairs, her legs nearly gave out. *At least we're going up and not down. Up and out of this dungeon.*

When they got to the top, however, they were not in the mansion but on another level of the cellar. There was a stairway to the right, but they walked past it and continued forward, making several turns. She tried to keep track of the turns and directions. *How many lefts and how many rights was that?* After a while, she became confused and lost count. She started to panic.

With every turn, it felt like she was being buried alive. *I'll never see Jaime again or my mother or Elena. Elena? She has to be looking for me. She'll get help.* Her hopes rose for the briefest of moments before she thought, *But what if they have Elena as well? What if she's down here somewhere? Oh God, help me. Please help me.*

They came to a stop. There was a door to the left, very solid from the looks of it. It had a small opening with a grill near the top. Angamuco fiddled with some keys, unlocked the door, and waved Ana in. It was a large room. Unlike the cell they had just come from, this was a finished apartment with paneled walls, a hardwood floor with rugs, a fireplace, two oversized upholstered chairs, and a table. In the corner of the room was a large wooden bed. Ana felt sick.

"Here we are, dear. Safe at home. I'll get a fire started then get you some supper. You must be famished. You'll find some clothes that should fit you and extra blankets in the wardrobe if you feel a chill. Should there be anything I've forgotten, please tell me, and I'll see to it."

Ana was sure his intentions were deplorable, but she was thankful to be in a regular room.

"You even have a maid. Her name is Consuela. She's quite amiable. A bit slow, owing to her age, but strong and dependable. You'll have to bear with her—she's deaf-mute—but she'll understand you. She can read lips, you know."

Ana was thinking of the food he had mentioned. She was starving and could only think of getting something to eat.

"Behind the panel divider in that corner, you'll find your bath and bidet. Consuela will bring you hot water."

Ana found herself saying, "Gracias."

This pleased Angamuco enormously. "Yes, I'll see about supper, and perhaps afterward we can have some wine and chat by the fireplace."

This went right past Ana. She was about to pass out from hunger and dehydration. Not too long after Angamuco departed, she did just that.

Benito was obsessed with the state of La Condesa's mansion. "I tell you, I walked up and down the canal at least four times to be sure it wasn't some sort of optical illusion."

The Monk, Diego, and de Anza were sitting in a pulquería by the dock. Diego told the Monk about the day's effort and explained they had nothing to show for it. Benito persisted with his observation.

"Well, it's not too far beyond my house. Let's have a look on the way back," said Diego.

"Good," said the Monk. He motioned to the bartender to send one more round and, looking back to Diego, said, "Priorities, Diego. Priorities."

"Tomorrow, we'll go to Tepetzinco," said de Anza. Then he added jokingly, "That is, if we survive the Pantitlan. What a joke."

"I wouldn't be too sure, Captain. A great number of boats have disappeared on this lake."

"I don't doubt that, but who's to say they were lost in an ancient whirlpool?"

"The Aztecs documented it, and it was an integral part of some of their rituals. I don't think they imagined it."

"The sergeant seemed to think it's real enough, and I consider him a rational sort of fellow," offered Diego.

"Tales told by his Indio mother," de Anza retorted.

The Monk tossed back the rest of his drink. "Well, I'm going with you tomorrow. We shall see."

"We're not going out there to find the Pantitlan, and, if there is such a thing, I'll see we do our best to avoid it," said Diego as he finished his first round. The waiter brought the second.

"I'm looking forward to a peaceful night at home and forgetting all this for one night."

Diego knew Elena would be waiting for him. *Why just tonight? Why not every night?*

They ambled back toward the plaza and stopped to witness the Monk's mansion phenomena. Diego and de Anza stepped back, then walked to the bridge and had another look.

"It's true," said de Anza. "I don't know what it means, but it's true."

"Pedro. You told us the records showed it was built twenty years ago and took two years to complete. Correct?"

"*Sí*, Diego."

"And the reason it took so long, at least according to the court recorder, was driving additional pylons to prevent subsidence. Is that also true?"

"Yes, Diego."

"Well, then, if that's true, I think we should confirm. Why is half of the building sinking nearly as far as all the others?"

"After looking again," Benito interjected, "I see cracks in the middle of the foundation. Without doubt, the southern end is sinking."

"Pedro," said Diego, "would you find out who the architects were and what they can tell us about the construction?"

"I have a colleague who works for one of the alcaldes *de corte*. He'll know where to inquire. I'll try to catch him tonight."

"Great! See if he can get the plans of the building and find out who the builders were."

"I'll ask," said Diego. He added that he needed to be home by six.

"Give my regards to Señorita Bautista, won't you, Diego?" De Anza said wryly.

"Right, I will. Both of you, just be sure you're at the dock again tomorrow by eight. Sergeant Trujillo and his men will be waiting with the barge."

"Looks like we're in for a bit of a storm," noted the Monk. "See you in the morning."

As they walked away, de Anza turned and said, "Take it easy tonight, Monk. I don't want to have to fish you out of the water tomorrow." The Monk kept moving, raised his arm, and waved without turning.

The Monk never noticed, as he cut across the baratillo,

that Yaotl was standing with his men in the plaza not too far from him. It was a few minutes past six, and it had started to rain.

"Are you sure she's there?" asked Yaotl.

"*Sí*, jefe. We followed her from her place. She went inside about an hour ago. We're told she doesn't have to be at the mansion until nine tomorrow. If the *fiscal* leaves first, we'll make our move."

"You're sure there's just the one woman in the house besides the girl?"

"*Sí*, just the maid. She has a room in the back on the ground floor. A rear door leads into a hall by the kitchen. I've checked the lock. There won't be any problem getting in."

It always happened, without fail. Each time Diego met Elena, his heart would jump into his throat at the sight of her. So it had been this evening. He took her into his arms and kissed her. *This is heaven. I never want to let go.*

They shared a light meal Maria had prepared. Afterward, they moved to the drawing room. Since it was raining outside, Diego lit a fire. They sat there together quietly, talking over the events of the day.

"Diego, I can't sleep thinking about Ana."

"I'm sure. I wish I had news, but the detail Felipe assigned hasn't turned up any clues as to her whereabouts. It's like she just vanished. I know that's not what you want to hear. At the very least, we haven't found any evidence of foul play."

She laid her head on his shoulder and stared into the fire. It had been nearly five days since she had last seen

Ana. “Do you think she could be dead?” she asked, tears in her eyes.

“Don’t think that. We can only go on the evidence, and as I said, there’s nothing to corroborate foul play. You shouldn’t lose hope.”

Diego told her of their failed mission to the islands and the plans for the morning. He laughed a little about Benito’s excitement over the level of the mansion.

“That’s true. Ana and I both noticed months ago. I can’t tell you why, though.”

“Poor construction,” answered Diego.

They sat there quietly, nested together on the couch, listening to the hypnotic rhythm of the rain tapping on the window. Warm and comfortable, they fell asleep, just as Diego wanted, in heaven.

TEPETZINCO

IT WAS STILL raining in the morning when Diego left home for the Alhondiga dock. Maria was in the kitchen, and Elena was dressing upstairs. Yaotl's men gave Diego five minutes to get some distance between himself and the house. Then they made their move, leaving one man on guard in case he returned. They moved their covered horse cart to a spot opposite the house in the alleyway, across from the back door.

The lock on the door to the rear of the house was old and broke easily. Two men entered the house and made for the kitchen as quietly as possible. Maria was standing at the kitchen prep table slicing vegetables when the first man came up from behind her, putting his right hand over her mouth and simultaneously taking hold of her left wrist with the other, bringing her arm around her back. She tried to scream Elena's name, but it was too muffled for her to hear. The paring knife was still in her right hand, and she brought it down as hard as possible into her assailant's right hip. Reflexively, his hand came down from her mouth to grab her arm and pull the knife away. She tried to scream again, but the second man silenced her with his blackjack with a sharp blow to her head. She fell straight to the floor, taking the knife with her.

"*Maldita perra!*" the first man said, keeping his voice low. Lucky for him, she hadn't cut an artery. Nonetheless, the blood flowed steadily from his wound, and his eyes searched the room for something to stem the flow. Pointing, he said, "Give me that towel, Jose. *Mierda!*" As the first man saw to his wound, the second bound Maria's hands and feet and gagged her.

"Daniel, are you all right?"

"I'll be fine."

The two men left Maria on the kitchen floor. Jose knew he'd be in trouble if she were seriously injured. Yaotl had instructed them not to hurt either of the women. The stairs to the second floor were across from them in the center of the courtyard under the portico. They moved swiftly and silently up the stairs. Now the question was which room. They split up, moving in either direction on the arcade, listening at each door as they went.

Jose heard a soft whistle and looked to see Daniel signaling him from the opposite side. Jose made his way around to the middle door. Daniel's ear was glued to the door. "Now we wait until she exits. We'll take her from both sides," said Daniel, taking the gag from his pocket.

As the door opened, and Elena stepped out, Daniel, grateful this one didn't have a knife, put his hand over her mouth while Jose pulled her arms behind her back to bind them. Elena opened her mouth as if to scream. As Daniel fumbled, trying to get a new purchase with his hand, she bit down hard on his little finger.

"Aarrgh!" This time he couldn't suppress the scream. Both men struggled to get her bound and gagged. She was surprisingly strong and fought like a wildcat. They finally succeeded. Jose threw her over his shoulder, and they made their way back downstairs and out the door. The rain-drenched horse cart was waiting in the alleyway.

They put her in the back of the cart and drew down the cover. They both sat on her to keep her from escaping. Besides swearing up a blue streak, Daniel was bleeding badly from both his hip and what was left of his right little finger. He looked down at the squirming hellcat beneath him and noticed Elena's turquoise bracelet. He bent down and pulled it from her wrist. "You won't need this any longer, dearie."

Elena screamed a muffled, "Bastardo! What do you thugs want with me?" She couldn't think of a reason for them wanting to take her. In time, it would become terrifyingly clear.

The Monk and de Anza were already at the dock as Diego walked up. They weren't speaking to each other, and, from the looks on their faces, Diego assumed words had been exchanged.

Sergeant Trujillo walked across the boat ramp to Diego and shook his hand. "Poor luck with this weather, Don Diego."

"Rain or no rain, we must make the run to Tepetzinco today."

Trujillo looked up. "The wind has picked up. I

wouldn't worry about waves. They only get a few feet high, even in the worst weather. But the way they act is strange. They go back and forth like water in a bathtub. I can't explain it, but it makes rowing difficult. It could be slow going for a lot of the trip."

Diego was concerned. He wanted as much time on Tepetzinco as they could get. "At least we have only one island to visit today. Are we just about ready?"

"*Sí*. The last of the gear has been stowed. You and your colleagues may board. Judging by the sound of their conversation earlier, they didn't seem too pleased to be traveling together."

They shoved off from the dock. Going out through the canal, which entered the lake further south than Diego would have preferred, was easy. It meant that, when they left the canal and entered the lake, they'd have to row east first and then north to the island.

Once on the lake, he understood what the sergeant was saying about the motion of the waves. The whole barge rocked, at first fore to aft, but, as they turned north, it was port to starboard. Diego was thankful he hadn't had a large breakfast that morning.

It took them a little over five hours to reach Tepetzinco. Twice as long as it would if the weather had cooperated. The rain continued to come down, and it was getting heavier and affecting their visibility. Diego was surprised the sergeant managed to find the island. They landed on the island's southwest end, angled to the northeast along its length. Like the water people of the southern islands they had visited, the Indios here made their livelihood from the lake. The largest concentration of Indios was in the only village on the island near their landing site.

It was one in the afternoon, but it may as well have been midnight. The clouds darkened the sky so much Diego could barely see. They decided to stay together in a single unit to search the village. Afterward, they'd do what they'd done on the other islands—fan out and comb the island in teams of two.

It was hard to estimate how large the population was. Most everyone was sheltering from the weather. Judging by the number of jacales, de Anza estimated as many as three to four hundred, a considerable village for water folk. Near the center was a large round mud brick *temazcalli* with heavy clouds of steam escaping from a small opening at the top. Next to it was a sizable oblong-shaped structure four times larger.

"What do you think, Sergeant? A council lodge?" inquired de Anza.

"I think there's a good chance. Pedro, Benito, Sergeant, we'll leave the men outside and the four of us will go in. With luck, there'll be some local authority inside, a chief. Benito, if you don't mind, you enter ahead of us. You're the only one not wearing a uniform. I don't want to scare them," said Diego.

Dressed like a Catholic priest, Sergeant Trujillo thought, *he might scare them more than a soldier.*

"Sure," said Benito, drawing the reed mat away from the entrance and stepping in.

Diego turned to Trujillo. "Sergeant, how do you say 'chief' in Nahuatl?"

"Tlahtoani," responded Trujillo.

Inside the lodge, Benito counted twelve Indios sitting in a semicircle at the far end of the lodge. They sat on blankets, smoking, as they studied Benito. A small fire burned between Benito and the men.

"Good morning!" Benito said in Nahuatl. None of them spoke, but they all nodded in response. "I'm here with some Spanish soldiers from the city. May I ask them to enter?"

The man sitting in the middle said simply, "*Quemah.*" Benito thought, *This must be the head man, the chief.* The Monk poked his head out and motioned for the other three to join him. Once inside, the chief bade them sit. They did, and the chief offered tobacco. They each drew on the pipe.

Diego spoke in broken Nahuatl. "We've come to search for a place of worship, a temple. Does something like that exist on the island?"

Two of the men said something neither he nor the others understood. They assumed it was dialect. Whatever it was, Diego could hear urgency in their voices.

The chief responded to them with a single word. Again, Diego couldn't understand, but it seemed imperative. The others quickly composed themselves and went back to staring blankly at their visitors.

"We have no temples here," said the chief. "There are only two structures on the island besides those in the village. These are the remains of the *achichiacpan* and the old, abandoned casa. Are those what you seek?"

Diego assumed he was referring to the *achichiacpan*, Moctezuma's bath, primarily built as a temple to Chalchihuidicue.

"Do you pray to Chalchihuidicue?" Diego asked, assuming all islanders did.

"We pray to the Spanish god," said the chief.

"Can you tell us how to find the remains of the casa and *achichiacpan*?"

The chief nodded. "They are both north and on the western shore."

Diego reached into his tunic and withdrew a satchel of tobacco. "A gift, Tlahtoani." Diego stepped forward and held it out to the chief. The chief took it and inspected the contents. Looking up to Diego, he nodded his approval. He was a man of few words.

"*Tlazohcamati*, Tlahtoani. My men and I will be on our way and trouble you no further." Once again, the chief nodded.

They weren't back in the rain long and were preparing to move north when one of the soldiers came up and spoke to the sergeant.

When he was finished, the sergeant turned to his three companions. "The corporal says that, while we were with the chief, several villagers approached the lodge, but, upon seeing them, turned and ran."

"I suppose they're a little frightened of the military after all," said Diego.

"Did you notice the reaction of the two men next to the chief when we asked about the temple?" De Anza remarked.

"Yes," said Benito. "He barked at them, and they immediately shut up."

Diego considered what the sergeant said and what they had just witnessed in the lodge. "Why so distant and tight-lipped?"

"Maybe the chief said what he thought you wanted to hear. However, he lied about the water goddess. The fishermen and island dwellers still make offerings to her, even if they profess to be Christians."

"Well, let's start the search," said Diego. "The ruins of the bath and this abandoned house are on the western shore."

"Why would there be a house on the island?" said Benito. "I wasn't expecting that. Do you suppose it's Aztec?"

"We'll find out," said Diego. "Pedro, you and I will take that side of the sweep. Sergeant, you and Benito anchor the eastern end. Report if you find anything." They trudged off. Luckily the island was mainly grassy with lots of shrub oak and only a thin layer of topsoil. Otherwise, it would have been a long, muddy slog.

They had walked for some time, and Diego was starting to feel disheartened. He thought, *What if we don't find anything here either? What should we do next? The Indios said it was only accessible by water. What else could that mean? Certainly not the floating gardens, the chinampas. They're too small and impermanent.*

Then, in the distance, he saw what must be the abandoned house, sitting on the slope away from the shoreline. Its contrast to the landscape was the only thing that made it visible in the heavy rain. Remarkably, it was a Spanish-style home. At one time, in the distant past, it had been a *casa grande*. As they got closer, he noticed it incorporated a few elements of Aztec architecture.

Built as a two-story wood-framed building, it had a stucco exterior and a tiled roof that rose from the right side to a roofline that followed an obtuse curve to the center of the building. The rest of the top was down a few feet and flat across its length. Much of the stucco had disappeared. Under the flat portion of the roof, a balcony occupied the entire length of the second floor, supported by five columns. Half of it had fallen in on itself.

Under the extended curved portion of the roof were two small windows midpoint to a formal entryway below. The entrance was constructed of solid stone blocks and stood out from the house. The size and shape were similar to small Aztec structures Diego had seen. It had a breadth of ten feet, rising to fourteen feet.

In the center of the lintel was a single embossment. It was round and irregular. Diego didn't recognize it but made a quick sketch and tucked it into the breast pocket of his tunic. They entered a small rectangular courtyard with a fountain in the center, surrounded by a second-story arcade, much of which had also collapsed. To the left was a series of rooms. The right seemed to have larger living spaces.

"Pedro, I'm not sure how safe it is to explore this much further. This house is very old and seems like it's been vacant for some time," said Diego.

"Yes, and with all this wind and rain, it looks like the whole thing might give way at any moment. I wouldn't risk going through the entire house. And, as you say, no one's been here for a long time."

"It looks like this large center room at the back is where the family would have congregated. Let's have a quick look and then move on."

"Agreed. We don't want to fall too far behind the others," said de Anza.

Diego was right. The spacious room appeared to be the living or great room of the house. The space was empty, and nothing was left in the way of furniture or decorations. The walls were barren, but two chandeliers hung precariously from the ceiling. Only the large fireplace at the back of the room remained.

"Not much to see here," said de Anza.

Diego scanned the room. "Wait. Come here. Closer to the fireplace."

They walked over, and as they got closer, they noted it was a solid stone block construction. There was nothing ornate about its design, but its size was quite generous.

Diego lit a match and, brushing away the dust from the mantle, held it close. "Words are chiseled into the stone, just below the top. See here? Pedro, can you read this?"

"It says, '*Surge et accipe cor.*' Is that how you see it?"

"Yes. Latin?"

"I think you're right, but I'm afraid I don't know what it means."

"Neither do I, but we can figure that out later. Let's get on our way." Diego jotted down the inscription, and they headed through the courtyard and the stone entrance.

"I'm still puzzled as to who built this house," said Diego.

"We can see if Padre Aranda is familiar with its history," said de Anza.

They resumed their search up and along the shoreline. The rain continued its relentless downpour. They'd been walking for about twenty minutes when Diego felt de Anza poking him on the shoulder. He had two fingers to his lips and whispered, "Listen. Just ahead and to the right."

They crouched down, and Diego listened, looking at de Anza. Both had quizzical looks on their faces.

"It's laughter," said Diego. They listened a bit longer.

"Laughter and giggling. A man and a woman. Laughing in the rain?"

"Let's get closer," said Diego. Keeping low to the ground, they crept forward.

"What's this?" said Diego, struggling to see in the heavy downpour.

"Looks like a stone wall."

Eyeing it closer, they saw it was about two feet tall and jutted from a rocky outcrop on the hill, extending down toward the lake, growing in height as it moved down the hill. Steam wafted above it from the other side.

Diego whispered to de Anza, "This must be part of a bath. I can't see much more."

The laughter and giggling were clearer now. "Wait! Do you hear that? Splashing!"

Simultaneously, they pulled themselves up and peered over the wall. They could see the wall as a part of a greater square edifice. If it had had a roof at one time, it was now gone. A blue-tiled expanse of floor was fifteen feet down from where they stood. At its center, rising two feet above the floor, stood the bath, a circle of stone fourteen feet wide, covered with intricate mosaics composed of green, white, and red tiles. A man and woman frolicked naked within it.

At the hillside end of the room was a broad eight-foot-high statue in a kneeling position. They presumed it was the water goddess, Chalchihuidicue. Hot water flowed in a channel below the hem of her skirt, leading to the bath and emptying into it. At the lake end of the room was a seven-foot-high opening in the wall.

"Well, we've found the bath, but I can't see any evil aspects to it. It doesn't appear that there are any other rooms, and I don't suppose we should disturb the occupants. What do you think?" asked de Anza.

"Agreed. It's interesting, but this is not the temple we're looking for. We'll go down and around."

They were about to proceed down the hill when Diego said, "Just a moment! Pedro, do you see that man?"

"*Sí*, Diego. Anything special about him?"

"Certainly! He's the missing steward from the reception. The one who served me the drug. What did Don Felipe say his name was?"

"Alejandro Hernandez," whispered de Anza.

They went down the hill and around the ruins to find a staircase hewn from rock that ran from a small stone jetty on the lake to the entrance of the ruin they had seen from the other side. The heavy rain masked the sound of their footsteps as they made their way up the stairs, into the ancient structure, then across to the edge of the bath. A woman screamed as the two uniformed men appeared at the side of the bath, swords drawn.

"Alejandro Hernandez! I'm detaining you for questioning by order of His Majesty, King Ferdinand the Sixth."

The man was dumbfounded as de Anza reached into the bath, grabbed him by the arm, and dragged him out.

"*Perdóname*, señorita," said de Anza with a broad smile to the woman hunched down in the bath, trying to conceal her nakedness. "Apologies."

De Anza said, "Should we take the woman as well?"

"I don't think so. But let's get her name."

Hernandez's clothes were nearby, and de Anza instructed him to dress and told the woman to do the same. They turned their backs. Once they had bound Hernandez, de Anza doffed his hat and made a long sweeping bow to the lady. Then, together with Diego and their prisoner, they left, leaving a perplexed and angry woman alone in the ruins of Chalchihuidicue's temple.

They continued up the shoreline, Hernandez in tow. Remarkably, with everything they'd discovered, they were still on track to complete their trek north and make the rendezvous with Trujillo and the Monk.

They met up with the rest of the squad standing by the barge moored on the northwestern tip of the island. "We caught a fish along the way," said Diego.

"Who is this?" inquired the sergeant.

"This is the steward who went missing after the reception. I can't say I appreciate his taste in champagne," replied Diego.

The rest of the team had nothing unusual to report other than the behavior of the chief's men, the people in the village, and those they encountered in the sweep. Upon seeing the soldiers, they had turned and run, without exception.

"Not a complete failure, though, gentlemen," said Diego. "We've got Hernandez, and between his presence and the villagers' reactions, Tepetzinco is worthy of another visit."

"Yes," said de Anza.

"Hopefully, not on a day like today," added Diego.

His point was well taken, for the weather was at its worst since their departure that morning.

"I'd like some time in that hot spring you spoke of," Benito said, laughing.

"Señores, we'd better be pushing off," pressed Trujillo. "It'll be getting dark soon, and it's already hard enough to see in this rain."

De Anza maneuvered Hernandez into a seat between himself and Benito as the rest of the squad boarded the barge.

"That everyone?" called the barge captain.

"*Sí!*" echoed Trujillo, and they were off.

The lake was doing its best to display the effect the sergeant had described in the morning as the waves sloshed back and forth at about two feet, tipping the barge to and fro as they went. The oarsmen were struggling. Their strokes were inconsistent, too shallow or too deep, as they rose and fell on either side. It was slow going as they fought to keep the unwieldy barge on a proper course.

Thirty minutes into their journey, Diego noticed an unusual sound above that of the sloshing waves. It started low but soon increased in volume. The sound reminded him of a rushing river. It came from the starboard side and continued to grow louder.

Everyone noticed at that point. Then they saw it. Ahead and to the right, they could see and hear the large swirling mass forming a vortex of ink-black water 150 feet across. Almost hypnotic in its motion, the choppy waves were swallowed by its racing flow, churning violently as they disappeared into its maw.

The current drew them closer. The distance lessened, and the current accelerated. Unless they could escape its pull, it would take them toward it faster and faster until they passed the maelstrom's unescapable threshold. Once crossed, the inevitable descent would begin, offering no hope of return.

"My God, it's true," said Benito.

They were all awestruck, all but the captain of the barge. He was barking orders to the helm and oarsmen, attempting to swing the barge off its current course to port. "Starboard oars! Pull hard. Pull for your lives. Portside, bury those oars! Helmsman! Hard aport!"

The sudden turn of the barge tipped the massive vessel to the left. As it righted itself, Hernandez took advantage of the added momentum, and, seizing de Anza by the ankles, flipped him overboard. Floundering in his greatcoat, weighed down by his sword belt, de Anza could barely keep his head above the choppy waters. Worse, he was on a tack toward the maelstrom with steadily increasing speed. De Anza was caught in a current yanking him into and around the whirlpool, away from the wheeling barge.

The Monk jumped up, hurriedly shed his cloak, grabbed the towline, and fastened it around his waist. He dove into the water and swam straight out toward the whirlpool. He hoped to meet de Anza as he completed his first and probably only revolution and catch him before he crossed the threshold. The Monk prayed hard that neither he nor de Anza would be sucked in before that. He had only one chance. To make this work, the Monk had to swim against the same current sweeping de Anza around and into the vortex. It took a Herculean effort to slow himself down to the point where de Anza could catch up with him. It was all de Anza could do to stay above water. It was almost dark, and the rainfall was still heavy. Visibility was down to a couple of feet. The Monk was counting on de Anza to collide with him, knowing he wouldn't see him until he was right on top of him.

Then, frighteningly, the Monk felt his feet pulled up and into the maelstrom. He was about to go sideways when de Anza smacked into him with tremendous force.

The Monk struggled to get a firm grip on him. De Anza's flailing attempts to keep afloat weren't helping matters. Then, he had him. The Monk managed to get one of his long arms around de Anza's waist. A jolt came as they were drawn into the whirlpool, and their swift descent drew the towline taut. It wrenched the Monk's torso violently, but he kept hold of de Anza.

The bargemen, seeing the line go taut, began to haul them back and out of the pull of the maelstrom. As the pull of the current lessened, they knew they had escaped the fierce draw of the vortex and were safe. At last, they came alongside the barge and were lifted out of the water and onto the deck. Diego started breathing again. They took the Monk's discarded cloak and threw it over the two of them. It was almost large enough to cover them both.

Regaining his breath, the Monk saw Hernandez flat on the barge's deck. Diego's first action after the Monk dove overboard was to introduce Alejandro's head to the butt of his sword. Seeing the Monk staring at the outstretched body, Diego said, "Since no one was watching him, I thought it might be better if he was kept out of the way while you two were enjoying your swim." He attempted a laugh, but it went short.

Benito could see how distraught he was. "Well, when I saw the captain going in for a dip, I found I couldn't resist." His broad smile warmed Diego's heart.

Thank God my two best friends are safe, Diego thought.

"It's certainly good to be back," said de Anza. As he stepped over the prone body, he accidentally planted his foot on Hernandez's ribs. He turned to the Monk. "Benito, I, well, I—" was all he got out. He extended his hand and offered it to the Monk.

"I'm sure you would have done the same for me in another life." They laughed as they shook hands, de Anza firmly grasping Benito's forearm with his other hand.

"I don't understand, Pedro," interjected Diego. "Why didn't you jettison your sword and belt? You didn't need an anchor."

"It was my father's sword. He gave it to me before he died."

"And you intended to return it to him personally?"

De Anza stared expressionless at Diego for a few seconds, then burst out laughing. Benito and Diego joined in.

Elena woke in an empty room that was barren save a table, chair, and the bed she was lying on. On top of the table were a porcelain basin, a pitcher of water, and a glass. She remembered bumping along in a horse-drawn cart, trying to breathe through a gag with her hands tied behind her back as two men sat on her legs.

The cart stopped. Elena was blindfolded and felt herself lifted out of the cart and carried somewhere. She had no idea where she was. She remembered being turned onto her back and how it hurt her arms that were still bound at the wrists. Someone pulled the gag aside and, holding her nose, started pouring a liquid down her throat until she had no choice but to swallow it. Then she was here, lying unbound on the bed.

Elena still couldn't fathom who would want to kidnap her and why. She went to the door, but, of course, it was locked. No sooner had she turned away from it than she heard a key turning in the lock. She stood there, fearful and angry, as the door opened.

"I've come with some food and fresh water."

She recognized the man as one of the two men who kidnapped her. "*Bastardo!*" she loudly exclaimed, grabbing the basin from the table and hurling it across the room at him. It barely missed as he turned to avoid it.

"Please. I'm sorry, señorita. I do what they tell me."

"They told you to be a criminal? A kidnapper? You're comfortable with what you've done?"

"Señorita, the man I work for doesn't take no for an answer. When he tells you to do something, you do it. No matter what it is. Please forgive me if you can."

"I can't. Put the food and water on the table and get out."

He quickly complied, desperately wanting to escape her wrath.

Jose was a criminal, no doubt, but he grew up knowing no other life. He had no trade or education, and even if he had somehow been given the means to apply himself in some other way, no one quit Alavaro Yaotl. A good man by nature, Jose was happy to be able to support his mother and younger sister. He had never known his father.

"Wait," said Elena in a less threatening voice. "What's your name?"

"Jose, señorita."

"Why was I taken?"

"I can't say. I mean, I don't know."

"Who do you work for?"

"That I cannot say. *Disculpas*, señorita."

"Jose, where am I? Where did you and your friend take me?"

"I would tell if I could, and it's better you not see my friend for a while. Between you and the maid, he's still in much pain. He'll heal, but that piece of his finger won't grow back."

"Maid? Maria? Is she hurt?"

Jose's head went down and, in a genuinely apologetic tone, he said, "I'm sorry. When she cut Daniel, he lost control of her, and I had to hit her to keep her from shouting."

"You killed her? *Bastardo!*"

Elena ran at him, but Jose quickly replied, "No! She's not dead. She was breathing when we left her." Elena stopped short, and Jose was a little relieved. He didn't want to tangle with her again. "I promise I'll find out how she is and let you know."

Elena glared at him. She was angry beyond words but recognized he was trying to be helpful. She watched him leave and heard him lock the door behind him.

She prayed, "Please, God, let Maria be well." Frustrated, she thought, *Well, I didn't learn much from him.* She looked about the room, searching for a clue to her whereabouts or a means of escape. There was a window, but as she pulled the drapes aside, she saw it was shuttered and locked. She tried to peer through the boards of the shutters, but the glass panes were clouded and obscured what little she could see. She would have to find a way to free herself. The question was how. Elena sat in the one chair in the room and silently resigned herself to being there a while longer.

Across town in the Mercado de San Juan, Daniel sat nursing his wounds, drinking pulque and cheap mezcal. One of Yaotl's men had sloppily tended to his injuries, stitching up the cut in his thigh and wrapping his finger with a dirty bandage. Since he was flush, for the moment, with the money he'd gotten for the kidnapping, Daniel ordered his fourth round and settled into his chair. Leaning it back against the wall, he watched the people walking through the marketplace and grumbled.

He caught sight of the Indio girl he'd seen many times before walking into the market. As she passed, he grabbed her by the arm and pulled her down onto his lap. "Hello, little Pepita. How are you today?"

The girl wasn't frightened. Though young, she had seen much of life and was used to this one's advances, which were proffered on a near daily basis.

"I've got pesos to share. Would you like a drink and maybe a quick roll?" said Daniel, laughing, with his arm around her waist and hugging her closer.

She could smell the liquor on his breath. "Not today, señor. I have washing to do."

"Ah, be sweet, my dearie. You can do your washing later."

Daniel remembered the bracelet in his pocket. It didn't have much value, so he figured he'd put it to work. "Look what I got here!"

Pepita saw the bracelet and went wide-eyed. It looked like a treasure to her. She reached for it, but Daniel snatched it away.

"Whoa, don't be so quick, dearie. What say we have a bit of fun, and when we're done, it's yours?" Aside from the alcohol on his breath, he smelled like he had never bathed or changed his clothes.

"But I have to do the wash, or I'll get in trouble."

"Come on now, dearie, won't take but a bit."

"Well, if I can have it, I'll finish the wash and come back."

Daniel wasn't that much of a fool, but he also knew it wasn't a king's ransom he was entrusting to her. He gave her a lecherous grin. "Very well, dearie. You do that. I'll be right here waitin' for ya." He let her off his lap and slapped her on the behind. Then she was off to do the wash, never to return.

Daniel ordered another round, and now he felt little pain from his injuries. He would continue to drink and eventually spend all of his money. Soon, though, he would no longer need the spirits to ease his discomfort. By the next day, gangrene would set in, and three days later, he would be dead from septic shock.

Cold and drenched to the bone, Diego unlocked the front door to his home. Thinking only of a hot bath and something to eat, he was surprised to see Don Felipe coming out of the drawing room and into the foyer. Not giving Diego a chance to say anything, he delivered the news. "Diego, my boy. Thank God you're home. I'm sorry, but something dreadful has happened. Maria was attacked by two men who broke into the house this morning."

"Maria? Is she all right?"

"Yes, she's resting. But she took a nasty blow to her head."

"Thank God she's okay. What did they steal?"

"Diego, prepare yourself. They took Elena."

Diego took the news like a punch in the gut. "How? Who?"

"We do not know who or why yet. They broke in

through the door in the rear and attacked Maria in the kitchen. She tussled with them, but they struck her down and left her, bound and gagged, on the kitchen floor. Maria regained consciousness as they took Elena out the same way they came in. It sounds as though she put up quite a struggle."

"Felipe, where is Maria?"

"In her room. I had the doctor look at her, and my maid, Señora Reyes, is sitting with her now."

Diego walked straight to Maria's room at the back of the house and knocked gently at the door.

"*Adelante*," came a soft voice he assumed to be Señora Reyes'. As he entered, he saw Maria lying on her bed asleep, the señora sitting next to her with her rosary in her hands. She nodded in recognition, raising two fingers to her lips. Diego moved quietly to Maria's bedside. There were no bandages, but she had a cool compress on her left temple that Señora Reyes had been refreshing regularly. Beneath it, he could see a small part of the dark, swollen bruise.

Anger and frustration welled up within Diego. He was outraged at seeing his longtime companion attacked and injured, and he was desperate to know where Elena might be. For the time being, he was impotent to help her.

He gently placed his hand on Señora Reyes' shoulder, whispered his thanks, and left the room. "Felipe, what are we to do?"

"I had my men canvass the neighborhood to see if someone witnessed anything or saw anyone loitering in the neighborhood. A servant in one of the other homes said he'd seen a horse-drawn cart in the alley behind the house at around eight on his way to the market. When he returned an hour later, it was gone. The grocer making a delivery at nine thirty discovered Maria. The back door lock was broken, and the door was open. There isn't much to go on other than what Maria told us. Two men, of medium build, in their twenties, entered a little after eight. One grabbed Maria from behind as she was working at the kitchen table. Maria planted her vegetable knife into the man's thigh in the scuffle. There's a fair amount of blood in the kitchen and a trail leading upstairs to your room and out the back door. The rain erased the trail from there. They likely used that cart to transport Elena. One other thing. We found what looks to be part of a man's finger on the first floor outside your room."

"I assume you've checked the clinics and hospitals in the city for similar wounds being treated."

"Yes, Diego, but nothing to report."

"I'll alert my informants to be on the lookout. What do you think the motive could be?"

"Ransom would be the most likely, but that presents a list of questions."

"What would those be?"

"Well, if it's a case of kidnapping for ransom, where would the ransom note go? To Elena's family, assuming she has one?"

"She does—her mother. Her father died some years ago."

"And what are we to think if you receive the note, Diego?"

"I think I see where you're headed with this."

"A vital question is, why kidnap Elena from your home and not her own?"

"Yes, Uncle. Regardless of where the ransom note goes, whoever kidnapped her had to know she was here."

"Which means, Diego, they know about your relationship."

Diego pondered the implications. Felipe was already there.

"It's not a kidnap for ransom, is it, Felipe?"

"No, I think not. This is about you, Diego. The kidnappers did this as a warning to pressure you. And if that's the case, it's quite probable someone connected to you or one of your investigations did this."

"I think you're right, but I'm not sure it was meant to be a warning. They thought I would accept this as a kidnapping for ransom. They hoped it would draw me off the investigation, at least long enough for the trail to have gone cold."

"Good point, Diego. Different angle but same conclusion. So, from all the active cases you have, which would warrant an action like this?"

"Only one, Felipe. The Plaza Mayor murder."

Felipe thought for a moment. Finding the dead man in the plaza and in such close proximity to the cathedral and viceregal palace had become news over the past week. Rumors and wild ideas involving everything from rebellion to satanic curses were spreading among members of the government and clergy. This needed to be resolved quickly.

"Diego, try to get some rest. I've sent a messenger to advise Benito and the captain of Elena's disappearance. Let's meet in my office tomorrow morning and regroup."

"Very well. Sleep well, and thank you for everything."

"Don't worry, Diego. We'll bring Elena home. Now get some sleep."

Sleep? How can I sleep? Oh, Elena. Where are you? Wherever you are, I pledge this: I will find you.

"Is my guest comfortable in her new surroundings, Giraldo?"

"I presume, *mi dama*. I, of course, haven't met with her."

"No, we wouldn't want that for her own good. It would mean her death if she found out where she was or who arranged her capture. What of the ransom note?"

"I've prepared something simple that covers all the necessary specifics," said Giraldo.

"Let me see it."

If you want to see the woman alive, go to the Cathedral of the Assumption this Sunday at eight in the morning. Place 500 silver reals in the hollow under the baptismal font of San Felipe de Jesus. Bring no one else, and be sure law enforcement is not within ten blocks of the cathedral. The woman will be released once the money is retrieved without incident.

"That will do. When will it be delivered?"

"This evening," said Giraldo.

"I assume one of Yaotl's men will retrieve the ransom."

"Correct, *mi dama*, and Yaotl will retain twenty percent for his efforts."

"Very well. Let's discuss this Sunday's sacrifice."

"Of course, *mi dama*. All of the preparations have been completed. Your daughter will arrive from Tepetzinco at nine. Six others from the island will be coming to participate, including the offering. High mass will begin at noon. The ceremonial elixirs have been prepared for you and the ranking celebrants. Your ladies-in-waiting will dress and prepare you at eleven."

"Very good. I've thought this over, and I've decided to offer up Isabel's lady-in-waiting to Xochiquetzal rather than the willing oblation from the colony."

A look of extreme apprehension came across Giraldo's face. "*Mi dama!* If we sacrifice the *fiscal*'s woman, the fictitious ransom plot will have been for nothing, and, in time, he'll begin to suspect other motives."

"You don't understand me, Giraldo. I'm talking about the stout little thing we have tucked away. It occurred to me that to have her heart ripped from her chest while her closest friend sits three floors up, oblivious to the proceedings, would be delicious."

"But you said I could have the little one. You said it was a gift."

"Oh, shut up, Giraldo. I'll do what I please. I don't care a whit what I said to you. Make sure she's delivered to the temple attendants Sunday morning."

"But you can't. She's mine. She's my wife!"

Dona Andrea shrieked with laughter. "You pathetic fool. Is that your fantasy, that you and the little mestizo are man and wife?" Eyes wild and glaring, she uttered a loud inhuman shriek, spittle shooting from her mouth, and slapped Angamuco viciously across the face, followed by a torrent of foul invectives. This was Dona Andrea's true face, the ugly and vile countenance of a monstrous harpy. Finishing her tirade, she commanded Angamuco to do what he was told.

Walking to his room on the second floor underground, Giraldo had tears in his eyes. *She's mine. She is my love, the one who loves me as well, mine to sit with and exchange our thoughts or to sit silently, content to be together.* He started sobbing, a piteous creature living in a fantasy he had created for himself. Now she had taken that from him, and, once again, he'd be lonely with no one to smile at or be smiled at in return. His tears dried as the anger grew in him. *Bitch. Vile whore. I will kill you.* As he calmed himself, his thoughts became more conspiratorial. *But how? Her death must be filled with the same terror and pain she has inflicted on others all her wicked life. Yes, it's a question of method and timing.*

He thought about going to Ana's room. As much love as he may profess, he was afraid and shrank from the task of confronting Ana with her fate. He was, at his core, a coward. Instead, he continued to conspire, considering the best methods to serve his cold and righteous revenge.

COMPARING NOTES

DIEGO, BENITO, AND the captain sat before Felipe de Carceres' desk. It was ten o'clock. Diego looked ragged. He hadn't slept. The evening before, when the captain and Benito had gotten word of the kidnapping, they both had rushed to Diego's home. They knew he would be inconsolable, but they did their best and pledged to do everything in their power to bring Elena home safely. Diego showed them the ransom note he had found slipped under the front door.

Don Felipe asked Diego, "Is Maria recovering? How is she?"

"Yes, thank you. She's feeling better this morning but needs further rest. Thank you again for Señora Reyes' kind assistance."

"She'll be there until Maria is back on her feet. My cook will take care of all the meals. She should be there now."

De Anza muttered an oath and said something about

what he'd do when he got his hands on the culprits. "And you, dear captain. I only just heard of your near escape from drowning. Are you quite all right?"

"I'm fine, Don Felipe, thanks to the tall man here. If it hadn't been for him, who knows what watery grave I'd be resting in now."

"It's a fantastic story, though, Pedro. The Pantitlan! My God! Long I've heard the tales. But to find it truly exists? Amazing."

"It's an amazing world we live in. There have been serious efforts to prove and disprove the Pantitlan's existence. Now we know. It may have something to do with the rainfall yesterday. In all my time in the valley, I don't think I've ever seen it rain so hard and so long without a break," suggested Benito.

"And the earthquake," said Felipe.

"Earthquake?" asked Diego. "What earthquake?"

"It was in the afternoon. It must have been while you were on the water, or you would have felt it. Diego and I spoke earlier this morning about the motive for this kidnapping. Have you both had a chance to read the ransom note?"

"Yes, Don Felipe," said Benito. "With 500 silver *reals* involved, the motive seems to be money."

"Or that's what someone wants us to believe," Don Felipe retorted.

"Why?" asked Benito.

"Because the idea that she was kidnapped for ransom doesn't hold together if you examine the facts," answered Diego. "First, the ransom demand was sent to me. That means someone had to know about my relationship with Elena. Then, as my uncle kindly pointed out, they could just as easily have blackmailed me—more easily, in fact, by threatening to reveal my relationship to the Audiencia. No abduction necessary."

De Anza asked, "What was the purpose of the kidnapping if not money?"

"It was done purely to distract me, Pedro. To keep me worried and busy solving the kidnapping and securing Elena's return."

"Distracted from what specifically?"

"From the investigation I was pursuing before the kidnapping—the murder in the plaza."

"And the poisoning at the reception," said Felipe.

"Felipe and I agreed this morning that new facts and circumstantial evidence suggest the two are connected."

"I've already given you my reasons for suspicion," said Don Felipe. "At that time, we didn't have enough to draw a firm conclusion."

"So, you two say La Condesa is behind both?" queried Benito.

"We strongly suggest it," said Diego. "She has a solid motive—marrying her daughter to one of the richest men in the world. As an influential member of society, she has access to Miguel Torres. And, if the good Sister de la Montes is correct, some of these same hallucinogens were used both on the dead man and in the 'love' potion. Then there is Alejandro Hernandez, who was involved in the poisoning attempt at the reception and was later found on Tepetzinco. That connects both crimes. All we need now is hard evidence." As he finished his argument, Diego slipped a cigarillo out of its pack and lit it. He took in a deep draw of the rich smoke.

"In any case," Felipe added, "I will arrange for the

money and have someone place it in the base of the baptismal font as called for in the ransom note. The cathedral will be bustling with churchgoers at that time. I assume that's why they chose Sunday. We'll comply with the demand not to have any law present, but I'll speak with Archbishop Salinas to ensure two or more of his diocesan priests are in attendance to watch over the font."

Looking at de Anza, Felipe asked, "What have we learned from interrogating Hernandez?"

"No new facts, but I believe he has suggested through his statements that both deeds are indeed connected."

"How's that?" asked Felipe.

"He hasn't directly implicated himself or anyone else in either of the crimes, but he demonstrates fanaticism while voicing his defiance, babbling on about his and their superiority and saying my men and I are only subhuman chattel to be exploited. What he means by that, I have no idea."

"Inferring, I suppose, that he is a member of this cult?" asked Felipe.

"Yes, I'm sure that's the case. And, if he is, that would connect him to both the murder and the poisoning," said de Anza.

Felipe stepped out from behind his desk and paced about his office. He turned to the three men. "I've taken a step to, in a way, confirm La Condesa's involvement. As you can guess, there'd be an enormous commotion if we were to call her in for questioning. The viceroy would have my head. Knowing this, I met with Miguel Torres yesterday to warn him and ask for his assistance."

"What did you expect from him? He's more than likely ignorant of these matters," said de Anza.

"No doubt," said Felipe. "I'm sure he holds no suspicions when it comes to the Montoyas. I had a hunch La Condesa would continue to pursue Miguel, and I was correct. Miguel told me she had invited him to tea tomorrow at her mansion. I'm sure she will again attempt to drug him, expecting to elicit the same response Diego exhibited. Then she'll sequester him in the mansion, which he would willingly submit to. A proposal of marriage would be secured. Then all that would be necessary would be to have the banns read at mass, and poor Torres would be locked into marriage by his sense of honor. I informed Miguel of our investigation and my suspicions. He has absolutely no interest in Dama Isabel and accepted the invitation to tea simply because it was de rigueur to do so."

"What else, Uncle, do you have in mind?"

Felipe smiled. "It won't provide hard evidence, but it's a small test to determine her complicity. Señor Torres has kindly asked me to accompany him to the tea as his guest. When we arrive, he'll make some excuse about my wanting desperately to apologize for my nephew's intolerable behavior."

"Wait a minute!" shouted Diego. "Intolerable behavior?"

"Diego, you must understand I have to play the deeply embarrassed uncle who's come begging her forgiveness on behalf of his nephew. Otherwise, she would be suspicious. My attendance will ensure Miguel's security. La Condesa would be foolish to make a second attempt in my presence. The test will allow me to judge her reaction when Torres walks in the door and I'm with him. My fondest hope would be that it provokes an outburst of some sort, but I would be satisfied if it prompts at least a look of suppressed anger or frustration. When do we plan to return to Tepetzinco?"

"Soon, and this time with a much larger force," said Diego.

De Anza turned to Diego and, in a hushed voice, said, "Diego, I have some thoughts on that."

"Excellent," said Diego. "Let's chat in my office."

Elena lay on the bed staring at the ceiling that had become familiar to her since waking up here more than a day ago. What would she have thought if she knew her best friend was in a more commodious cell directly beneath her? She tried to focus, but her thoughts kept revolving from Diego, to her mother, to Ana, then back to Diego. Ana, she assumed, had been taken, and so had she. *Is there a connection? It would be an unlikely coincidence if we were both kidnapped, so there must be a connection.*

The key turned in the lock, and she was on her feet in a split second. *Who will this be?* The door swung open. Standing there was a young woman, a chambermaid by the looks of her. The same guard at the door when Jose brought food leaned in and said in Nahuatl, "Be quick about it."

The girl made a half turn toward him and quickly nodded. She went about her business, straightening up the room and exchanging the towels she brought with the used ones next to the bed. Elena thought, *Not much work covering this room. She'll be out in less than a minute. It's nice, though, to see someone for a change.*

As the girl was stacking the plates on the table and preparing to leave, the desperate Elena decided to try and enlist her help. She hoped the girl was just what she appeared to be and unaware of Elena's kidnapping and imprisonment. She walked silently to the girl's side. "What's your name, dear?"

The girl curtsied. "Pepita, señorita."

"Pepita, do you know the Palacio de Virrey?"

"*Sí*, señorita."

"And where it is?"

"*Sí*. Some days, when we don't have to work, we take our lunch there and watch the soldiers parading in their uniforms and the ladies with their beautiful dresses."

"Then I beg you, Pepita. Go there and ask for Don Diego de Santiago. Tell him you've seen me and where. He will reward you generously. Please!"

Pepita gave Elena a frightened look. At that moment, the guard leaned back in. "I said make it quick. Let's go!"

The girl gathered the towels and used dishes and scurried out through the door, which abruptly closed. With the throw of the lock, Elena was alone once again.

The Monk sat in the library at the Colegio de San Ildefonso. Padre Pablo Aranda sat across from him. "I never thought Pedro's one visit would blossom into a series of visits. I'm so pleased."

"It's my pleasure, Padre. I've read some of your histories. You are truly gifted with the ability to breathe life into the past and with an engaging style."

"Thank you, my son. Only another Jesuit can flatter a Jesuit so convincingly."

"Padre, I hope someday I can devote as much of my time to learning as you have. Sadly, for now, that is not the case. I've come to take advantage of the colegio's fine library and perhaps steal a few minutes of your time."

"No need to steal, my son. It is yours freely," said the padre.

"As I mentioned, Diego Santiago, Captain de Anza, and I were on Tepetzinco searching for the temple that allegedly exists there. The natives informed them of an old, abandoned house. That was interesting in itself. I was hoping you might know its history, who built it, and when."

"Interesting. Was it a Spanish house or an old Aztec dwelling?"

"Spanish, Padre."

Aranda thought for a while, then said, "I am unaware of it, but I'll review some of the other histories and see what I might find."

Disappointed, Benito looked to the next item on his list. "Hmm, that's too bad. There was one other curiosity related to the house. Diego observed a symbol above the entryway." Benito passed the sketch Diego had made across the table to the padre. "We haven't been able to determine what it represents."

The padre pushed his spectacles further up his nose and squinted at the drawing. He rose and walked over to one of the bookshelves. After scanning the volumes for a minute, he pulled one down and opened it. Bringing it back to the table and thumbing through the pages, he found what he was looking for. "Yes, yes. I believe this is what Don Santiago saw." He slid the open book over to the Monk. "Your friend sketched a depiction of the heart of Copil."

"I see. Yes, Padre, I'm familiar with the myth of Tenochtitlan's founding and the part Copil's heart played in it."

"Precisely, my son. And you know it was on Tepetzinco where Huitzilopochtli had him relieved of it?"

"Yes. So if the symbol above the door represents Copil's heart, what, if anything, do you think that might tell us?"

"Well, Benito, I suppose whoever built that house had a passing interest in the ancient Aztec codices, or in human sacrifice. You see, the act of removing Copil's heart was symbolic, if not the literal first Aztec human sacrifice."

The padre's gallows humor amused the Monk. "So you're saying that whoever lived there practiced these rites?"

"Possibly."

"Then this may be further evidence that Tepetzinco is the temple's location."

"How old would you say this house was, Benito?"

"I didn't see it, but Diego said it was near ruin and they feared being trapped by a collapse. So I would guess over a hundred years. Maybe more."

"Did they discover anything else in this house?"

"Just some writing on the mantel. That's my other reason for visiting the library today. My Latin is good, but I wanted to confirm the translation. According to the texts I read, '*Surge et accipe cor*' translates to 'arise and take heart.' I can't make much of that."

"A motto of some sort? Perhaps for a family or an organization?" said the padre.

The Monk went on to tell him the other observations Diego's team had made on the island—the villagers' behavior, the discovery of the missing steward in the *achichiacpan*, and their encounter with the whirlpool.

"*Dios en el Cielo!* The Pantitlan." The Monk could

see the childlike wonder in the padre's eyes. He told himself this was the sort of thing the old man lived for.

"Envy is a sin, my good Benito, but I would give anything to have seen that."

"In all truthfulness, I can tell you I was impressed."

The padre returned the book to the shelf. "Can I assist you with anything else today, my son?"

"No, but thank you. You've answered all my questions."

"Then, Benito, may I ask you a question?"

"Certainly."

"I don't mean to offend, but I'm aware of your history and truly regret the pain you've suffered. Please tell me why you continue to wear the cassock when you are no longer a member of the order."

The Monk was caught off guard by the question and had to think before he responded. "It's true I am no longer part of the community, a community I once respected and loved deeply. My work was everything to me, and I believed wholeheartedly I was doing it to serve God. I was cast out by men and did not accept it was God's judgment. Nonetheless, I could no longer serve within the church. At the same time, I could not see myself as part of the secular world. So I continue to wear my 'work clothes,' so to speak, and carry on with my labors, serving humanity in the name of God. I don't pretend to be anything other than a man. I do not proselytize, but I minister to the needs of the less fortunate of his children."

The padre thought over Benito's reply and said, "God bless you, my son. Know you are never out of his sight, and he knows, as I do, the good work you do. Adiós, Benito."

"Adiós, Padre."

"Idiot!" La Condesa was livid. "How could you let her into the room?"

The man was trembling with fear. He knew too well what La Condesa was capable of. "I'm sorry, *mi dama*. She cleans that suite of rooms every day. I didn't know."

La Condesa shot a look at Angamuco standing in the background and then back to the guard standing in front of her. "Get out! Giraldo, stay here."

The man left the room. La Condesa turned to Angamuco. "I know the guard is one of us. What of the maid?"

"She's just an Indio girl. She's worked for us a little more than a year."

"I want her dead. Don't let her leave your sight until it's arranged. We can't risk her mentioning our guest to anyone. Do it tonight."

"*Mi dama*, I had word from the island this morning. The *fiscal* was there searching with troops. He asked about structures on the island that could pass as temples. They must know something. The people there are worried."

"He knows nothing. Our spies tell us that the day before they searched all the other islands. Better that he had his look and came up empty. They won't be back. Advise my daughter to ensure the entrances to the tunnels and sanctuary are secured."

La Condesa's ancestors had engineered the current and larger entrance to the underground. The new network access was spacious enough to allow whole wagons to move in and out—storerooms in the temple complex held enough food and weapons to last through months of siege if necessary. In two hundred years, they had built a fortress into the rock with living quarters to house the entire population of the sect if need be. Along with the guns everyone had been trained to use, eight cannons could be wheeled out to defend the island from invasion.

"There is one other piece of unfortunate news," said Angamuco. "They captured Alejandro at the temple to Chalchihuidicue. He's in the palace jail."

"Has he divulged anything?"

"I don't think so. He's one of your most devoted followers. But if they use more persuasive means of interrogation, he may."

"I want him dealt with as well. Bribe a guard, send an assassin, however you want it done. Just see to it. We can't afford exposure of any kind."

"Yes, *mi dama.* I will see to these matters immediately."

Two more murders, Giraldo thought to himself, *and the words flow from her mouth as easily as if she were ordering breakfast. A young girl and a loyal follower. No sign of remorse for either of them or sense of loyalty to her dedicated follower. I'm sure, if need be, she will dismiss me in the same fashion, without a second thought.*

Aloud, he said, "I'll have Yaotl deal with the maid. An unfortunate misstep on her walk home landed her in one of the canals. Not too close to the mansion. Other operatives in the palace can ensure Alejandro is dispatched quietly during the night. In the morning, they'll find him on the floor of his cell or hanging from its rafters." Then he whispered, "His reward for complete devotion to his mistress."

"Pedro, it was only yesterday you nearly drowned. Are you sure you want to go back?"

"Diego, we've searched the island from end to end and didn't find this temple, and there were fourteen of us. I'm sure it's there, which means it's hidden somehow. So we'll try once more. This time we won't announce our presence or bring a contingent of soldiers. Sergeant Trujillo and I have decided we'll go by ourselves."

"How do you plan to get there unnoticed?" asked Diego.

"We'll take a common reed canoe and land on the island's northeastern shore. The sergeant and I will wear native clothing. We should pass as villagers as long as we keep our distance."

"I'd feel better if we went back with a small army."

"Yes, I hear you, and we will at some point. I'm confident we'll find something as long as they feel they aren't being watched. Then we'll be better prepared for our next move against Tepetzinco. We'll arrive at dusk and move down the shoreline until we reach the village. We plan to reconnoiter for three or four hours. Then we'll return to the city. There's nearly a full moon and not a hint of rain in sight. We'll be back by midnight."

"Very well, Pedro. Be careful."

"I will, my friend. I'll see you in your office tomorrow morning at eight."

WE KNOW

ANA HAD THOUGHT of overpowering the old Indio chambermaid, Consuela, but on each of her visits, she was accompanied by a guard who waited just outside the door until she was finished. Ana was feeling fully rested now. She'd had plenty to eat and had bathed and changed into clean clothes from the wardrobe. She wondered who had worn them before her and if she were still alive.

Angamuco had returned only twice since she'd moved to her new accommodation. He continued acting the gentleman and made no untoward advances. He merely sat and chatted about his favorite music (which she was unfamiliar with), the weather, or what they had eaten for dinner, but mostly how lovely Ana looked. *That was almost two days ago*. Ana still had trouble with time. She was ignorant of the exact time and could only guess what day it was.

She sat in one of the oversized chairs by the fireplace, thumbing through the pages of one of the books left on the shelves. She could read, but not very well, and she skipped over some words as she went. Then she heard footsteps and saw Angamuco at the door peering in the grated window.

"Hello, my dear." He turned the key in the lock. As he entered, Ana noticed he limped demonstrably.

"Have you hurt yourself?" asked Ana.

"No. It's just a reminder I'm given from time to time of a childhood illness." He sat across from her at the fireplace.

She had to stop herself from staring at his face. For some reason, it was paler than before. It had a sallow yellow color similar to the beginning or end of a bruise. She thought it must be another manifestation of the illness he mentioned.

"I have exciting news for you, my dear. La Condesa regrets the way we've treated you and would proffer a suggestion."

Ana was almost afraid to ask. "What would that be?"

"In recompense for the trouble you've gone through, she would put you on your way."

"You mean set me free?"

Angamuco replied with a tilted smile. "Exactly that, my dear. And as added assistance to get you back on your path, she will provide you with the sum of 1,000 pesos—500 as you depart and 500 more after six months—provided you do not speak of your incarceration or say anything that may harm the reputation of Dama de Montoya, her family, or her servants." He placed his hand on his chest and bowed slightly as he said "servants."

"Why?" she blurted out, immediately regretting she had asked.

"My dear, over the years, I've completed many tasks for La Condesa and have been a loyal steward of the family. I asked for this one favor from her, and she agreed. I've grown quite fond of you, my dear, and genuinely wish what's best for you."

He's lying, she thought. But keeping her made about as much sense as letting her go. After all, a thousand pesos would buy La Condesa a fair amount of insurance she wouldn't go to the authorities—that is, if they would believe her anyway. It was the word of a servant woman against that of a *condesa*.

She asked, "May I leave now?"

"I'm afraid not until tomorrow, Sunday. La Condesa wished to apologize in person and planned a special treat. Unfortunately, she is in Michoacán and will not be home until midmorning." Ana was anxious to get out of her prison as quickly as possible. *One more night. One more night and I will be free.* The anticipation of being reunited with her mother, Jaime, and Elena overwhelmed her, and she could think of nothing else. *To be with my friends. To be in the sunlight again.* Intoxicated by these feelings, she thanked Angamuco again and again but could not bring herself to embrace him.

"I'm happy to see you this way, my dear. Of course, please take the dress you're wearing, and, if you'd like to finish that book, take it along. One of La Condesa's footmen will collect you in the morning."

"I am happy, so very happy. You are a kind man."

Angamuco swallowed hard. "Thank you, my dear. Now I must be on my way. I have several matters to deal with."

"Oh, señor!"

Angamuco stopped and turned around. "Yes, my dear."

"I wanted to ask. You mentioned La Condesa has a special treat."

"Yes, that's right, my dear. Thank you for reminding me. La Condesa would like you to attend mass in her private chapel tomorrow. She insists you receive the sacrament."

By the time de Anza managed to crawl into bed Saturday morning, it was already four. As tired as he was, he got little sleep. His mind was still reeling with the discoveries he and Sergeant Trujillo had made over the past twelve hours. It was too fantastic to believe, beginning with their arrival on the island.

"Sergeant, we can hide the canoe behind those tall reeds," de Anza had said.

"Aye, Captain."

Together they pulled the boat ashore and around the thicket of reeds. The trip took a little over two hours with the two men rowing. The canoe was much faster on the water than the cumbersome barge they had come in the day before.

"No sign of the Pantitlan this trip," said the sergeant, keeping his voice low.

"No, thank God. Benito seems to think it was a fluke we came across it yesterday. He proposed a combination of heavy rain, wave action, and the earthquake sparked the whirlpool."

Trujillo chuckled. "Good. From now on, I'll know better than to cross the lake in those conditions."

De Anza felt naked without his sword but even more

so without his beard. He had sat staring at the razor in his bath for ten minutes before he committed himself to removing it. To hide the better part of his hirsute body, he wore a blouse and pants of woven maguey. Enough of the Indios wore them that he could get away with it. Trujillo didn't have the same problem and simply wore a *maxtlatl* and huaraches familiar to the island population. Both carried knives strapped to their waists.

As planned, they walked down the shoreline toward the village. They climbed the hill to conceal their approach and to give themselves an overall view of the village. Besides the tall grass and occasional scrub oak, there wasn't much cover, so they kept low to the ground and crawled the last ten paces to a small cliff face overlooking the village with its stretch of jacales and reed lodge houses. As before, they estimated the community numbered from three hundred to four hundred inhabitants. A few hours of daylight remained. They would observe while there was still light. Once night came, they'd go in for a closer look.

It took almost an hour for them to catch on to a curious traffic pattern in the village. The sergeant noticed it first. "Captain, see that lodge over to the left at the base of the cliff?"

"What about it, Sergeant?"

"There seems to be quite a bit of traffic going in and out."

"Interesting. It's not the council lodge. That's near the edge of the village on the west end. What do you think it's for? Storage perhaps?"

"I don't think so. Except for a few, they aren't carrying anything in or out. What's curious is that, since I've been watching, more people have gone in than come out—a substantial number more. I started counting at one point, and, in that time, I counted fifty Indios entering the lodge and only four coming out. It must be getting crowded in there."

"Yes, I make it to be around thirty feet wide and twenty feet deep. Let's keep an eye on it, Sergeant. Once it's dark, we'll find a way to get a look inside. Wait a minute. There's a face I remember. It's the Tlatoani. Look, he's going in just now."

"Official business, no doubt, Captain. Unless we've stumbled across the village pulquería."

After an hour observing, it was nearly dark. Then they saw something unexpected. In less than a minute, upward of a hundred villagers left the lodge, spreading out in various directions. *Curious*, thought de Anza.

"How do we want to do this, Sergeant?"

"Why not just walk right up and go in? I didn't see a guard. Of course, he could be stationed inside the entrance."

"What say we create a diversion? A few minutes ago, I saw them lighting torches near the center of the village. Can you grab one of those and set one of the other lodges aflame? One close to the lakefront. We want them to run to the fire, but we certainly don't want to burn the entire village down."

"I can do that."

"Good. With luck, the entire village will be distracted. I'll duck into the lodge and have a look. If everything goes well, we'll meet back here. If we're discovered, head for the canoe."

"Got it. Good luck, Captain."

Trujillo got into position. De Anza followed and hid behind a cart not far from the lodge. Foot traffic was still heavy, and de Anza was thankful for that. Three or four minutes later, he heard shouts in the distance. Then he saw the flames, above and behind the other jacales, at the far end of the village.

Now it seemed the entire population was in the alleys and passageways, shouting and running toward the burning lodge, carrying buckets to retrieve water from the lake. De Anza saw two men exit the lodge. *I guess now is as good a time as any.* He sprinted from his hiding place to the entrance of the lodge.

Cautiously, he pulled aside the woven reed framework that covered the entrance and crept in. Expecting to see someone inside, he instead found the lodge empty. Two torches planted in the ground by the back of the lodge illuminated the space. There were no partitions, just one large room. Then the shadow of the light next to the torches drew his attention. On either side of the two torches, the dirt floor was smooth, unmolested, but between the torches and running from the back of the room to the entrance where he was standing were footprints in a well-worn path. The flickering light and its angle delineated the two.

Aha! More than meets the eye. De Anza started to walk down the center to the back wall. That's when he felt it. He turned and looked at the entrance. The door was where he'd replaced it. Yet there was a cool draft blowing through the room. He continued to the back wall and realized the cool draft wasn't coming through the door. It was coming from behind the wall. He placed his hand on the reed wall and could feel it.

De Anza knew he didn't have much time, so he frantically searched for some lever or device that would move the wall aside. Impatient, he grabbed two handfuls of reeds and pulled. A six-foot section pulled away easily. He slid behind it and pulled it back into place. He wasn't prepared for what he saw next.

Before him was a tunnel that ran about thirty feet to an opening at the other end. The tunnel was much broader and taller than the small section of reed he'd pulled away to access it. As he made his way through, he saw it led into a circular open space at least 150 feet across with a domed ceiling that rose more than half that distance in the center.

It was like standing in the largest dome in Christendom. In the center was a round platform level with the floor with light rails crisscrossing the surface. It was a movable round table like those the British built, a roundhouse for directing light rail cars. On the near side of the tunnel were two large oak doors at least a foot and a half thick with cross-hatched iron plates.

De Anza supposed the doors were there to secure the entrance if need be. Looking around, he saw three tunnels with rails extending into them. One had a railcar parked on it. To his immediate right was a stable carved out of the rock holding twelve draft horses whose purpose he was sure was to pull the cars through the tunnels. But to where? To the left was a similar structure crowded with hundreds of wood crates and barrels secured behind iron bars.

He walked over to get a closer look. *A storeroom of some kind? No. An armory.* There were racks of Charleville muskets, long-armed muzzleloaders, flintlock pistols, and three-pounder field artillery. He couldn't see into the back of the room. *With those and the tall stack of powder kegs right in front of me, they could start a small war if they wished to.*

De Anza made one other curious observation. The massive dome and each of the tunnels was lined with dozens of torches, but there was little smoke. He thought all of it was carried away by the same breeze he felt when he entered. They even had a means of ventilation. It must have taken decades to build out. Though the rail tunnels were lit, he couldn't see an end to any of the three.

I haven't time to explore, and the sergeant no doubt will be waiting for me. De Anza walked back through the tunnel, moved the section of reed wall aside, and found himself in the lodge. As he walked to the door to exit, a large Indio entered. He stared at de Anza for a few seconds, then shouted, "*Amahquihqueh*?" in Nahuatl, which Anza took to mean "who are you?"

The man continued to stare, speechless, at de Anza for a few more seconds. Then he let out a scream and charged straight at him. De Anza did the same, minus the screaming, and hurtled toward the Indio.

The Indio had his arms above his head, prepared to land a crushing downward blow just before they collided. A split second before he could execute this move, de Anza, catching the man off guard, shifted his weight and stiff-armed him in his left shoulder. The Indio spun round and fell to the ground. De Anza didn't stop. Crashing through the door, he raced as fast as he could out of the village to his rendezvous with Trujillo. He made it up the hill and found the sergeant at their earlier vantage point.

"Whatever you did, Captain, you've stirred up a hornet's nest. Everyone is out and about. We should be going."

"No doubt, Sergeant. They'll start searching soon. Let's go."

Both men took off in the direction of the canoe. Thanks to the nearly full moon, they could see their way clearly, but so could their pursuers. Although they had a slight lead, the men chasing them knew the lay of the land, and that lead could evaporate quickly.

Along the way, de Anza told the sergeant what he had seen in the lodge and beyond.

"That explains why we couldn't find the temple. It must be underground as well," said Trujillo, catching his breath as they marched along the shoreline. At this pace, it took them only forty minutes to reach the spot where they'd concealed the canoe.

"Captain! Get down!" whispered the sergeant.

De Anza did so and, looking ahead, saw two Indios standing next to the reed bed where they had concealed the canoe. They were bent over, inspecting the canoe. "What should we do, Captain?"

De Anza grinned. "Get our canoe and leave post-haste." Then, taking a more serious tone, he added, "Be nonchalant. We're just two more Indios searching for the intruders. Only one man saw me, and I don't think he's either of them. How's your Nahuatl?"

"Fluent, but it may be a different dialect from what our friends here speak."

"They have spears. I don't see knives or bows."

"Neither do I," said the sergeant.

"Then we just walk straight toward them and you say, 'Have you found him?' They don't know there are two of us, which may help. Once we're close enough, they'll recognize we're strangers. We must get close enough that throwing the spears isn't an option. Have your knife at the ready."

They started walking, keeping their heads bent down. When they were close enough to be recognized, Trujillo asked if they had found the intruders. "*Otiquimipantili?*" The taller of the two Indios replied in the negative as de Anza and Trujillo kept advancing in their direction. Then de Anza heard the shorter of the two shout the familiar "*Amahquihqueh?*"

De Anza, brandishing his knife, charged at the man. Trujillo followed suit. The first man lunged at Trujillo. He deflected the thrust with the hilt of his knife but still caught the tip of the spear as it glanced past his right side just above his waist. In close now, Trujillo slashed upward with his blade and cut deep in the man's right bicep. He screamed in pain as he let loose the spear with his right hand, leaving him with a feeble hold on the spear with his left.

Meanwhile, de Anza's man was directly in his path, and, as they met, he lifted his knee squarely into the man's loincloth. Bent over and in agony, his spear fell to the side. De Anza kicked it away into the water.

Holding both men at bay, Trujillo took the other man's spear and chucked it into the lake. The injured men sat on the ground, defeated and expecting death. Instead, Trujillo reached into the canoe and produced a rope. "Never leave home without it." The sergeant cut four short lengths to bind the men and one more to fashion a tourniquet.

"I think we can leave these two here. How's that cut on your side?"

"Looks worse than it is, Captain."

"I think it's about time you call me Pedro, Luis."

Smiling, Trujillo said, "Only when the men aren't present, Pedro."

De Anza smiled back as they got into the canoe and pushed off from the shore. "Quite a night, Luis. Wait till Diego and the Monk hear about this."

De Anza finally fell asleep, but for only a few hours before he had to bathe, dress, and meet Diego in the offices of the Audiencia. He was far from tired, however. He was wide awake despite being hunted on the island, the life-and-death struggle with the two Indios, and two hours rowing a canoe. He was fueled by adrenaline and eager to tell Diego and the others what he and the sergeant had—no pun intended—unearthed.

He arrived at the palace to find Diego already in the office smoking a cigarette and poring over the night log he had retrieved from the front desk when he got in over an hour ago. The man looked worn and haggard. *I doubt he slept at all*, de Anza thought.

"Buenos días." De Anza knocked on the open door as he entered.

"Buenos días, Pedro. Please come in. Have a seat."

De Anza sat, lit a cigarillo, and leaned back in his chair.

Frustrated, Diego said, "We still don't have a damn thing, not a single clue as to her whereabouts."

"Diego, have faith. We'll find her."

"You're starting to sound like Benito."

"Did someone mention my name?" Standing in the doorway, Benito Avila was surprisingly alert for this time of day.

"Buenos días, Benito," said de Anza. "Did you spend the whole night at the library?"

"No, but I was up late reading. Padre Aranda loaned me one of his histories of the Aztecs I hadn't read yet."

De Anza purposely stayed away from any comments about his apparent sobriety. "I'm glad you're here. We're missing Felipe, but what I have to tell you can't wait."

"He's just down the hall. Let me fetch him," said Diego. "His tea with La Condesa and Miguel Torres isn't until eleven." Diego stood, walked out the door, and started down the hallway.

"He's in a bad way," said de Anza.

"I could tell," said Benito.

"I don't think he's slept since Elena went missing."

A minute later, Felipe de Carceres appeared at the door. Diego followed him.

"I'm afraid I have some bad news, my friends," Felipe said in a somber voice. "This morning, the jailer found Alejandro Hernandez dead in his cell. He hung himself with his belt."

The three men paused at the news.

"I thought jailers took belts and shoes away from prisoners," said Benito.

"They do," said de Anza. "What's more interesting is Hernandez didn't have a belt. When we arrested him on the island, all he had was a pair of pants, a shirt, and huaraches. He was murdered."

"I'll initiate a full investigation," said Felipe.

"One step forward, two steps back. He was our best chance to unravel all this, and someone walks into the Royal Palace and kills him. My God! What's the use?"

"Calm down, Diego," said de Anza. "Besides, I think I've got something that will put us back on track."

Suddenly Benito broke out laughing. "Good Lord, Pedro! I just noticed. What happened to your beard?"

"I ran into a razor."

"I see."

"It was necessary for my disguise for the trip to Tepetzinco with Trujillo last night."

"You should keep it that way," said Diego, feeling better after a laugh. "It suits you." "Funny how you don't notice things staring you right in the face," said Benito.

"Perfect segue." De Anza started to give his account of his and Trujillo's exploits.

"That's it! You've found it!" cheered Felipe.

"We found an underground citadel, not the temple, but I'm willing to bet a year's salary it's there," said de Anza.

"Pedro, we owe you and the sergeant a debt of gratitude. You think we should go back with an army?"

"I think so. A large army, Felipe. We found a sizable store of ammunition and guns, even artillery. Judging by how entrenched these people are and their capacity for violence, I would anticipate a significant struggle."

At that moment, Sergeant Trujillo appeared at the door.

"Buenos días, Sergeant," said Diego. "The captain here was just telling us about your visit to Tepetzinco."

"Yes, it was quite an adventure."

"Pedro said you were wounded."

"Just a scratch, Don Santiago. I'll be fine. But I didn't come here concerning Tepetzinco." "What is it, Sergeant?"

"We found the body of what looks like a mestizo woman in the canal by the Roldan bridge this morning."

Diego leaped from his chair.

"We're still working to identify her, but she was wearing this."

The sergeant reached into his tunic and brought out a bracelet with azure turquoise stones strung together on twisted silver strands. Clasps at either end secured it to a simple leather tie.

Diego fell back in his chair. Felipe thought he recognized it. The Monk was sure.

"Diego," started Benito.

"She's dead," said Diego.

"Who's dead?" asked Trujillo.

De Anza signaled him not to pursue it.

Diego, oblivious to whom the question was asked, stared blindly and answered, "Elena."

They gave Diego some time to get himself under control.

"Diego," Felipe said softly, looking at him to be sure he had his attention. "We don't know it was Elena they found. I hate to say it, but I think you should accompany the sergeant and see for yourself." He paused. "I'll go with you."

"So will I," said Benito.

De Anza chimed in. "We'll all go."

It was a mournful walk, and no one spoke as they made their way to the Punta de Roldan. It took them past the Montoyas' mansion, where de Carceres would be sitting for tea later in the morning. Diego walked alone, a little ahead of the others. They hung back, knowing he had no appetite for discussion. As they walked along, the Monk told them Padre Aranda had identified the symbol on the

Tepetzinco house as a depiction of the heart of Copil and gave them the translation for the Latin above the fireplace.

A boy came running at them from the opposite direction, yelling all the way. "Don Santiago! Don Santiago!" Esteban looked as ragged as ever and very excited to see Diego. He nearly slammed into him. "Buenos días, Don Santiago, are you well?"

What was Diego to say? Seeing the boy in all his youthful exuberance lightened his heart.

"I am well, *hombrecito*. And you?"

"*Estoy bien*! Gracias. Are you on a case?"

Diego thought of what to say to the boy. "Yes, yes, Esteban. I'm on a very important case."

"Can I help? Is there something you wish me to investigate?" Esteban's countenance beamed with pure anticipation. Diego remembered how the boy had told him how kind Elena was to him and confessed that someday, when he was older, he would like to marry Señorita Elena.

Diego was on edge now and had to find a way to jettison the boy before they reached the Roldan. He couldn't let Esteban see her. *Not now. Not like this.* "Esteban, there may be some action, and I don't want you hurt. Go to the baratillo, and I'll meet you there later. *Bueno?*" Esteban's excitement disappeared, and he bowed his head. He didn't say anything, but Diego could see he was crestfallen. "*Bueno?*" Diego repeated.

"*Bueno*," said Esteban. He slowly turned and walked toward the baratillo.

Diego's heart was breaking. He was praying to God that this was some mistake. Perhaps Elena had dropped the bracelet or it was stolen by her kidnappers, who had sold it to someone else. He went on and on, turning over the possibilities in his head.

And then they were there, at the bridge on the Roldan. It was a busy city port, a tradesman's marketplace where goods from all over the valley and the rest of Mexico found their way into the city to be sold or bartered. Boats that brought vegetables from the *chinampas* would turn around after being reloaded with tools, fabrics, and other dry goods.

Sergeant Trujillo spoke to the soldiers who were first to arrive after the body was found early in the morning. He finished talking to them and walked over to Diego and the others. "They placed the body in the storeroom on the other side of the bridge."

The group walked over the bridge and, after being acknowledged by another soldier at the door, they were shown in.

In an empty corner of the two-story warehouse was a table. Bright sunlight from one of the two windows lit the scene. A white linen sheet covered the corpse. "Once we're finished, they'll move the body to the mortuary," said Trujillo.

Diego could barely move but managed the few steps to the table. The sergeant made eye contact with Diego, signaling to confirm he was prepared. Diego nodded. The sergeant lifted one corner of the sheet, exposing the deceased's face.

"It's not Elena!" Diego almost wept for joy. "Thank God! This is not Elena Bautista."

"No, it's not," said a small voice. Esteban, walking to the table, said, "Now I know why you wanted me to meet you at the baratillo. It's not the señorita. But I know who it is."

Miguel Torres had allotted forty-five minutes to complete all the requisite social obligations, bowing, hand kissing, chitchat, comments on beauty, dress, and the overwhelming charm of La Condesa. Then, with one last bow, he'd be gone. He was intrigued, though, and after hearing what Carceres told him, he was hesitant to drink anything, let alone tea, which he characterized as a snobbish British affectation. Felipe had assured him that, although that was probably the plan, they wouldn't dare now that both men would be present.

Having been announced to the master of the house at the entry hall, they were shown to the west parlor by La Condesa's private secretary, where they were told La Condesa would receive them. Looking about, Felipe thought, *I could fit half of my home in just the entry hall.* As they followed the secretary to the parlor, Felipe noted that, while the mansion's exterior was similar in style to many buildings in the city, the interior spoke more to the rococo fashion that had come into vogue in Europe. They passed from the hall and into the parlor through the twelve-foot white-and-gold doors. There, on opposing settees, were La Condesa and Dama Isabel.

Felipe locked his gaze on La Condesa's face as the secretary announced them. La Condesa was in the process of returning her teacup and saucer to a table between the two settees. She turned slightly and, seeing two men at the threshold, fumbled with both dishes, releasing them an inch or so above the table. They didn't break, and only a smidgen of tea was spilled. If she wished to exhibit the decorous image of a noblewoman about to entertain guests, that effort was cut short then and there. She quickly recovered, but Felipe had seen what he had hoped to see.

Still somewhat flustered, La Condesa greeted them. "Don Torres, Don Carceres. How pleasant to see you both." Both men bowed. Torres walked to her, and still sitting, she proffered her hand. Torres gently took it, bent again, and lightly pressed his lips to the back of her hand. Turning, he repeated the process with Dama Isabel.

"My ladies, thank you so much for admitting me to your home. I fear I may have breached protocol slightly, but I wanted to see Don Carceres for a few minutes. I must leave for my home in Cuernavaca immediately afterward. I'm hosting the viceroy in the country for a day or two of hunting."

"Not at all, Don Torres," said La Condesa with a practiced smile. Speaking to him and half looking at Carceres, she said, "I too like to hunt."

Felipe came forward and took his turn bowing and hand kissing, then said, "It is both a pleasure and an honor to visit with you today."

The two men sat, Torres beside La Condesa and Felipe next to Isabel.

Felipe said, "I have to tell Madam I am deeply impressed with your home and how you've successfully combined the classic with the new."

"Yes, I too am impressed," said Torres. "You'll have to refer me to your architect."

"I'm afraid my husband managed the design and construction of the mansion. Poor Renato passed on shortly after its completion. However, I'm sure there are several other very accomplished architects here in the city."

This was a bald-faced lie. Renato de Montoya died in

Michoacán before the construction of the mansion. His death was La Condesa's great emancipation and the impetus for leaving the country house and moving permanently to the city.

"Ah, Count de Montoya. Descendant of the original conquistadores. Is that true?" said Felipe.

"Oh, yes, quite true. Gaspar de Montoya reported directly to Cortes. Like him, Renato was a great and good man." She paused and then sighed. "My only love. I was a child bride, and he was the only man I've ever known." Another lie. "There's a portrait of him in the library. Would you care to see it?"

"Oh, yes, indeed," said Torres.

A minute later, they were standing in the library admiring the life-sized portrait of Count Renato de Montoya y Michoacán. *This is delicious. If these fools only knew what lay beyond that portrait.*

"A handsome man indeed," said Felipe. Turning to Isabel, he said, "A pity you never had the chance to know your father, Dama Isabel."

Isabel replied with a yes, thus doubling the words she had spoken since their arrival.

"Is that a family motto painted at the top of the portrait?" asked Torres.

"Yes," said La Condesa. "It goes back to Gaspar's time."

In astonishment, Felipe raised his eyes and read the words "*Surge et accipe cor.*" *Good God!* All at once, he leaped to the final connection. *The house on Tepetzinco, the engraving on the mantel. Copil's heart above the door. In the painting, it was stitched in gold on Renato's blouse.* He wanted to run and tell the others but couldn't. Struggling to contain himself, he tried his best to be nonchalant. Then he remembered what the two fugitive acolytes had said about the cult's high priestess. *She was both beautiful and regal.*

"Esteban, please understand. I know how close you are to Señorita Bautista, and, well, if it had been Elena, I didn't want you to see her that way."

"I know you think of me as a child, Don Santiago, and I suppose you are correct. But I am a boy born on the streets, and they have been my home ever since. I have often gone to sleep in some corner of the city only to wake up to find one of my compadres had died in the night. Death is always with me."

Diego thought this was sad but true. "At least, Esteban, we can be thankful this ill-fated woman was not Elena."

They had all returned to Diego's office except Don Felipe, who had gone to meet Miguel Torres ahead of their appointment with La Condesa.

"Esteban, you know Benito. I am Pedro de Anza. I'm a captain in the king's service."

"Yes, Captain. I've heard of you, mostly from the *doncellas* who linger in the market."

"Ahem. I see. Well, it's my pleasure to know you. Diego here has mentioned you and how much assistance you've provided him in the past. You mentioned in the storehouse you can identify this poor woman we saw."

"Yes, Captain, but she's hardly a woman. She looks older because she worked in the mines of Michoacán for years. You don't age well in the mines. I think she was eighteen. She's been in the city for a couple of years and lives in a tenement with six others by the Mercado de San Juan."

"I see. And what was her name?"

"She was called Pepita."

"And her family name?"

"She didn't have one. Like me, she had no parents. People just called her Pepita."

"Tell me, Esteban, do you know where she worked?"

"No, Captain, but I can show you where she lived. One of the others there will know."

De Anza turned to the others. "There's no time like the present, and it's not far. I'll go with Esteban. We'll return within the hour."

"Perfect," said Diego. "It's twelve thirty now. Don Felipe should return from his appointment at about the same time."

Dona Andrea was brooding once more. "By the great mother. That ass! Twice we've failed to subscribe Don Torres to our cause, unwilling as it may have been. How could he have brought that son of a whore Carceres? I can't fail a third time. With his means, we can not only safeguard the continuity of the sect but expand its reach and power." She pondered her next steps for a few minutes and then rang for Giraldo.

Giraldo had been with Gabriela all morning. The breach on the island was severe. La Condesa had been informed but not fully briefed. He heard the bell and began his ascent from the temple. The question now was whether to proceed with the sacrifice tomorrow. It could be done, and total secrecy was assured, but perhaps they should focus on the Tepetzinco matter.

"Giraldo. Preparations are in order?"

"Yes, *mi dama*."

"Good. We don't want any issues this late."

"*Mi dama*, Gabriela and I thought it might be wise to postpone the ritual and concentrate on the security issue on the island."

"Out of the question! I can see you proposing such lunacy, but Gabriela should know better. The issue with the incursion on the island is precisely why we should go forward. The breach is a sign of Xochiquetzal's displeasure. Tomorrow is the full moon and the feast of Tepeihuitli on the calendar. Xochiquetzal is honored in the ritual. We'll decide what course to take concerning Tepetzinco after the goddess has been appeased."

Once she gets caught up in the dogma, Giraldo thought, *her fanaticism shows. A true believer. She's insane*. To bring her back down, he offered a few words of pandering. "Of course. The goddess requires appeasement. Why not offer her the apostates tomorrow as well? Surely it would register your devotion, and she would bless you in return."

She gave a thoughtful look. "Giraldo, for a weasel of a man, you sometimes surprise me. Yes, we'll offer the three. The two Indios first, then the stubby mestizo."

"I told the mestizo we are going to free her tomorrow, but I told her that she would first attend a Christian mass in the morning so you could show your sincere regrets. She should go quietly to the chamber adjoining the temple, where she will be prepared. There, I'll give her something to quiet her down."

"Giraldo, I retract my assertion. You are not a weasel. A weasel is warm-blooded. You are more of a reptile. Be sure whatever you give her to ensure her compliance doesn't dull her senses. She must feel every cut, every slash that parts her skin from her body before we take her heart and offer it to the goddess. Even better, she should live to see Gabriela don the skin to perform the ritual dance of praise." As La Condesa said this, she seemed to float off, her eyes expressionless. Giraldo recognized his opportunity to exit and quietly stepped away, leaving her behind in her unholy reverie.

Don Felipe de Carceres ran up the stairs to the second floor of the Audiencia and down the hallway. Out of breath, he reached Diego's office and walked in without knocking. The office was thick with cigarette smoke hanging weightless in the center of the room. Still breathing hard, he stood for a moment, then blurted out, "La Condesa is the witch!"

They all stared at him as if he'd lost his mind until Diego said calmly, "We know. The dead woman in the canal has been identified as an Indio named Pepita. De Anza confirmed her current employer with her roommates about an hour ago. She works—worked—as a chambermaid at the mansion de Montoya."

Now breathing normally but feeling a bit deflated, Felipe told them of Renato de Montoya's portrait with the family motto matching the one found in the abandoned Tepetzinco house and Copil's heart. "At the very least, the Montoyas lived there and, in all probability, built it centuries ago or more."

Diego interjected in a highly animated voice, "What's most important is she has Elena. We must go there, kick the door in, and find her."

"Patience, Diego," said de Anza. "If we do that, we may never find her. We are too few, and she could easily be spirited away while we're still in the entry hall. No, we need to surround the mansion, covering all the possible entrances and exits before we go in. And we'll need enough men to fan out to every corner of the mansion before we begin a systematic search."

Felipe interposed. "Wait. I don't disagree with anything you two have said, but if we go in there now, swords drawn, the viceroy will have us on the first ship to a country none of us has ever heard of. She is nobility, and although the Audiencia is the highest legal authority in Nueva España, we still report to de Guemes. It's over our heads."

"Very well," said Diego. "We'll get the viceroy's approval."

"And I'm sure he'll give it to us, but we need to catch him. He leaves for Cuernavaca today," said Felipe.

Diego was up in a flash. He snatched his sword from the table and ran out the door. The Audiencia and the viceroy's offices and residential quarters were on opposite ends of the Palacio de Virrey. He dashed down the stairs to the interior courtyard and ran across to the opposing corner, back in, and up to the office of the viceroy's private secretary, Alfonso Delgado.

"Sir, I'm Diego Santiago, *fiscal de crimen*. I must see the viceroy immediately. It's a matter of life and death."

Delgado gave Diego a guarded look. "*Buenas tardes*, señor. I remember you from last week's reception. You accompanied Carceres. Are you feeling better?"

"Yes, fine. I'm here on behalf of Carceres. I must speak with the viceroy. As I said, it's urgent."

"Yes, well, I fear you just missed him. He left for Cuernavaca not ten minutes ago."

Wasting no time, Diego said, "Gracias, señor." He ran out of the office toward the stables in the back of the palace, hoping he might catch the viceroy leaving in his carriage. He stopped at the top of the stairs and looked out the window. There he was, or at least it was the viceroy's carriage, leaving the stable and headed for the gate at the other end of the building.

Diego had one chance to catch the viceroy before he left. That side of the palace had one long service hallway that spanned the length of the building. Across from where he stood was an unassuming door that accessed the hall. He ran to it, opened it, and began his quarter-mile sprint across the building.

Luckily, the carriage was not moving too quickly through the yard. Diego had to get ahead of it before it reached the other end. He slammed through the door at the end of the hallway and found himself in a hall mirroring the one he'd just run from. He looked out the window. He was above the yard and next to the gate. The carriage was just a few yards away. He drew his sword and, using the butt end, smashed the window's glass. Praying he gauged the distance correctly, he leaped out of the window and down onto the carriage's roof as it passed beneath him.

He had estimated the distance correctly but had not taken into consideration the carriage roof, which was, to his surprise, made of fabric. He fell straight through it, hit the floor of the carriage compartment, bounced back up a bit, and came back down onto the seat opposite the viceroy.

Sheepishly, Diego said, "*Buenas tardes*, Your Eminence."

Serene, the viceroy coolly replied, "Santiago."

Relocated to the viceregal offices, the viceroy sat at the head of an impressive thirteen-foot walnut trestle table with a carved apron and scrolled supports. Befitting his station, all his furniture was of exceptional quality and imported from Spain.

Felipe, Diego, and the rest took their places around the table, with Esteban standing at Diego's side, feeling very out of place in the grand office.

The viceroy turned his head to Carceres. "Felipe?"

"Your Eminence, I regret this interruption, but we need to move quickly to prevent further loss of life, rescue a kidnapped señorita, and bring down a fanatical murder cult. Because of the personalities involved, we could not move without your permission in advance."

"And who are these personalities, Felipe?"

"One is La Condesa de Montoya y Michoacán."

"You're joking."

"I wish I were, Eminence, but we believe she is behind the poisoning of Diego here at your reception and the murdered man found in the Plaza Mayor. In all likelihood, many more."

Felipe described the timeline of events, the poisoning, the suspected plot to ensnare Miguel Torres, the Indios' story of the cult, the discoveries on Tepetzinco, and the multiple proofs implicating La Condesa.

"Good Lord, Felipe. Hundreds of years and right under our noses. Do they have an army out on that island?"

"Based on what the captain found, I wouldn't assume otherwise," said Carceres.

"Captain, my palace force sits at about 220 infantry and one hundred mounted cavalry. Is that correct?"

"That's correct, Eminence, plus the twenty-three halberdiers," said de Anza.

Guemes said, "Let's draw from there. How many men do you need? We can go to the Milicias Urbanas de Ciudad if you need more. They have eight times that."

Diego looked over to de Anza. "Pedro, what did you find out about the men who built the mansion?"

"None are alive. Worse, the plans they submitted are missing from the archives."

"Then we'll have to go with what Don Felipe can tell us about the interior and what we can see from the outside."

They returned to Diego's office and sat for the next two hours outlining the assault on the mansion de Montoya. They spent the rest of the day mustering the troops and briefing the officers. When they were ready, they planned to spring the trap in the morning. Diego hoped it wouldn't be too late.

THE MANSION

Ana had been too excited to sleep because today was the last day. In the back of her mind, she was wary of Angamuco. Yes, he'd been nice, but he was also the one who had left a painful bruise on the back of her head. Soon, though, she surrendered to blind hope because, in the end, she wanted it to be true that she would be going home, putting this all behind her.

Beneath the mansion de Montoya, in the silence and the absence of light, rested the half-buried remains of the Huēyi Teōcalli. Today, as on other days for the past twenty years, the light would return to the Templo Mayor, and it would serve once again as the instrument of Xochiquetzal's dark power.

Braziers would be set aflame, illuminating the two steep staircases between three balustrades leading up to a final platform high above. Large braziers on stone pilasters at either end of the high platform would burn bright, revealing two temples. To the left was the temple dedicated to Tlaloc, the god of rain, and on the right was the temple of Huitzilopochtli, the god of war. Their colors of ocean blue and rust red flickered in the light.

In front of Huitzilopochtli's temple lay a stone altar six feet long, five feet wide, and forty inches high at the center of its curved top. This was the sacrificial stone. There beside it was the *cuauhxicalli*, a stone vessel carved in the shape of a eagle waiting to receive the victim's beating heart once the priestess had ripped it from the writhing body of the sacrifice—the offering to Xochiquetzal.

Once done, the victim's body would be thrown down the stairway, where, at the bottom, the large round *coyolxauhqui* stone lay. Carved in deep relief and brightly painted in red, blue, and yellow was the image of Coyolxauhqui, the murdered sister of Huitzilopochtli. Like his sister, the now lifeless body would be beheaded and dismembered. The skull would be cleaned, made bare, then added to the skull rack, the *tzompantli*, its meaty limbs to be devoured in ritual cannibalism with the remains fed to the animals. This was how the goddess mother's followers had performed the ceremony for the past 230 years, both in Cuicatl's subterranean Capoltic Teopancalli, the dark temple on Tepetzinco, and now here, in the Huēyi Teōcalli, hidden beneath the city.

The captain's men, a force of one hundred, were assembled in the courtyard of Palacio de Virrey. Three blocks away from La Condesa's mansion, arms, horses, and wagons were staged in the stable yard. It was ten in the morning. Captain de Anza was preparing to brief the men.

"To prevent escapes, we've assigned four teams of six men and four mounted. You'll set up on the mansion's four corners. Each of you knows your team assignment and position. You are to detain any person attempting to escape. Three teams of eight are assigned to search the mansion, one team for each of the three floors. You will immediately deploy to the floor and corner you're assigned and begin your search. *Fiscal* Santiago and I will lead two teams of eight into either side of the cellar. Twelve dragoons will position themselves at the front of the building along with the cannon squad. You all have your instructions should you find anyone or anything suspicious. Sergeant Trujillo and six men will coordinate movement from the main hall. The remaining men will be held in reserve to the rear of the dragoons. Everyone in the building at the time of entry will be detained and brought to the main hall. We are particularly interested in La Condesa Dona Andrea. She and her daughter Isabel are to be treated with respect. You can use whatever force you deem necessary to detain anyone else."

Elena had just finished dressing when she heard a knock at her door, followed by the key turning in the lock. The door swung open, and she saw Jose carrying a tray. One of the regular guards could be seen sitting in the hall across from her door. She hadn't seen Jose since Friday when he came to tell her Maria was recovering and expected to be up and around soon.

"Buenos días, señorita. I thought since it is Sunday I

would bring you something good for breakfast—*huevos ahogados* with fresh tortillas, *jugo verde*, and coffee. My mother was raised in the countryside and learned to make eggs this way. I hope you like it." He set the tray on the table and moved back by the door.

It smelled delicious, and while she hadn't been starved, the food they were serving her had been on the low end of ordinary.

"Thank you, Jose, and thank your mother for me."

"*Sí*, señorita." Then, looking behind him at the guard, who was not paying attention, he turned back to Elena and spoke in a low, soft voice. "Señorita, when you're finished with the eggs, please look at what's beneath the plate."

He quietly backed out through the door, pulling it shut as he did. She heard the lock turn. She went to the table and sat. Unable to wait and as hungry as she was, she was too anxious to see what lay on the underside of the plate. Carefully, she lifted the plate and peered beneath. *My goodness! A key.* There was only one possibility. *It must unlock this door. But what about the guard?*

She wondered what she could do to prompt the guard to abandon his station. *I know. I'll shout I'm ill and need a doctor.* She assumed he would come in and check on her before doing anything, and she was prepared to act the part if it was called for. Then, after he left, she would count to twenty and try the key. She resolved to try just after lunch, when some of the staff would be taking their afternoon siestas. *That might work, but once I'm on the other side of that door, which way do I go?*

The attendant Giraldo had promised finally arrived. Ana heard the light tapping and saw him through the barred window. He was a young man of twenty-five to thirty with dark black hair and an appealing smile. Since she would be attending mass, Ana had put on the most attractive but conservative dress she could find in the wardrobe. She rose from her chair, walked to the door, and waited while he let himself in. She noticed something odd. *He must be wearing a shirt without a collar.* Then the door opened.

The man was tall, muscular, and naked save for a loincloth. Ana only had time to silently mouth her surprise before he grabbed her arm and pulled her out of the room.

"What are you doing? Who are you?" Before she could say she was attending mass with La Condesa, she realized she wouldn't be. He dragged her down the hallway, roughly at times if she was slow or showed any resistance. Ana wasn't entirely resigned to the fact yet, but she knew she would die this morning.

After making several turns, they descended one flight of stairs back to the level on which her first cell had been. They arrived at the end of a hallway and another oaken door. He opened the unlocked door, and they walked through.

The room was large, with cabinets running the length of two sides. Several chairs and what looked to be four pedestals were centered in the room. Six Indio women stood to one side, two of whom approached Ana. The women each took one of Ana's hands and guided her to a spot near one of the pedestals. They began to undress her. Ana didn't resist. What was she to do? Six of them and the tall Indio were still standing by the door they had entered. She blushed with embarrassment as he was enjoying the show.

Once Ana was completely naked, the women removed her hair tie and had her stand on the pedestal closest to her. They dressed her in a green skirt with various geometric patterns in red and a broad, beaded belt of turquoise, gold, and red coral shell. The *huipil* was similar to the skirt. A necklace of thin gold discs, three rows strung smallest to largest, hung around her neck.

They painted her face red from the nose to the top of her forehead, around her eyes in black diamonds, and two jagged Z-like symbols in green on both cheeks. Finally, they fitted her with a crown of flowers and quetzal feathers with two green horns.

That was when the tall Indio brought her a goblet and instructed her to drink.

"What is it?"

"Just something to relax you. Señor Angamuco provided it."

At that, Ana snapped and ran for the door, but she didn't stand a chance. Throwing himself in her path, the powerful Indio stopped her dead in her tracks. She just about bounced off him and fell to the floor. He straddled her chest and held her nose with one hand. He waited until, gasping for breath, she opened her mouth, and he poured the liquid down her throat. Whatever it was, it burned as it went down. She struggled a few moments longer, then slowly started to slip away.

Ana was awake but unable to move without assistance. They brought her to her feet. She was surprised she could stand because, no matter how hard she tried, she couldn't manage to walk or raise her arms. The two Indio women guided her to one of the chairs and sat her down. She wanted to cry, but she couldn't. Nothing, however, stopped the anguish from mounting in the pit of her stomach. She couldn't think. All Ana was aware of now was fear, desperation, and an overwhelming sense of isolation.

Two more guards entered the room. In tow were Flaquita and Manolito, her original cellmates. Their arms tied behind their backs, they had their clothes unceremoniously stripped from their bodies. Both were fitted with loincloths, Flaquita with a simple *huipil*. Once this was done, the three of them were taken through another door in the back of the room.

They were amazed by what they saw next. Their first impression was one of wonder. They were, they thought, in a subbasement of the mansion, but now they were outside. Going from a much smaller room into this enormous open space tricked their senses. For here stood a building almost as large as the mansion above, a bright white temple with statues of animals, painted symbols, and colorful flags. A breeze on their cheeks added to the illusion. They would never know that the current that chilled their skin and gave life to those colorful flags was an ingenious ventilating system devised for the vast subterranean network on the island. Soon though, they would notice the light from the braziers dimly reflected on the walls of an enormous underground cavern. Once the priestess began to speak, they could hear the hollow echo of her words from behind them.

Growing up, Ana had heard her mother speak Nahuatl. She heard the priestess speaking Nahuatl, but it was an arcane, unfamiliar dialect. It was true Nahuatl without the influence of 250 years of Spanish colonialism. The priestess stood in the smaller temple to Huitzilopochtli atop the pyramid as she spoke. Of the three, only Ana was ignorant of the drama playing out in front of them.

The high priestess stepped forward, and Ana, looking up, saw the masked figure of a woman dressed as an Aztec goddess walking to the front of the upper platform. The woman was beautiful and regal, wearing the feather headdress of the ancients and a fearsome red-and-black mask with a wide grin of yellow teeth and white bone piercings on the lip, septum, and ears.

What couldn't be seen was Gabriela, daughter of La Condesa and heir to the sect. She was standing in the back of Huitzilopochtli's temple, robed with headdress and makeup but utterly naked beneath her robe. She was waiting for act three of this morning's rite, when Ana, the ritual's surrogate Xochiquetzal, would have her skin stripped from her body. Gabriela would don it, like an animal hide, and perform the sacred dance of their ancestors as Ana's heart was taken from her.

Also unseen was Angamuco. Hidden from the congregation, he had secreted himself in the temple of Tlaloc. He could come and go as he pleased during these ceremonies. *Mi dama, you thought you were the only one who knew of these passages built during the mansion's construction. Well, so do I.*

Two attendants walked to either side of the priestess as she stood there, stark still. They reached up, both taking hold of a corner of the mask. They gently lifted it away, revealing its wearer. Even with the makeup, La Condesa was easily recognizable. Ana thought, *Maybe this is a dream. If it is, oh, please let me wake up.*

La Condesa, the priestess, raised both her arms as if praising some god, and simultaneously came the loud and frightening beating of drums, rattlers, shakers, and a single note from two high-pitched flutes. As quickly as the cacophony had started, all became quiet again. Two other attendants walked over from the base of the pyramid. Both were naked save for their loincloths and ceremonial skull masks topped with turkey feathers. Each took hold of one of Manolito's arms, dragged him over to the temple, and began ascending the steep white steps where the priestess stood waiting. Manolito guessed what was to happen. He'd heard of it on Tepetzinco. He twisted and kicked to free himself, to no avail. The two Indio attendants were far stronger, and nothing would stop him from being frog-marched up the stairway.

When he reached the top, he saw the priestess had moved behind the curved stone altar and was holding a deadly-looking obsidian blade. He began to scream as two additional attendants grabbed him by the ankles and lifted him onto the cold altar stone. They held him in place as the priestess lifted the sacrificial blade and then brought the knife down, buried to its hilt just below the sternum, then in quick fashion, cut down to the navel.

Reaching in and up under the ribcage, she grasped his heart, ripped it from his body, and held it, still beating, high in the air as her offering to Xochiquetzal. The priestess placed the heart in the *cuauhxicalli* and wiped the blade clean with a cloth. Dismissively, the body was thrown down the staircase to be placed on the *coyolxauhqui* stone. There, the attendant made an incision between two vertebrae in the neck, deftly decapitating the body.

Flaquita was still screaming. She hadn't stopped since they took Manolito away. Ana wanted to scream, but she couldn't. Her lungs and mouth wouldn't obey. She'd never seen such horror in her life. Then they came for Flaquita, who was desperately clinging to Ana. They tore her away, still screaming. Ana did the only thing she could do. She fainted.

It was one o'clock. Elena thought she couldn't wait any longer. She'd been holding the key Jose had given her for over an hour in anticipation of what she'd do next. Then she heard and felt an explosion.

Thirty feet below Elena, the mansion's two massive, eight-inch-thick front doors splintered into a thousand pieces. This was the result of a three-kilo cannonball, shot at close range, traveling four hundred meters per second. The thunderous sound could be heard over a mile away, loud enough even to resonate below ground in the temple chamber, catching the high priestess and her cohorts by surprise.

The priestess's hands were bloody, having dispatched both Manolito and poor Flaquita. Knife clutched in her hand, she had been preparing to do the same to the now-revived Ana lying supinely before her. La Condesa did some quick thinking. There was no longer time to complete the rite as intended, and Ana would be worth more alive than dead if they were under attack from the authorities. She set the knife aside and stepped back into Huitzilopochtli's sanctuary to consult with Gabriela.

Then came the sound of a second explosion, but it came from within the temple, not from without. La Condesa turned and saw one of the four altar attendants dead on the ground. A pistol ball had blown a sizable hole through his back. The other three were fleeing down the staircase. One, slipping in the blood, tumbled the better part of the way.

There, holding two pistols, one spent, was Giraldo de Angamuco. "Just keep back."

"Giraldo, you fool, what are you doing?"

"I've come for the girl. You told me I could have her."

"Idiot. Put down that gun at once!"

"You haven't sensed the change in our relationship, have you, dear *condesa*? Or should I say whore of Satan? The girl and I will be leaving now. And, from what I've seen upstairs, you'll want to be leaving as well."

Dona Andrea was speechless, unused to being spoken to in that way, especially from the toady Angamuco. Angamuco helped Ana down from the altar, took her hand, and turned to leave. Impulsively, he turned back to La Condesa and plucked the topaz from her navel. "In case I need some spending money." He and Ana disappeared into Tlaloc's temple.

"I fear the toad is right," said Dona Andrea to Gabriela. "Get everyone into the escape tunnel and take them to the boathouse on the Canal de la Viga. From there, you can get them to the island. I'll be behind you. First, I have to collect our other guest. We'll need the insurance." Gabriela nodded and ran off to execute her mother's command.

This is it, thought Dona Andrea. *I've been found out.* Even though she needed to act now and act quickly, Dona Andrea took a moment and sat down on the temple's steps, not to reflect, but, as was her nature, to adapt to the challenge. *I can't escape. I can't hide. They've taken my home, and I'm sure they'll be coming to the island soon and in force. The legacy can't die. The true religion of Cuicatl must continue.*

After the explosion, Elena heard an unending stream of footfalls outside her door. It had just started to die down. She reassessed her "I'm sick" ploy, which seemed unworkable, but she had to try. She didn't know what had caused the explosion and wondered whether her guard was still at his post in the hallway. Then it hit her. It was so obvious. *I'll just call out to him and ask about the explosion. If he doesn't answer, I'll use the key. I may not have another chance.*

She summoned her courage. "Hello! Hello! Is everything all right? What was that explosion?" She waited. Nothing. *Okay, Elena.* She placed the key into the lock and turned it slowly, hoping to make as little sound as possible. She heard the lock click. She opened the door. To her surprise, she had a visitor. There in the doorway stood a bare-breasted woman with a painted face, a crown of feathers, an evil-looking knife in her belt, and a pistol in her right hand.

They'd been in the mansion for fifteen minutes. Diego and de Anza regrouped at the cellar stairwell, having searched all four corners. "All we found were storage rooms and a lot of dust," said de Anza.

"I'm afraid we came up with pretty much the same thing," confirmed Diego. "Still, there's something odd about this cellar."

"Odd?"

"Yes. I counted thirty paces from the back wall of my side to this spot. What would you say it was on your side?"

"I would imagine about the same."

"The mansion sits on an entire city block. These rooms account for only a third of that."

"I'd agree. So what does that tell you?"

"It tells me one of two things." Diego pointed back into the darkness he'd returned from. "Either the other side of that back wall is nothing but dirt, or—"

"There's another cellar," said de Anza, finishing his sentence.

The two squads returned to the main floor via the stairwell. They looked for similar access across the hall, but found none.

Diego addressed the squads. "All right. Teams of two! Fan out and search for other cellar access. Call out when you find it."

Two went to the back and two to the front of the building. The rest took the rooms on either side of the hall. Diego and his man entered the first room on the left side of the hall. Clearly it was a library. Aside from the door they came through, there was no other exit. Diego scanned the room, bookshelves, fireplace, and portraits. He imagined they were family members—ancestors, judging by the dress of some. One in contemporary garb stood out—the full-length portrait of Renato de Montoya.

"Private! What's your name?" he said to the young soldier beside him.

"Ortiz, señor."

"I mean your first name."

"Mateo, señor."

"Mateo, please find the captain and ask him to join us. There's something he'll want to see. On the double!"

The soldier ran out of the room as Diego turned back to the portrait.

The soldier returned with Captain de Anza.

"Pedro, this is the portrait Felipe told us about. Recognize the Latin?"

De Anza looked up. In Latin at the top of the painting, above Renato de Montoya's head, were the words "*Surge et accipe cor.*" *Arise and take heart.* He thought back to the island. "I wonder if that house is still standing. It felt like the whole place was about to crash on top of us."

"Now we know it was built and occupied by the Montoyas. It must hold secrets going back to the origins of the cult. I'm worried, Pedro. I thought we'd find Elena by now."

"We'll find her, my friend. Let's keep searching. Let's check with Trujillo and see if he heard anything from the other teams."

Together, they looked away from the portrait and started for the door. De Anza stopped abruptly, placing his hand on Diego's forearm. "Wait!"

Diego looked at de Anza, wondering what had piqued his attention. "What is it? Did you see something?"

"Stand still. Do you feel that?"

Diego stood motionless. "Yes. Yes, I do. It feels like a breeze."

"Diego, it's what I felt in the village lodge house on Tepetzinco. The breeze was coming from behind the reed wall." De Anza turned, searching with his eyes, and walked slowly to the wall. "It's the same breeze the ventilation in the cave produced, a positive pressure that pushed clean air through the passageways." He put his hand out and felt for the current. "It's the portrait. It's coming from behind the portrait." He ran his fingers around the large frame, feeling for some catch. "Got it!" he said excitedly.

He pushed down the latch, and the large painting gave way. It swung toward him. The breeze was more pronounced now. They saw the stairway descending from the small platform.

"Mateo!" Diego shouted. "Ask Sergeant Trujillo to send men and lanterns."

The private raced out the door.

Once the men and lights had arrived, they started down the stairs to what turned out to be the first of three subbasements. They all but accounted for the missing space they'd sensed in the first cellar. On the first level, they found prison cells and furnished rooms. They were all empty with no sign of Elena. The next level yielded similar results.

The final stairwell went twice as far down as the first two, where they met the shocking proof of the sacrificial cult. The network of chambers was stocked with artifacts and supplies used in the rite, including one room containing costumes, jewelry, headdresses, masks, and ancient weapons.

They made their way down the hall to a door. Passing through it, they followed it a short distance to a second door. Opening it, they entered the temple chamber and were horrified by what they saw. Braziers, still burning, lit the blood-stained staircase, and, at the base, two decapitated heads, a man's and a woman's, were lying on the floor. The man's body had been dismembered. The stench of death hung heavy in the air.

"God in heaven!" said de Anza.

"I'm sure he is, but he's not here," said Diego, as the two men took in both the splendor and the horror of the Templo Mayor.

"What twisted evil provokes such actions?" said de Anza, turning away from the scene. "Come, Pedro. We have to know if Elena is here."

Diego's heart was pounding as he and de Anza climbed the blood-drenched staircase. When they reached the platform, they found it to be an inch deep in blood. More still dripped from the altar stone. Then they saw the *cuauhxicalli* containing the two hearts. De Anza thought of what Padre Aranda had told him. "Pedro, evil exists in this world."

Diego couldn't look away. He felt as though he was going to be sick when he heard the whimpering. It was coming from the other temple at the far end of the platform. He glanced over to de Anza. He heard it too. They moved slowly across the platform.

Huddled in a back corner was a woman crying. She was dressed in a bizarre costume and had red, black, and green makeup on her face. Next to her was the crumpled body of a man. Diego recognized him as someone at the viceroy's reception the night he'd been poisoned. He remembered because, frankly, the man's ugliness made him unforgettable. He was still breathing.

Angamuco and Ana had made it through the secret passageway to where he had first entered it. He slid the panel aside, and there, standing before him, was La Condesa. Before he could raise his musket and fire, she had thrust her blade into his abdomen with a hateful look, pulling it sideways, cutting like a razor as it went. La Condesa took his musket and walked away. Fearful of another encounter with La Condesa, they retreated to the temple. He could go no further and collapsed there.

Diego and de Anza looked down at the strange couple.

Giraldo knew he was dying. Ana's emotions were a mixture of fear, shock, and, strangely, an amount of pity for this terrible man who, after all, had rescued her from a hideous death.

"Now, don't you worry, my dear. You'll be just fine. You go with these two gentlemen, and they'll take care of you."

Ana started to cry.

"No, no, my dear, don't be sad," said Angamuco. "Now you are free of this ghastly nightmare. Be happy because, in a way, you saved my life."

The old man looked up at Diego. "I know who you're looking for. They will have undoubtedly taken her to the island." Then, with a grimace of pain, Angamuco reached into his breast pocket and took out the topaz. Handing it to Ana, he looked at her and said, "Here, this is for you. You never know, my dear, when you might need some spending money." Sitting there, he remained looking at her but never spoke again.

"Pedro, you heard that. We've got to get going."

Then he heard the girl say, "Don Santiago?"

He looked down at her and helped her up.

She said, "You're Señor Santiago, aren't you?"

"Yes, I am. I mean, that's me."

"I'm Ana, Elena's friend."

"Ana, do you know where Elena is?"

"What do you mean? I've been locked up here for I don't know how long."

Diego realized Ana didn't know Elena, too, had been kidnapped, so he didn't pursue it. Ana didn't need more bad news. "Come on. Let's get you out of here. It's time you went home." Diego lifted her and carried her up and out of the cellar, back into the sunlight.

"Diego, if we want to get Elena back safely, we can't just run off to the island. We've got to plan. Just as we did with today's operation."

De Anza and Diego were standing in front of the mansion, contemplating their next steps. They'd sent the Lopez woman home to her mother. Since Ana was utterly unaware of Elena's abduction, she couldn't offer further information. She did tell them of her strange interrogation by La Condesa, of being clubbed unconscious, and her whole story to the point where they had found her with Angamuco.

"Once again, you're right, my friend. It's just I feel so helpless, and you've seen for yourself what these people are capable of doing."

"You're a man of action, Diego. It's hard for you to stand by, but I'm afraid that's the wisest course of action. Remember, we've got the viceroy and the whole army on our side."

Diego smiled and put his hand on his good friend's shoulder. "What would I do without you, Pedro?"

Together, they started back to the plaza. It was four o'clock when they returned to Felipe's office in the Audiencia. The five of them, now to include Sergeant Trujillo, were comparing notes.

"How many people did we round up, Sergeant?" asked de Carceres.

"Seventeen, if you count the servants. We don't think

they're connected to the cult, but we'll check to be sure. That leaves only five that we're suspicious of."

De Anza chimed in. "They must have had some escape route we haven't found yet. The passage the girl and the old man used goes to other parts of the mansion but nowhere else."

"I told Pedro I'd seen the old man at the reception that night. We can surely say La Condesa is responsible for everything—the plaza murder, the poisoning, and both kidnappings."

"Add two more murders to that, Diego," said de Anza.

"One other thing," said Trujillo. "I recognized two of the five suspects as members of Yaotl's gang. He's also mixed up in this in some way."

Felipe stood, called for his assistant, then said, "I'll arrange for dinner to be brought in with plenty of coffee. We've got an invasion to plan."

They worked late into the evening plotting their attack on the island.

"We know the island's geography well enough, but we haven't a clue about the tunnel networks and where they lead," said de Anza.

"That and their firepower. From what you've told us, Pedro, it's fairly impressive. It's not like breaking up a gang or staging a raid on some hangout. It's preparing to go to war," said Carceres.

"The key is access to that underground roundhouse through the lodge. I'm sure there must be other entrances, but that seems to be where they have all their stores. If we take that, it's just a matter of time before they lose the means to continue and possibly surrender," remarked Trujillo.

After four hours of working out tactics, it was decided they'd attack in the morning. There was still the issue of Elena.

"Once the attack begins, Elena is as good as dead," said Diego.

They all looked at him, knowing he was right.

"Then we must go ahead of the main force before the attack begins." It was Benito.

"Agreed," said de Anza.

"I must go as well," said Carceres.

"Felipe, no," said Diego. " You are too valuable."

"You mean I'm too old."

"I concur with Santiago," interjected Trujillo. "Señor de Carceres, you'll be needed to authorize the resources and coordinate the attack."

Felipe conceded. "Very well, Sergeant, you're right. There's much to do, not much time."

"Benito, Pedro, we'll meet at the dock at nine. I'll have the boat and gear ready. Felipe, Sergeant, we'll see you on Tepetzinco."

Diego walked into his kitchen to find Maria preparing dinner. Whatever it was, he could smell it cooking on the stove, and it smelled delicious. He made a point to announce himself given her recent experience.

"Hola, Maria. I see you're feeling better. I'm glad to see you doing what you like best."

"Who said I like this? You pay me to do this. I'd much rather be out dancing. Young man, do you have a brain in that head?"

Speechless, he looked at her glaring back at him with a stern face.

Then she broke out into a broad smile and, with a roaring laugh, said, "Welcome home, Dieguito! Of course I love to cook. You think I would do it just for you?"

Diego walked over to her and hugged her. "Shame on you, Maria. It's good to see you well again. I'm afraid I don't have much time for dinner tonight. I'll be leaving again shortly."

"Elena?"

"Yes, we think we know where she is. We're going there tonight."

"I'll make you something quick to take with you. I have a feeling you'll need all your strength."

"Maybe something for Benito and Pedro as well?"

"*Sí*, something for them as well."

Benito walked across the plaza, into the western barrio of San Juan Moyolta, and past the *mercado*. As he stepped up to his door, he was surprised to see he had a visitor.

"Sor Juana? This is a surprise. I mean the time. They unlocked the door for you."

"Benito, if only your head were as smart as your ass."

"Okay, that was uncalled for, but I am surprised."

"I heard about the raid on La Condesa's mansion. They used a cannon to blow open the front entrance?"

"We wanted the element of surprise."

"I came to see." She collected herself. "I came to see if you were all right."

"I'm fine, and we found the missing girl, Elena's friend. She's a little shaken up but unharmed, for the most part.

I think, though, she may have nightmares for some time to come. Regretfully, we didn't find Elena, but we know she's on the island. One of La Condesa's men spoke before he died."

"And you're going there?"

"Yes. Tonight."

"It will be dangerous, won't it?"

"Perhaps."

"Then I want you to take something with you." She reached under her habit and took out a silver crucifix.

"I don't know," said Benito with a hint of reluctance.

"Please. For me." When Benito didn't respond, she said, "Benito?" Tears came from the corners of her eyes and down one cheek.

Benito stared into those tearful eyes, and, with two fingers under her chin, he gently lifted her face and kissed her tenderly. They embraced.

Benito said, "Okay. For you." He took the crucifix. She started to walk away, her hand still in his, and slowly they parted.

Benito asked, "I'll see you tomorrow?"

"You better," she replied and disappeared into the night.

LUGAR DE OFRENDA

"I DON'T NEED A gun, Diego."

"Benito, you'll have to defend yourself."

"I brought my staff. It's served me well in the past." Benito reached out with it and lightly tapped Diego on the shoulder.

"Well, then, stay behind us. Not that we're much cover for that bulk."

De Anza and Diego both had two flintlock pistols, one M1752 long rifle, and their swords, accompanied by military-issue combat knives.

Benito chuckled. "Don't hurt yourselves with all that."

De Anza, lowering himself into the boat, asked, "So what's the plan, Diego?"

"Somehow, we have to gain entry without being noticed. We can't go through the village lodge. That will be guarded and reinforced now that they're expecting us."

"Without another way in, we may have to attempt it," said de Anza.

Benito took his oar and pushed off from the dock.

As they rowed down the canal toward the lake, Diego said, "I was thinking of our search in the mansion this morning and finding that the portrait of Renato de Montoya was the door to the underground. We wouldn't have discovered that had you not noticed the current of air flowing from behind it."

"Just like the reed wall at the back of the lodge. Are you thinking we search for out-of-the-ordinary breezes?"

"In a way, yes. But in one specific location. Think of it. The abandoned house on the island is hundreds of years old. Why would the Montoyas choose that site to build a house?"

"Perhaps because there's something there, like access to the tunnels."

"That's what I'm postulating, Benito, and I think I know where in the house."

"The fireplace!" said de Anza excitedly. "The inscription above it, exactly as on the portrait of Renato de Montoya and the heart of Copil, the same as above the door."

"Yes, the house probably grew impractical for the cult's needs. It's been crumbling for some time now. When we saw it, there was no sign it was occupied or in use. The access may still be there."

"But its disuse is also an argument there's nothing there at all," said de Anza.

"If there aren't any objections, we'll try that first," said Diego.

They grew silent for a time and continued to row. At one point, Diego broke out the bread and sausages Maria had packed. Since none of them had eaten since breakfast, the food was consumed with enthusiasm.

As they grew nearer to the island, Diego became more and more concerned with the timetable. It was just about eleven. In five hours, two contingents of fifty soldiers each would land on either side of the island half a mile north of the village, move south, and hold for the artillery salvos. A third contingent of fifty soldiers would land at the island's far end, and, staying on high ground, make their way south. They'd sweep for other islanders and protect the rear to either side.

At six, the naval attack would begin. Four barges would approach from the south and line up with the village. Each of the four barges was fitted with two falconet swivel cannons firing heated round shot. After three warning rounds, inhabitants would have five minutes to clear the area before the cannoneers commenced with a full barrage.

Blasts of fire-red grapeshot would set the jacales and lodges on fire as they ripped through them. The troops would descend on both flanks and secure what was left of the burning village. Two falconets would be brought ashore to support a piece of six-pounder field artillery that would be employed to pummel the outer cliff face hiding the roundhouse. Once they broke through, and with any luck, stray shot from the falconets would strike the powder magazine. Then a force of one hundred men would rush the tunnels. In that scenario, Elena would be dead before they reached her. That left Diego seven hours to locate an entrance to the tunnels and find Elena.

They landed just below the baths dedicated to Chalchihuidicue, where they had captured Hernandez. They pulled the boat in and off the shore, concealing it with brush.

Diego told Benito, "The house isn't too much further south from here, sitting on a bluff not far from the shore."

Because of their last visit, Diego was worried the house would be guarded. They had kept low and so far hadn't seen a single soul. Then the house was there in front of them, much more visible than when the torrential rain had obscured it. The color of the white stucco had gained a bluish tint thanks to the full moon. It seemed quiet and peaceful enough. It would appear to be a pleasant summer retreat if it weren't for what they knew of its history. They crawled up the bluff, wary of a sentry or lookout. When they reached the top and looked across the small yard, there wasn't any sign of humanity.

"I may have been wrong, my friends," Diego whispered. "It must not threaten the sect if this has been left completely unguarded."

"Not necessarily, Diego," whispered Benito. "This place or its parts are close to two hundred years old. What if its significance has been forgotten over time and the natives, superstitious, don't come near it?"

"I sincerely hope that's the case, Benito."

De Anza took the lead, crossing the yard and moving to the archway under the symbol of Copil. The others followed. Again, through the entrance to the courtyard, there was no sign of life. They walked through the yard and under the portico on the south side of the building to the great room. Each of them carried a small lantern, and they paused to light them before entering the darkened room. The fireplace stood at the far end. As they crossed the room, a portion of the ceiling chose that moment to come loose and crash to the floor. "Good God! I just about jumped out of my skin," said de Anza.

The three of them stood shoulder to shoulder, facing the enormous fireplace. The inscription was visible, but they had to look for it. They checked for any mechanism that might actuate a door or a panel. Nothing. They felt for drafts or currents of air emanating from behind the bricks, the corners, and the floor—still nothing. The opposite was true. They could feel a large draft of air being sucked into the chimney.

The first thing Diego noticed was that the fire grate was missing from the hearth. That was not unexpected; it was an abandoned house, after all. What was surprising was the swath of moonlight painted on the floor of the hearth. Diego ducked under the mantle and stepped into the hearth. The first thing that made him think was the capaciousness of the firebox. All three of them could easily fit in there with room to spare. He looked up. Sure enough, he could see the outline of the chimney top. *That's odd. I shouldn't be able to see clean through the flue to the top.*

He knelt. "Pedro, Benito, come in here and have a look."

Soon the three of them were shoulder to shoulder again, now looking up as Diego had instructed.

"See? There's no damper or smoke shelf. You shouldn't be able to see straight up and out."

"The house is falling apart. The damper may have just fallen away. I agree the flue should at least be stepped, but who knows who built this place and what they knew about chimneys?" argued de Anza.

"Well, do you notice the other missing item?" asked Diego, affecting a somewhat smarmy tone. De Anza and Benito both shrugged. "There's no soot, no discoloration in any of the brickwork, including the floor of the fire-pit. This fireplace has never been used. It must serve another purpose."

Benito inspected the brickwork. Indeed, except for some dust, it was as pristine as the day it was laid. Benito's height became an advantage. He noticed below him how the brickwork was staggered up to a point about three feet above him. Then it flattened out.

"Diego, hop up here and look at the back wall above me."

Diego held onto the Monk's shoulder and, using the offset bricks, climbed up.

"My god, could it be that simple? It's open, but I can't feel the draft flowing in or out of it." He grasped the ledge and determined it was a wall about five inches thick. Using the bricks again as footing, he pulled himself up. "Hand me my lantern."

De Anza picked it up and relayed it via the Monk. Diego took it and raised it to the opening. As he pulled himself over the wall, his feet found the floor his lantern had revealed. "I think we've got it. It's a rounded tunnel going back further than I can see. There's also a rope ladder next to the wall that looks like it hasn't been used since King Charles I. I wouldn't try it."

"Not to worry," said de Anza. "I took Sergeant Trujillo's example and brought a good length of strong rope."

Tossing the rope up to Diego, Benito supported de Anza's climb. There wasn't anything to tie the rope to, so the two men held tight, bracing their feet against the wall, as the Monk hauled himself up.

What the three of them saw now was, with some improvement, the same tunnel Cuicatl had discovered and built her jacales around 233 years before. What they were about to see was beyond their imagination.

"No time to waste," said Diego.

They started inward along the tunnel, reaching the first cavern, the site of Cuicatl's original temple. It was dark except for the light of their lanterns. Diego lifted his lantern and was startled by the exaggerated stone face of an Aztec god standing before him. Which god it was, he wasn't sure. The statue stood six feet off the ground, and, as he looked beyond it, he saw other figures. The walls were covered with mosaics of the same god performing different rites. All involved excising human hearts. He got the same sick feeling he had in the temple under the mansion.

"Look," said de Anza, standing on a large dais across from them. "This must be the altar."

Benito walked up to it and ran his fingers over the top. "It's dusty. No one's used it for a while. Why would they abandon it?"

"I'm not sure, but we should be moving on," said Diego.

"Right," affirmed de Anza. Their hearts sank when they got to the other end of the cavern. It was a dead end. There was a tunnel, but it was blocked with a uniform, smooth gray substance. Whatever it was, it was hard as rock.

"They blocked the passage?" said de Anza.

"It explains the dust on the altar stone, and the fact Diego didn't feel any kind of draft at the entrance," said the Monk. "We had it right up to this point. But why wall off the temple?"

"I think I know why," said Diego. "Come over here."

Diego was standing by the wall opposite the altar,

holding his lantern up to the wall. A crypt had been carved out of the rock. A hollow, four by four by six, was chiseled out of the rock five feet above the floor. It contained a hexagonal glass coffin tapered at the bottom. Below was a separate black stone tablet showing an image in relief that matched the statue they saw when they first entered the chamber. Next to that, the name Cuicatl I was etched into the stone and, below that, "*Surge et accipe cor.*"

"It's walled off because this is her tomb."

"The queen bitch herself," said de Anza. "What do we do now? Turn around?"

Benito leaned against the rock wall. "Let's not give up that easily. I think I know what they used to fill in the exit. If I'm right, we have a chance of breaking through it."

"What are you thinking, Benito?" asked Diego.

"A manufactured mixture of lime, volcanic ash, or sand. I think this may be the former."

"Okay," said de Anza. "How does this help us?"

"The Romans used something like this thousands of years ago to build the Colosseum. I'm guessing this is made using a method less sophisticated than their recipe. My second guess is that the wall isn't meant to keep people from entering. It's more like a memorial and maybe not that thick."

With that, the Monk walked back to the blocked passage, picking up a more diminutive version of an Aztec god as he went, more likely a demigod. He raised it to shoulder height and ran toward the barrier, crashing the ugly little figure into a spot just north of dead center. It didn't entirely give way but noticeably caved inward.

After two more attempts, there was a hole in the wall the size of their lithic friend.

"Good show, Benito!" cheered Diego.

Then they were stunned to see light coming through the opening. The Monk cleared enough space to pass as the other two retrieved their gear. Once to the other side, they saw a tunnel lit by torches spaced about twenty feet apart on alternate sides.

Diego spoke first. "I'm not sure how often this is frequented, but there has to be someone who maintains these torches at the very least. Keep an ear out as we go. We need to remain hidden until we've located Elena." Then he thought, *We haven't much time left. God, guide us.*

Keeping a good pace, they reached a point where the tunnel branched in two directions.

"Which way?" queried de Anza.

"Felipe and I assumed this may happen," replied Diego. "My working logic is the village was south of where we entered the passages. Each time we come to a branch in the passage, we'll default to the one that leads the truest south. I understand we might subsequently take a turn east or west along the way, but at least we'll be consistent in the direction we take at these branches."

He reached into his pocket and brought out what looked to be a pocket watch. "This is what we'll use to determine our choices." Flipping open the top cover, he addressed the lower half of the device, which he held parallel to the ground as he turned his body left and right.

"What are you doing, Diego?" asked the Monk.

"Felipe gave this to me before we left the Audiencia. It's a portable bearing compass. It should work underground as long as we don't run into any large iron deposits, and we shouldn't." He paused a moment, consulting the device, then pointed to the tunnel on the right. "This one."

They encountered two more branches in the tunnels. Both times, they went with whichever one pointed truest south. At the last branch, they went left, and the torches disappeared.

"I guess there are limits on how many they can keep lit," said Benito.

"I hope this isn't an indication we took a wrong turn," said a somewhat doubtful Diego.

They kept going, however, and didn't turn back. Not long after, they heard a low roar. The sound grew with each step they took. They couldn't see the source, but they correctly guessed it was the sound of rushing water. By the time they entered the chamber that held the source, the roar was thunderous, the temperature had risen, and they were starting to sweat.

Off to the left was an incline, and at its bottom, they could see, through the lantern light, steaming water rushing by at breakneck speed. They could also see that they witnessed only a portion of a potentially much larger flow hidden behind the rock face above it. Turning their attention back to the path before them, they saw it had been leveled and finished with paving stones with a low wall on the river side of the walkway. As impressive as all this was, they had no time for gawking.

They traveled on, continuing to take their southbound turns as they went. They had been walking for an hour when they saw the light ahead. It wasn't a branch they encountered this time. They emerged into a much larger tunnel, its sides finished with the same material used to block off Cuicatl's tomb.

An estimated twenty-five feet wide, it also had a small-gauge rail running down the center.

"The compass says we go right here," said Diego.

"This must be one of the three tunnels that leads to the roundhouse and the village. We should move fast now. Chances are someone will come along at any moment," counseled de Anza.

They started to trot, keeping to one side of the passage. Soon they reached the roundhouse. Diego and Benito marveled at the size of it. It was entirely man-made, carved out of solid rock.

"That one six-pounder may not be a match for this, depending on how thick the outer wall is," said Diego.

"Doesn't matter. All they have to do is secure the entryway. It's wide enough for the men to rush and not be in a tight bunch," said de Anza.

"Good. We can't waste time. Which of the other two tunnels do we take?" queried Diego.

"I say right up the middle. There's less of a chance the other side might bypass some central complex the way this one did," offered Benito.

"As I said, no time. Let's go."

"One quick second." Benito walked over to the gated armory. "These bars are enough to keep a body out but wide enough for me to grab one of these." Reaching in, he got hold of a small keg of black powder and lifted it through the bars. Then he turned, smiling, and said, "I did say I didn't need a gun, but this could prove handy. Let's go!"

They didn't have to go far before reaching the central

railway's terminus and another turntable with two railcars sitting on it. Beyond that were two immense wooden doors fifteen feet high and ten feet wide with iron braces and plates. A smaller iron door was positioned at the bottom and middle of the left one. It was locked.

They heard voices coming from the direction of the roundhouse. It was hard to distinguish, but it sounded like three male voices talking together and getting louder.

"Quick, into the railcars," instructed Diego in an urgent whisper. They speedily obeyed, Benito in one, Diego and de Anza in the other. Luckily, they each had canvas tarps helping to conceal their newly loaded contents. De Anza heard the same Nahuatl dialect they'd encountered on their earlier visit to the island as the villagers jovially continued their discourse.

Perhaps an early morning crew. They certainly sound fresh, thought de Anza. The voices rose and fell as they passed by. Then Diego, hearing the jangle of keys, peered out from under his canvas cover.

Three men in village dress were standing by the small access door. One searched for the appropriate key on a large key ring. Their backs were to the railcars as Diego and de Anza lifted their cover and deftly exited. Benito followed suit.

They were not big men and didn't look like soldiers or carry themselves as soldiers would—they were most likely workers. Diego waited until the one man had the key he'd been searching for in the lock. Then he tapped him on the shoulder with the point of his sword. The three turned, and Diego could immediately tell they were frightened and, best of all, submissive.

Allowing the man to complete his task and open the

door, Diego, de Anza, and Benito each took a man and guided them through. They were stunned by what they saw. Over the past two hundred years, the sect had carved a vast gallery stretching more than 300 feet into the mountain. The vaulted roof soared thirty feet above them. Below them, it was another fifty feet to the cavern's floor. The atrium was over a hundred feet wide. The entire space reminded Diego of the Aztec and Mayan architecture he'd seen and read about, but the construction was of giant carved blocks rather than earthen mounds overlaid with stones.

On each corner and in the middle of each side of the ceiling were inverted stone pyramids with no visible means of support. The walls, also of carved stone, stepped down to the mezzanine open to the lowest level and supported by ten large columns with carved stone capitals of serpent and jaguar heads. At the bottom was a pool of steaming water surrounded by an arcade. A causeway bisecting the pool's length ran from end to end, with a circular dais at the center.

Water fell from the mezzanine from the mouths of eight stone serpent heads. The steam gave all the walls a sheen, reflecting light from the giant fiery cauldrons surrounding the colossal atrium at each level. Rising from the far end of the causeway, a broad staircase climbed to a temple structure with massive bronze doors, each decorated with copper plates with reliefs of Xochiquetzal. Above the doors, a gigantic figure of Xochiquetzal's head overlooked the space. The mezzanine and the arcade levels were surrounded by squared portals, fifteen on each side.

"This place is going to get busy over the next hour. These three were just the first of many. Time is running low. I make it four now," worried Diego.

"I wonder why there are so few guards and we haven't seen other people," remarked de Anza.

"I don't think they considered a threat from underground," Benito answered. "If you looked just outside, there'd be a sizable number at the lodge and the village borders. As far as why we haven't run into anyone, I'd guess they regard this as sacred ground restricted to a small group of priests or shamans. Commoners are allowed access only for rituals, festivals, and work duty. It's amazing what they've built here."

"They did have two hundred years," de Anza retorted.

"Still, it's amazing for a village of three, maybe four hundred," said Diego.

"I wouldn't be surprised if they followed the Aztec practice of kidnapping slaves to do the work, only to sacrifice them once their toils are completed," said Benito.

Turning their attention back to Elena, Diego said, "It's time we interrogated our three new friends."

Diego didn't believe in torture, but he was desperate. There were too many doors and not enough time before the bombardment began. He saw de Anza bending over in a conversation with their three prisoners.

"Diego, this is Eztli, Itztli, and Meztli. They call themselves techs. They are responsible for what they call the complex, keeping it in repair and building new tunneling works."

Eztli spoke up in perfect Spanish. "We were chosen from the community to be educated in various useful arts—architecture, hydraulics, metalworking. We were taught at the university in the city. Our families remained on the island. If we spoke or ran, they would be killed.

That is the way. Others are trained in different disciplines. We all live under the yoke of the religion."

"Do you know anything about the burnt offering left in the city a few weeks ago?" asked de Anza.

Eztli replied, "We know of it. The man you speak of was imprisoned with two others as recusants by the enforcers. They are the protectors of the faith, bred to be low in intelligence and high in brawn. They are thugs the priestess uses to keep the population in line. The priestess sacrificed him in the temple of Xiuhtecuhtli."

"I helped the other two escape," added Itztli. "They were just young people, innocents."

"After the sacrifice," Eztli continued, "she had the offering taken there to strike fear in the Indios. She desires to grow the sect beyond the island. Fear is the weapon she wields."

"Then you know where they're holding a young woman brought here just yesterday?" said Diego, desperation in his voice.

"*Sí*, all the prisoners are kept in one place."

"Please take us there. We'll do everything we can to rid you of your oppressors," promised Diego.

Now they were six. They followed Eztli down one of the dual stairways to the mezzanine and then to the bottom floor of the atrium. Motioning them to follow, Eztli ran ahead. "It's the last portal to the right of the grand staircase."

They ran across the back side of the pool to the arcade formed beneath that side of the mezzanine, then forward toward the other end of the atrium. They ran past rushing streams of water emerging from the eight serpent sculptures, plunging from above to the central pool—the cacophony made by all eight streams crashing into the pool at once reverberated through the hall.

They came to the last portal, a rectangular opening seven feet tall and four feet wide that was a tight fit for the Monk. As they entered, they were thrown into darkness. The last light from the atrium grew dim. They lit their lanterns and moved ahead.

"Why is there no torchlight in this passage?" asked de Anza.

"There will be soon. The high priestess insisted no light should be seen coming from the portals. 'These are the passages to dark secrets,' she would say."

At last, they came to a juncture where they'd be visible to the guard if they proceeded.

Diego queried Eztli. "How far, and how many guards?"

"Thirty or so feet to the right once we enter the passage. There's typically only one guard. He's just the gatekeeper. The passage runs straight, so he'll see us once we enter."

De Anza asked if there were any sort of alarm.

"No, but he does have a weapon."

"I've got this." De Anza turned the corner and broke into a sprint. The guard at the end of the hall was half-asleep and didn't notice his charge until he was almost on top of him. He reacted too slowly to parry the upward swing of the rifle butt catching him under the chin. He went down and would not get up for some time. The others were right behind him. The cell door was made of cross-hatched square iron bars opening into a sizable space carved out of rock.

"No one's here!" Diego said, his heart sinking.

"I'm sorry, my friend," said Eztli. "This can mean only one thing. She is condemned to die today."

"When? Where?" Diego quickly asked.

"Normally in the morning. It will happen in either the grand temple of Xochiquetzal or the temple of Xiuhtecuhtli."

As they spoke, de Anza took the key from the guard's belt, dragged the guard into the cell, and locked the iron gate, throwing the key to the other end of the hall.

"We've got to know which one, Eztli. Is there a way to tell?" asked Diego.

"I dare not ask any of the priest attendants. They're too suspicious." He thought a moment longer and then was struck with the answer. "I can ask the watch captain! He knows about all movements within the complex. He's a lazy lout who sits at his post all day and is too thick to question why I'd like to know. He should be on duty soon. Best you stay here. This is as good a hiding place as any. It shouldn't take me too long. I'll be back soon."

Diego thought, as did de Anza and Benito, that this was taking a chance. Could they trust this man they'd known for less than an hour? He could easily betray them and be back with a contingent of guards.

Eztli suspected their doubts. He looked at the three Spaniards and, putting his hand on Diego's arm, said, "You worry I'll come back with an army." Looking to his comrades, he continued. "We have lived with this evil all our lives. We have families. This can't go on. Have no worry. I will see the watch captain and return posthaste. If I do betray you, you can kill Meztli and Itztli." He laughed, but somehow the humor was lost on his companions.

"Very well," said Diego. "Go. We haven't much time."

Elena sat on the temple floor, chained to an iron ring pivoting on a spike driven deep into the rock beside her. She was sweating profusely. The temperature in the chamber was over one hundred degrees. Any hotter or given more time, she would pass out.

The temple to Xiuhtecuhtli and the opening to the lava flow was not as it was when Cuicatl had discovered it many years ago. Six of the seven fissures were covered by a stone platform evenly planed across the entire chamber, with steps rising to it at the entrance. A circular opening twelve feet in diameter now sat above the seventh fissure, giving access to the exposed lava tube below.

The most innovative feature was the mechanical delivery system a not-too-distant ancestor had developed. To be able to remove the heart after dropping a victim into the pit, the victim had to be retrieved at the proper time. This could be difficult for several reasons. First, once the victim was introduced to the pool of lava, it was quickly consumed by the intense heat. If the timing was wrong, only a portion of the votive would be left to fish out. Then there was the whole problem of the fishing out. What instrument could hold a firm grip on the offering without destruction? Last, the nature of a lava flow was that it flowed, albeit slowly, but at the same time, subduction was dragging the body down. Her ancestor had come up with an ingenious way to overcome these issues.

The supplicant climbed a set of stairs to a stone platform some eight feet above and forty-five degrees to the right of the pit. There awaited a cage sitting atop a steel table fitted to a carriage. The carriage rode on two ladder racks with squared holes, meeting with the squared teeth of the carriage wheels, descending one step at a time. At a fixed point in its approach to the bottom, the carriage tipped and dropped forward, depositing the cage into the pit. The top of the cage was attached to a thick chain, which was attached to a wench above the well. The slack in the chain went taut as the cage hit lava. After its contents were incinerated, it could be conveniently hoisted out in time, body intact and ready for excision of the heart. The travel time from top to bottom was one minute. This was La Condesa's favorite feature as it allowed for a mounting sense of terror throughout the process.

Alone in the chamber, Elena waited, trembling with fear in anticipation of her death.

Eztli returned not ten minutes later. Though Meztli and Itztli knew he had been kidding, they were relieved at his arrival.

"The high priestess has called for attendants to be stationed in the temple of Xiuhtecuhtli. The watch captain had other news as well."

"News of what?" asked de Anza.

"Groups of *ejecutores de la fe* are stationed on high alert in and around the village. She ordered squads of them to patrol the complex. They could arrive at any time."

Shoulder dropping, de Anza asked, "How many?"

"The squads are made up of ten men each, and he said five squads."

"We can't fight that. We're too few," cautioned de Anza.

"Agreed," said Diego. "It means we must get Elena and get out of here as quickly as possible. How do we get to this temple, Eztli?"

"It's through another passage leading off from this side of the atrium. Not far."

"Before we go, we agree we use the way we came in as our escape route?" said Benito.

"Yes," said de Anza. "It's unguarded, and I'm not sure anyone knows it exists. The wall to the tomb was put up hundreds of years ago."

"I just wanted to be sure. I've been talking to Meztli and Itztli. They know a faster route. They're both familiar with the underground river. It provides water to the atrium and the temple of Chalchihuidicue on the island's shore. The river has its beginning deep below us. Heated by volcanic action, it rises to the surface through small cracks. The one we passed along the way is an actual river with no exit. It moves back or to some other channel where it cools and descends—a sort of loop. I think the rock face above it curtails its ascent. Without it, the river below it would rise and flood the passageways, turning this entire complex of tunnels and chambers into an underground reservoir. I propose we remove that impediment."

"And how would you propose to do that?" asked de Anza.

"With a couple more of these," he said, raising the powder keg, "and a fuse placed at the top of the rock face. I've talked it over with Meztli and Itztli. They'll get what we need and meet us in the river chamber."

Diego's eyes rolled to heaven. "Why not? Now let's get going!"

They ran back to the portal on the atrium. Meztli and

Itztli split off for the armory while Eztli guided Diego, de Anza, and Benito through a series of passageways to the fire temple.

Eztli, ahead of the others, stopped suddenly, instructing the others to do the same. He shushed them and turned an ear toward the passage ahead of them. Soon the others heard it too—the low bass of drumbeats accompanied by the high squeaky sound of flutes and rattlers.

Eztli darted ahead of them. "We must hurry. They've begun."

"So, my dear Elena. Are you intrigued by my little toy?" La Condesa was standing next to her, Elena still chained to the wall.

Elena looked at La Condesa with nothing but scorn in her eyes. She said nothing.

"Come now, my sweet thing. This is your special day. I'm sorry we didn't get to know each other on a more intimate level." She bent down and stroked Elena's cheek. "But you are common, after all, and unworthy of my special attention. Oh well, the only pleasure I will get from this little exercise will be to imagine the bewilderment Diego Santiago will feel when he finds your smoldering and unrecognizable remains on his front doorstep. Maybe as a gift I'll have your heart placed in a jar by your side."

Elena spat at her and, summoning her resolve, simply said, "*Puta!*"

Wiping the spittle from her face, La Condesa slapped Elena and was about to hit her again, but she regained her composure, stood up straight, and laughed. "I'd like to think you will enjoy this. But I'm sure you won't."

She turned and walked to a small pedestal overlooking the pit, which cast a bright crimson glow upon her figure and countenance. Along with the musicians, seven attendants were in the chamber. Two took Elena by the arms and hauled her up to her feet. One unshackled her wrist, and then they marched her forcibly up the steps to the stone platform and the waiting steel cage. She struggled to no avail as they pushed her into the cage, dropping the barrel bolt down into its sheath and throwing the latch, fastening it shut. Surrounded by a steel plate, it was out of Elena's reach.

La Condesa—nay, the high priestess—raised her right arm high and commanded, "*Xipehua*!"

The drums sounded anew, followed by the piercing shriek of the wood pipes and the rattling of the shakers. The attendants removed a square steel rod beneath the carriage cogwheels, unlocking them. Then they threw a lever, releasing a counterweight, and the worm screw began to turn. The platform started its descent. A loud metallic hammering sound was heard as the large steel teeth of the cogs turned and fell into place on the next rung of the ladder rack. This announced each drop to the next step as the carriage descended. A countdown to death.

Two blasts from Diego and de Anza's long rifle sounded, and the two attendants fell to the ground, mortally wounded. The remaining five, armed with war axes, rushed de Anza and Diego. Two fell back from the force of the half-inch musket balls from Diego and de Anza's pistols.

As they were tangling with the three attendants, Benito ran to Elena, now midway through her descent.

At first, he took hold of the cage and tried to pull it from the moving carriage, but rails around the bottom of the carriage kept it in place. *Clang* went the platform as it dropped another step. *Four to go*, thought Benito. He was well below the cage's center of gravity, so lifting it was out of the question. Benito attempted it anyway, in vain. *Clang*. Three to go.

On the other side of the chamber, Diego and de Anza were hotly engaged in a battle with the high priestess's three remaining attendants. They were having a difficult time of it. The attendants' ancient battle-axes, while little more than clubs, had razor-sharpened lengths of obsidian embedded around the upper third of them. Their swords had only a slight advantage in reach, but attempting to parry a twelve-pound battle-axe was a nonstarter, so they had to dance quite a bit.

De Anza sought an opportunity to land a cut or jab against their foes. He found one and, lunging toward an Indio, landed a deep cutting jab to his wrist. The man dropped his axe but foolishly attempted to retrieve it with his other hand. That was what de Anza had been waiting for, and he lunged forward, delivering his blade precisely between the third and fourth rib on his left side, piercing his heart. He was dead before he hit the floor.

Meanwhile, Diego was doing his best to fend off the other two. Now the odds were even as de Anza came in on the fight.

Benito tried desperately to halt the carriage's advance, pushing as hard as he could. But even with his near herculean strength, weight, gravity, and the torque of the mechanism's drive defeated him. *Clang*. Two to go.

Benito looked up at Elena. Though stoic and silent, she

couldn't hide the pleading in her eyes. Benito was frantic, but he could do nothing to stop the machine's relentless advance. When the carriage reached the bottom, it would meet the immovable stop, tilting it forward and dropping the cage with Elena into the fiery red-orange iridescence of the lava flow. Its low throaty rumble beckoned, seemingly demanding its due.

Clang. One to go. Benito found himself asking God for help. A prayer. Something he hadn't done since he left the life he used to cherish and hold sacred. Sor Juana crossed his mind. Then it hit him. The crucifix! Feverishly, he fumbled through his robe, and pulling it out, he jammed it between the currently engaged gear and the next. The cogs groaned along with the straining worm screw. Hundreds of pounds of pressure bore down on the cross. Miraculously, it held, and the carriage came to a halt.

Still seeking the upper hand with their opponents, Diego and de Anza were given a gift. When the high priestess witnessed the failure of her much-loved mechanism of death, she let out a howl of anger. Unfortunately for her two minions, they turned momentarily, distracted by her cry. In that instant, Diego and de Anza struck. Diego wounded one man in the leg, and de Anza mercilessly opened the other's abdomen with his sword.

They ran to Benito's side. Climbing the steps to the platform, Diego made his way down the greased rail to Elena, still trapped in the cage. He looked it over, but there was no apparent locking apparatus. All the while, the priestess bellowed curses and death threats from her podium. Finally, Diego saw the bolt at the top and back of Elena's steel prison. Throwing the latch, he shoved the bolt up. The cage door swung open. Almost causing Diego to lose his balance, Elena jumped into his arms, eager to escape the horror. They looked into each other's eyes. She had known Diego would save her; he knew this was the woman he loved. Still, they were far from safe.

Seeing the two in their embrace sent Dona Andrea into a rage. She cursed them, stepping backward at the same time, preparing to make a break down the passageway behind her. Completely unhinged, she swore at the four watching from the far side of the rumbling lava pit. They noticed she was stepping back as they looked on, guessing her intention.

Her tirade suddenly stopped midsentence, as if she was searching her mind for what to say next. A faint glint of metal appeared just above her navel, followed by a drip of blood that, within seconds, turned to a torrent. Her belly arched forward, and she tried to vocalize but managed only a long, guttural "ugh" and dropped to her knees.

Their eyes followed her as she toppled forward through the opening on the floor and into the lava flow. They heard the frantic screams of her attempt at escape. The sound of her cries diminished, replaced by the low rumble of the molten rock descending back into the bowels of the Earth, taking her with it.

Mesmerized, their attention returned to where she had been standing to find the figure of a woman in the contemporary dress of a Spanish señorita, holding a long saber at her side. It was Dama Isabel de Montoya y Michoacán.

She stepped down from the podium and walked over to the four, who were still shocked by what they had just witnessed. "I was five when I saw her kill my father. There was a storm with lightning and loud thunder. I was frightened, so I ran to their room. They didn't hear me when

I entered. My mother was sitting on my father's chest, cooing to him softly. She reached behind her back and drew out a long black dagger. Still cooing, she brought it forward. Tilting it up, she drove it down through his eye, using the butt of her hand to ram it home. I swore someday I would kill her, and today was that day. Now you must go. You were seen. Gabriela will be here shortly with the *ejecutores de la fe.*"

Amazed at the transition, Elena took her by the hand. "Dama Isabel. You can't stay here. You'll be in danger."

"Thank you, Elena, but you need to understand my family. Gabriela is the oldest and has been groomed to inherit the sect all her life. She will not harm me. Now she can advance to the position of power she has always craved. She knows I have no interest and that I present no threat to her."

Eztli emerged from his hiding place at the bottom of the stairs. "She's right. We must leave quickly." He ran ahead, probably motivated by the fear of what would happen to him should the ascendant high priestess capture him. His defection would mark him and his allies for a death he didn't want to contemplate.

They kept up as best they could. The plan was to meet at the underground river. Benito hoped Meztli and Itztli had been successful in their mission and would be there with the additional black powder. He admitted to himself he was only guessing what it would take to bring the rock face down and divert the full power of the river into the passageways. He also wondered what the effect would be once the water reached the temple of Xiuhtecuhtli.

Diego thought, *If only we'd had Eztli with us earlier in the morning*. He had guided them through the labyrinth and arrived at the river chamber in a quarter of the time they'd taken without his aid.

Once they were all together, Benito reviewed his plan. "Eztli, will you help me plant the charges? The rest should make their way through the tomb to the house and from there to the boat. I have no idea how this diversion will manifest itself. It could be that nothing happens. It could also be something unexpected. Best everyone gets as far away as they can."

Diego took Elena's hand. Smiling, he said, "We'll be right behind you. We'll be home before supper." He kissed Elena, and de Anza led them out of the chamber.

Benito thought he should place the charges at midpoint in the chamber just where the roof came into contact with the rock face. He hoped the explosion would be focused in and down, away from the ceiling. It was also a spot where a natural rock ledge would keep the charges in place while they ran. Getting them to the ledge would be tricky, as would keeping the fuse from getting too damp from the steam rising from the open flow. The shelf they would use to get to the ledge angled down along the rock face, finishing toward the end of the chamber three feet up from the floor. It was still slippery, but fortunately, the flow submerged a couple of feet before the end of the chamber, giving them a relatively dry space to get across to the wall without falling. That would not be the case with the ledge as they made their way up to place the charges.

"I'm the tallest one. I'll go first. You can hand me the kegs, and I can wedge them in one at a time. Be sure to give me the barrel with the fuse last."

An explosion came out of the tunnel. A musket ball whistled past Eztli's head and ricocheted off the rock wall. They heard the voices and footsteps of at least a dozen *ejecutores de la fe* coming up the passage. This time, they carried more than battle-axes. Diego loaded his pistol and fired one shot, dead center, down the passage. The clamor abated, but they knew they were still advancing, albeit more cautiously.

Benito had the second keg jammed into place and motioned to Eztli for the third and final charge. A single *ejecutor* rushed into the chamber but fired blindly. Diego cut him down with his sword. Benito took a match and touched it to the end of the fuse. It ignited immediately. They had twenty seconds to exit the chamber and make it to safety before the blast.

They ran for the chamber exit that led to Cuicatl's tomb. But Benito turned to look and saw the fuse was no longer lit. He knew that if he were to ignite it once more, there would be no chance of escaping before all hell broke loose.

He felt someone grip his shoulder. It was Diego. Eztli was standing beside him. "Benito, let's go!"

"I can't, my friend." Benito reached past Diego and relieved Eztli of his torch.

"Benito, no!"

"Go on, Diego. I can do God one more favor. Look in on my brood in the marketplace for me. Especially *pequeño* Esteban." He started to mention Sor Juana, but stopped himself and simply said, "*Vía con Dios,* mi amigo." He turned and made for the ledge.

Tears streamed down Diego's face. He knew he would not dissuade the Monk. Diego took Eztli by the arm and said, "Come, we have to move fast."

Diego and Eztli were entering the tomb when the deafening blast reverberated through and around the remnants of Cuicatl's temple, knocking them both to the ground. They made it to their feet. Eztli looked around, astonished at what he saw. Still, he did not hesitate to rush out of the tomb as fast as his legs would carry him.

Diego led him to the entrance to the passage and lowered him down through the fireplace. As they ran out of the house, they heard what sounded like thunder and then a violent crash of water took out the side of the hill and much of the rear of the house with it. Falling down the bluff, they moved up the shore just in time to see a second rush of water pick up the rest of the house and carry it out into the lake. Within a minute, it had submerged entirely, leaving no evidence it had ever existed.

Diego ran north along the shore. Eztli was close behind. Dawn was breaking, and the rays of early morning light swept across the water. As he looked south, he could see the brigantines approaching the island. Straight out from him were several barges. *That would be the troops. I wonder if they saw the destruction of the hillside.* Out of the corner of his eye, he saw hundreds of canoes moving out into the lake. It was the villagers fleeing.

"I'm sorry, señor. I warned my people they should escape. I guessed your companions would be coming in force."

"I'm glad you did, Eztli."

They approached the boat that had brought Diego, de Anza, and the Monk here the evening before. It seemed like that was years ago. De Anza was standing guard with

Elena, Itztli, and Meztli next to him. Diego thought he had little to worry about at this point. He was relatively sure the entire complex was underwater. When Elena saw Diego and Eztli approaching, she ran into Diego's open arms. They held each other, not wanting to let go, not speaking. The danger had passed.

"Diego, where is Benito?" asked de Anza.

Diego was lost for words. He made his way around the boat to de Anza's side and, without speaking, looked him in the eye, his hand on his shoulder. De Anza could read the rest in his face. He lowered his eyes and asked, "How?"

"As he always did. Thinking of others. We better get going."

They barely fit in the canoe, and they wouldn't have save for Benito's absence. They were out on the lake when they noticed the waves stood still, the water seemed to lower, and they were being carried back toward the island. Rumbling emanated from beneath them.

Then they saw something no one expected. A detonation louder and more profound than any cannon blast brought the water around them up in the air. It hung there for a moment. They clung to the canoe as the wall of water obstructed their view. Then it came down, and they saw the island disappearing under the water, leaving behind an enormous cloud of dust. When everything had cleared, most of the island was gone. All that was left was a strip of the hillside about a mile long. The village was gone, but oddly the temple to Chalchihuidicue remained intact. The passages, the magnificent atrium, the black temple with its legacy of torture and death, and Cuicatl herself all were buried for the rest of time.

REGRETS AND REWARDS

"I THINK THIS IS my favorite time of year," said Elena as they all sat at the table in Don Felipe's dining room having lunch. "The weather is cool but not cold. The sunsets are beautiful, and the sky is clear and full of stars at night."

Señora Reyes came into the room with a luncheon guest beside her. It was Ana. Elena jumped up and ran to her dear friend. They hugged each other, both shedding tears. "Oh, Ana. I was so worried about you. Your mother, Jaime, all of us were."

"And I you. We must thank these brave caballeros for saving us."

"And one more." Don Felipe lifted his glass. "Benito de Avila. Gone but forever in our memory." They drank in silence, each with their private memories of the Monk. After he finished, Don Felipe looked down at his glass in sadness and deep sorrow and nodded respectfully. Then he turned and threw his glass into the fireplace, followed by them all.

Bringing everyone back, Don Felipe said, "Well!" He turned to de Anza. "What plans do you have, Colonel?" De Anza stared at him, blank and uncomprehending. "It seems as though the viceroy thinks you're not busy enough. He'd like to see you tomorrow morning." Then he added with a broad smile, "Eleven o'clock. Don't be late. Congratulations, Pedro."

Everyone stood and clapped, each offering their congratulatory sentiment. Diego gave his friend a hearty handshake. "Well deserved, my friend. You won't have time for my petty crimes any longer."

"Don't be so sure, Diego. We still have the matter of Alavaro Yaotl."

"Indeed, indeed," replied Diego, slapping his friend on the back.

"And you, Diego de Santiago." Felipe paused. "You're fired."

Diego's jaw dropped.

"It's sad, I know, but things being what they are, there is no way for you to do the honorable thing."

Felipe looked at Elena. "You'll be so kind as to see me in my office next Monday to sign your contract as a special consultant to the Audiencia. Fifteen years non-cancelable, 12,000 pesos annually with a performance-based upward adjustment of five to ten percent."

Flabbergasted, Diego said, "I don't know what to say."

"Say anything you like, except uncle." They both laughed.

Don Felipe took Elena's hand and put it in Diego's. "I forgot. There's a signing bonus of 5,000 pesos. You know, to cover any near-term expenses."

A VISITOR FOR SOR JUANA

"SISTER, THERE'S A military officer at the convent entrance asking to see you." Puzzled, Sor Juana Ines got up from the pew where she was kneeling and followed the other sister out of the chapel.

Captain de Anza stood nervously at the gate as Sor Juana approached him. "Buenos días, Captain. Is there something I can do for you?"

"Buenos días, Sister. My name is Pedro de Anza. I worked with Benito de Avila. I believe you assisted us with investigating both a murder and a poisoning."

"Yes, yes, Captain, that is true. I did."

"Well, I am proud to say I was a friend of Benito's and admired the work he did with the less fortunate of the city. He was a good man."

Sor Juana pictured Benito in her mind. "Yes, Benito was a very good man."

"Sister, I'd like to know what I can do to help continue his work. I'm not a religious man and don't know where to start. If you don't object, I thought you could advise me."

Juana thought for a moment. "Captain, I have no objections at all, and it's very kind of you to think about continuing Benito's work. I would be happy to advise you." *It's as though Benito sent this man to me. I was lost, thinking of my dear Benito. I know I'll miss him for the rest of my life. Doing this will keep me close to him.* Then she repeated aloud. "Yes, I would be more than happy to advise you."

SORORAL CONCERN

June 1757 Michoacán

“DO YOU HAVE to go? You’re my sister, and I love you.”

“I can’t stay here. I love you too, but there’s nothing for me in this place.”

“But we’ve always been together since we were children, and you followed me here after we escaped the island.”

“Look, you’re happy here, and that’s fine. But I’ve tasted other ways of living and experienced other possibilities. It’s too isolated here. I need to see the world. Meet other people.”

“You mean people other than me and what I’ve built here. What we’ve built here.” Hurt, she rose from the little white table where they’d been sitting on the veranda, walked to its edge, and looked out over the rolling green countryside.

Her sister, still sitting, called to her, "Gabriela. I do love you."

With a sigh, resigned to the fact that life would never be the same, she replied, "I know you do, Isabel. I'll miss you, my sweet one." She resumed her place at the little table. She reached across it and took Isabel's hand. With sadness in her eyes, she said, "You'll come to today's ceremony?"

"Yes, Gabriela. But this will be the last time."

AUTHOR'S NOTE

I endeavored to be as authentic as possible when employing Nahuatl terms, but Nahuatl Classico, spoken by the Aztecs when Tenochtitlan fell, is an extinct language. These words represent my best effort to present accurate translations of those terms from Classico and the modern Huastec dialect spoken in the surrounding regions today.

I have also taken the liberty to revise some geographical aspects of Mexico City and Lake Texcoco, such as the size and distance of Tepetzinco from the city and the route of the *Acequia Royal* and Roldan canals, in order to support the narrative.

Though some historical characters contemporary to the story, such as Hernan Cortes, the Viceroy, the King of Spain and certain others are represented, the central characters in the story are completely fictitious—as is the story itself.

JR

GLOSSARY

(Nahuatl, Spanish, Latin, and French Terms)

Acequia Royal	Royal Canal
achichiacpan	Natural spring
acordada	Special judicial commission
adelante	Come in, come forward
adios	Bye
affaire de cour	Love affair
alcalde	A judge or chief administrator
alcalde de crimen	Criminal judge
alcaldes de corte	A judge in the Audiencia's civil division
amahquihqueh	Who are you?
amiga	Female friend
amigo	Male friend
aristocrata	A member of the aristocracy
Audiencia	The royal court in New Spain and highest authority for matters criminal and civil
auto de fe	Act of faith
axolotl	A salamander found in Lake Texcoco

Ay! Venga!	Oh! Come on!
ayuntamiento	City hall
baratilleros	People of the baratillo
baratillo	Street market dealing in cheap or secondhand goods
barrio	Neighborhood
Basílica de nuestra Señora de Guadalupe	The Basilica of our Lady of Guadalupe
bastardo	Bastard
bievenido	Welcome
buenas dias	Good morning
buenas noches	Good evening
buenas tardes	Good afternoon
caballero	A Spanish or Mexican gentleman
cabrón	Shithead
Cachopin	Nahuatl pronunciation of the Spanish slang, Gachupin, a derogatory term for a recent Spanish émigré
capa	A loose outer garment without sleeves, covering most of the body
Capoltic Teopancalli	Dark temple
casa grande	Mansion, big house
casta	Social caste
catechumen	A novitiate receiving instruction prior to baptism
centavos	Cents
chinampas	Artificial floating islands used for agriculture

cigarillo	Cigarette
claro	Clear
clinica medico	Medical clinic
cochineal	A crimson-dye-producing insect
Coligeo San Ildefonso	College of San Ildefonso
compañeros	Friends
conquistadores	Conquerors
Coyolxauhqui stone	Round raised platform where victims of sacrifice were decapitated and Coyolxauhqui dismembered
criollo	Creole
cuaquepi	Insane
cuauhxicalli	Stone vessel to hold the hearts of sacrificial victims
dama	Lady
Día de Los Muertos	Day of the dead
Dios en el Cielo	God in heaven
Dios me salve	God save me
disculpas	Apologies
doncellas	Maidens
Ejecutores de le fe	Enforcers of the faith
el diablo	The devil
el jefe	The boss
encomienda	A grant of land
estoy bien	I'm fine

fiscal del crimen	Criminal prosecutor
gachupín	Derogatory term for a recent Spanish émigré
gracias	Thank you
hildago	Gentleman of rank
hola	Hello
hombrecito	Young man
huaraches	Sandal
huevos ahogados	Eggs poached in salsa
Huēyi Teōcalli	Great Temple
hupil	A sleeveless blouse
informantes	Informants
jarra	Jug
jugo verde	Green juice made with apples, nopal, kale, celery, and pineapple
La Condesa	The countess
la modista	The dressmaker
Libellus de Medicinalibus Indorum Herbis	Little Book of the Medicinal Herbs of the Indians
loco	Crazy
lugar de ofrenda	Place of offering
maldita perra	Damn bitch
mantele	Tablecloth
matones	Thugs
maxtlatl	Loincloth
mercado	Market
mestizo	Mixed race

mi dama	My lady
mierda	Shit
misioneros	Missionaries
moja dama	My lady
Nueva España	New Spain
ocotl	Pine
oidor	Judge
otiquimipantili	Have you found them?
padre	A priest, father
Padre Santo	Holy Father
Palace de Virrey	Viceroy's palace
Pantitlán	Nahuatl for "between two flags" and the site of a deadly maelstrom
Parian	Market
pequeño	Little
perdóname	Forgive me
peso	Basic monetary unit of Mexico, and several other Latin American countries, equal to 100 centavos
petates	Mats woven from palm leaves. Multi-purpose but most commonly used as bed rolls
Portal de Mercaderes	Merchants' portal
pulque	An alcoholic beverage made from the fermented sap of the maguey (agave) plant
pulqueria	An establishment that sells pulque
puta	Bitch

Quemah	Yes
Quetzal	A brightly colored bird found in the tropical highlands of the Americas. Some have tailfeathers as long as thirty-five inches.
quinto real	The king's twenty; a tax
Real y Pontificia Universidad de México	Royal Pontifical University of Mexico
Regimiento de México	Mexico regiment
sanbenito	A penitential garment, sacred cloth, worn by thoses condemed by the Inqusion during and after their *auto de fe*.
sangra pura	Pure blood
señor	Mister
señora	Lady
señores	Sirs
señorita	Young unmarried woman; miss
Surge et accipe cor	Arise and take heart
Teatro Comedias	Comedy theater
tecuitlatl	Spirulina
temazcalli	Sweat lodge
Templo Mayor	Main temple
teōpixqui	Priest
teixiptlatini	Impersonator
tianguillo	Night market

tlalpehua	Begin
Tlahtoani	Chief or leader
tlazohcamati	Thank you; much appreciation
tletlahuitolli	A fire bow
tzompantli	A rack to holding skulls, victims of sacrifice or war
Valle de Mexico	Valley of Mexico
vamos	Let's go
Vaya con Dios	Go with God
wattle and daub	A woven lattice of wooden strips called wattle is daubed with a mixture of clay or mud
xipehua	Begin
xocolatl	Colonial Spanish derivative of the Nahuatl 'chocolatl' hot chocolate

AUTHOR BIO: JAMES RYAN

James Ryan is a retired business executive living in Northern California. He spent thirty years traveling throughout Asia, Europe, and Central America over the course of his career, as well as living and working in France, Switzerland, and throughout the United States. Along the way, he acquired a deep appreciation for a diversity of cultures, their histories, and their mythologies. Temple Legacy is his first novel.

Made in the USA
Las Vegas, NV
01 July 2023

74144529R00166